The Underground Man

Mick Jackson

The Underground Man

PICADOR

First published 1997 by Picador

an imprint of Macmillan Publishers Ltd
25 Eccleston Place, London SW1W 9NF
and Basingstoke

Associated companies throughout the world

ISBN 0 330 34955 4

1 3 5 7 9 8 6 4 2

A CIP catalogue record for this book is available from
the British Library.

Typeset by CentraCet Limited, Cambridge
Printed and bound in Great Britain by
Mackays of Chatham plc, Chatham, Kent

The Underground Man

From His Grace's Journal

*

I have no idea how an apple tree works. The quiet machine beneath the bark is quite beyond my ken. But, like the next man along, I find Imagination always willing to leap into Ignorance's breach...

The tree roots, I imagine, play a major part – managing somehow to soak up the richness of the earth. I picture this richness drawn slowly up the trunk, pumped out along every branch.

No doubt the sun and rain are also involved, their warmth and moisture in some way being essential to the constitution of the tree. But how the richness of the earth, the sun and the rain come together to produce (i) a perfect blossom, then (ii) a small apple-bud – well, that remains a mystery to me.

*

Locate a local apple tree. Visit it daily through the summer months. Note how the bud slowly puffs itself up into apple-shape. See how it slowly takes a breath. The weeks roll by until its own increasing weight finally forces the fruit to fall. You will find it on the ground, all ready to eat. This whole process is utterly dependable; has a beginning, a middle and an end. But I am not satisfied. Far from it. Plain baffled is what I am. All sorts of questions remain unanswered. Such as

... who taught the tree its apple-conjuring? And ... where does the fruit's flavour come from?

*

I have on my estate one of the largest orchards in the whole of England. My Bramleys and Orange Pippins bring home trophies and silver cups. Each year, as the summer grinds to a close, I watch the carts being led down the drive. Their wheels creak and judder under the weight of the baskets. Every one is packed to the brim. I sometimes stand at the gate to the orchard and watch them dreamily trundle by. Sooner or later, an apple takes a tumble. I pick it up. I study it. But am never any closer to understanding how it came about.

O, how wonderful to be an apple tree – to know one's place in the world. To be both fixed and fruitful. To know what one is about.

*

Woke at dawn this morning, after a wearying night's sleep. Blew down to Clement to fetch a sack of corn and twenty minutes later we were both of us striding out along the Sloswick path to feed the deer. The day was bright and fresh enough, certainly, but had about it a brittleness, as if it had been wrought from glass, and though the sky was perfectly cloudless I sensed a chill in the air which rang silently all about me and warned that autumn was on its way. This proceeded to fill me with such foreboding that I became quite distracted and had to leave Clement to attend the deer alone.

As a young man I imagined growing old would be something like the feeling one has at the close of a long and satisfying day: a not unpleasant lassitude, always remedied by a good night's sleep. But I now know it to be the gradual revelation of one's body as nothing more than a bag of unshakeable aches. Old age is but the reduced capacity of a failing machine. Even my sleep – that beautiful oblivion always relied upon for replenishment – now seems to founder, has somehow lost its step. My fingers and toes are cold the whole year round, as if my fire is slowly going out.

Made my way home via Cow-close Wood where I spotted the lazy dipping flight of a single magpie. Spat twice, raised my hat, said, 'Good morning, Mr Magpie,' then looked around to make sure my little ritual had not been observed by anyone. I do believe I grow more superstitious with every passing year. Once upon a time, I would have thrown a stone after the bird. Now I cower like a frightened child.

A hundred yards further down the lane, rounding the corner by Horses' Graveyard, I came suddenly upon a huge and tatty crow, perched on a rotting tree stump, with his little legs apart. I was less than ten foot from him before I registered him and the shock of it brought me skidding to a halt. He eyed me, I thought, most malevolently, like some squatting devil in his black raggedy cloak. I distinctly felt my sphincter slacken, my testicles shuffle in their sack.

That awful crow stared right at me; its gaze seemed to penetrate my skull. By now, my mind was furiously sending out instructions – to turn and run, to get well away from that bird – but my body, I discovered, was weirdly stuck, as if caught in a spell. (As I sit here at my desk with my feet in my slippers I can muse over how but a minute before I had dealt quite satisfactorily with the single magpie ... had known how to counteract its little load of bad luck. But with the crow I was utterly defenceless. I had no antidote for that bird at all.)

Coming so dramatically upon it had left me breathless. My mind's slate was rubbed quite clean. And yet my own voice whispered distantly to me, insisting that if some effort were not soon made to remove me the crow might hold me in those woods until the end of time. So I did all I could to encourage my legs into action and found that some blood still shifted weakly in my veins. I inched my foot out along the ground until, at last, it became a tiny step; tentatively put some weight on it, then began the whole interminable process again. All the while, that damned bird kept his evil eye on me. But by concentrating my mind on my own creeping feet and doing my utmost to block out his vicious gaze I began slowly to edge my way past him until, in time, I had put between us an extra yard ... two yards ... finally, three.

Now I have never been especially athletic (and, even if I had, those days would now be long gone), but as soon as I was a dozen steps past that bird I broke into a frantic, rickety trot. I turned only once – to be certain the little winged monster wasn't after me – and as I did so he let out a terrible 'Caw' from his throne. Then he spread his oily wings and pumped them; rose, banked and disappeared into the trees.

I would not claim to be especially mindful of bird lore and the symbolic meaning attributed to each one but I am in no doubt that that crow most assuredly meant me harm. It had created around it an almost paralysing field of malignity; I am sure any other man would have felt it just the same. Such a small and common creature, yet its evil filled the whole wood up.

When I got home I found that Mrs Pledger had grilled for me my favourite smoked bacon and she looked most put out when I failed to raise a forkful to my mouth, but it was all I could do to get a cup of sweet tea down me and make my way back up to my rooms. I was deeply shaken by my crow-encounter and reckoned I might have caught a headchill along the way. When he returned, I asked Clement to be good enough to dig out my old beaver hat and give it a brushing down – a sure sign that summer is at an end.

✻

*

Slept right through till eleven when I was woken by Clement as he tended the fire. Felt much improved on yesterday, if a little muddled. Bathed, put on my thick tweed trousers and a brand-new Norfolk jacket. Strapped myself into my good brown boots and tried to comb some sense into what remains of my hair.

I have been going bald now for well over thirty years; was still quite a young fellow when I first found a little nest of hair in the lining of my deerstalker after a particularly vigorous stroll. Thereafter, I brushed my hair less frequently (and with a good deal more care), vainly hoping to slow the whole terrifying process down. I thought perhaps my strolls' exertion might somehow be to blame or, more specifically, the heat they generated under my hat. I don't mind admitting it took me quite a while to come to terms with the facts before me, one day managing to convince myself how it was all in my imagination and that I wasn't going bald at all, the next day suddenly certain I would be an egghead by a week Friday and that my life was not worth carrying on.

But there are, it seems, a hundred different ways of losing one's hair and I should perhaps be grateful that the manner handed out to me was one which takes a good long while. My hair made a slow, almost imperceptible retreat from my forehead, while at my crown a small circle of exposed scalp gradually grew. Two carefully positioned mirrors were required for me to observe the decay as, year by year, these two clearings made their way towards each other. Eventually, a thin channel of flesh connected them up, which then widened from generous parting to a broad pink trough, until, at last, all that remained was an occasional startled baby-hair on my otherwise bare cranium.

Even now, there are days when I am sure it is all over, that the damage is finally done. But closer inspection always obliges me to concede that new corners of my scalp continue to come to light and that the spread of flesh goes on. It is not an unbearable burden. My days of real vanity are gone. I no longer fret about it. There is simply more face to wash, less hair to comb.

The hair which still clings to the sides of my head is white, like lambswool. It sprouts out around my ears and in a rude manner behind. In order to scotch the inevitable comparisons with the proverbial coot, I have long sported a full moustache and beard, also white but a good deal more muttony, which seems to me to restore some much-needed equilibrium.

After five minutes' oiling and tinkering my head looked little different to when I started out. To perk me up I undertook twenty gentle knee-bends and trimmed my moustache then had a glance in the full-length mirror.

I have heard me described as a wiry man, which I interpret as meaning 'held together with wires' and seems altogether quite fitting and fair. Now, whether I have more wires in my body than the next man or whether it is just that mine are more on display, I could not say, but they are clearly at work at every junction of my frame – most noticeable in my arms, legs and neck. When I walk or bend or even grimace they can be seen twitching under the skin like tense lengths of twine.

Where my neck and torso come together is usually a regular network of root and vein. Of late, however, I have become uncertain whether all these wires are properly attached. Some appear to have grown quite slack; one or two to have come away from their housing altogether. On a bad day I worry that somewhere inside of me an essential spring might have snapped, to dangle and rattle about in me for the rest of my days.

I have also recently noticed how, in wet weather, I have a tendency to creak – there's no denying it, it's plain for all to hear – so on damp days I stay in by the fire and play Patience or Bagatelle. All the same, I think 'wiry' still just about does the job – even if the wires are not as taut as they once were.

*

OCTOBER 5TH

*

I was returning down the West avenue this morning, with autumn's grim carnage all around, when I came across one of my gamekeepers walking the most gargantuan dog. A terrific beast, it was – some sort of long-haired pepper-and-salt mongrel with a two-foot tail and an insolent gait. A donkey of a dog. Well, the keeper and I struck up a conversation about the weather and suchlike. Meanwhile the dog appeared to listen most intelligently, furrowing its brows as we carried on, so that I half expected it to share with us its own considered opinions and maybe put us right on the odd point or two. I complimented the keeper on his fine creature and asked what he fed it on and I recall him saying how, as a matter of fact, it belonged to his wife's brother and thrived on Lancashire hotpot – a large bowl, three times a day. Well, I was most impressed; especially after hearing how the keeper's young niece and nephew often went riding on its back with never a grumble from the dog.

I stroked its huge head – as big as a bison's! – and felt a lovely warmth spread across the palm of my hand from the thick rolls of dogflesh. I could have happily spent the entire morning marvelling at the beast but the keeper seemed eager to be about his business so we drew our brief exchange to a close. He raised his cap, made a clicking noise from out the side of his mouth and gently tugged on the dog's leather lead and that great solemn creature seemed also to nod its heavy head at me before turning and ambling away.

Once the dog had picked up a bit of momentum I saw how the keeper had trouble keeping up, and in no time they were fifty yards away and apparently still gathering speed when a thought occurred to me. I called after them, which sent them into something of a spin, and I hurried over to where they had come to rest. It took me I should say maybe three or four attempts to properly get the idea out – I tend to become tongue-tied when my mind is all fired up – but managed finally to articulate my offer of having a saddle made up in the dog's measurements so that the keeper's niece and nephew might sit upon it without fear of falling off. Personally, I thought this a first-class idea – a dog in a saddle, very good! – but the keeper kept his eyes pinned to the ground and politely declined. So we said our goodbyes all over again and I let them carry on their way.

I have always been very fond of dogs. Cats have much too high an opinion of themselves and generally make for poor company. Are, on the whole, utterly humourless and always wrapped up in their own thoughts. Some days I reckon all cats are spies. Dogs, on the other hand, are reassuringly foolish and always game for a roll-around. Over the years I should say I have owned several dozen dogs – of all temperaments and shapes and sizes – and while I retain a good deal of affection for each of them it is fair to say I have been besotted only with one.

About twenty years ago, on my birthday, good Lord Galway of Serlby presented me with a beautiful basset-hound pup. At that time his was the only pack in the country (brought over from France, I believe) so that they were valuable and unusual to boot. Immediately recognizable by their stout little legs, concave back and baggy ears, something about their appearance suggests that they have been knocked together out of odd bits of various other dog. The simplest task – such as walking – can prove very troublesome for a basset-hound. It is as if they have been poorly designed. Their coat is always most generously tailored and none more so than on the pup handed me that day. He had on him enough flesh to adequately clothe another two or three dogs besides – the majority of it hanging off his face – and though he was, at the time, no more than a few months old he wore the immutable basset expression of Lifelong Woe.

His eyes were all red and rheumy, as if he had tried washing away his miseries with port wine, but his tail stood to attention like the handle on a water pump and the look of utter disgust with which he regarded my dinner guests enamoured him to me straight away. Being presented with a great ribbon around his neck, to the accompaniment of whoops and cheers, was, apparently, a humiliation almost too great for him to bear. It was his doleful expression, his deep disdain which first stole my heart away, whilst simultaneously, and so vividly, calling to mind my father's long-departed brother, Leonard.

(Uncle Leonard was some sort of military man. My one abiding memory is of him sitting alone in the Games Room, quaffing great quantities of Scotch whisky while his cigar smoke slowly filled the room. The little finger on his right hand was missing, which he once told me was from his having bitten his fingernails as a boy. He died at Balaclava in '54, kicked in the head by a horse.)

The likeness between dog and dead uncle was so startling that I wondered if there was not, after all, some grain of truth in this notion of reincarnation – the upshot being that I named the dog Uncle on the spot, which seemed as acceptable to him as it did to me.

From that day forward we got along famously, were constant companions, and I don't doubt we made quite a spectacle as we took our daily constitutional: me in my brightly coloured waistcoats, which I favoured at the time, and proud Uncle in matching collar and coat, zigzagging beside me and scouring the ground with his plum of a nose.

I can only hope that he was happy, for he never lost that forlorn and put-upon look, but he was animated enough and most affectionate, which I took as signs of contentment, and when he slept he did not kick or twitch as many dogs do. On our cross-country walks his great flapping ears would gather up all kinds of rubbish, and I would like nothing more than to be picking them clean today. But one spring morning he spotted a rabbit in a nearby field, chased it into its burrow and got himself stuck. I ran back to the house like a madman, stood in the hall calling for servants and spades, but by the time we had returned and dug down to him the poor fellow had suffocated. I carried him home, with all the servants trailing behind and buried him in a quiet corner of the Italian gardens the following day.

Out strolling years later I would find myself idly talking to him, as if he were right there by my side and us still the best of friends. Even now, if I have grown sleepy in a fireside chair and decide I must go to bed, I might whisper, 'Come, Uncle,' without thinking, as I rise.

Some essential part of him stays with me; persists down all the years. Somewhere deep inside me his tail still wags. He never seems to tire.

*

✳

The last tunnel is all but completed – heady days indeed.

When Mr Bird entered the dining room this morning, a roll of papers tucked under his arm, he had about him his usual unassuming attitude but his features were all aglow. I noticed how he was a little ... *nervy* ... and how his eyes flashed about the place, which was enough to get me quite giddy with anticipation myself. Down the years Mr Bird and I have got to know each other very well and he is fully familiar with my love of maps and charts, but as he rolled out onto the table his latest set of plans I would be hard pushed to say which of us had more difficulty standing still. A mustard pot, a cup and a saucer were employed to hold down the curling corners of the map. Then Mr B. and I stepped back a foot or two to take the whole picture in.

In the very centre of the map stood the house in miniature (a good likeness, I have to say, done in pen and ink) accompanied by all the stables and outhouses – each clearly labelled in italic script. The whole estate was etched out around the house, with the woods and drives all carefully marked in. As we both stood there looking dumbly down at the map Mr Bird discreetly produced from his breast pocket a small pencil stub. He raised it to his mouth, gave the lead a little lick and, with a precision any surgeon would be proud of, marked out the first tunnel, as I looked anxiously on. The squat little pencil travelled east from the house, coolly dissected the lake, crept right up the Pudding Hill and came to rest in the outskirts of Worksop town.

Mr Bird pushed himself back on an elbow and looked up at me. I nodded back at him, encouragingly. A faint whiff of sweat hung in the air between us and it occurred to me how our hushed exhilaration had somehow managed to evoke the rare stench of horse-heat in that large cool room.

In the minutes which followed Mr Bird proceeded to pencil in a further three tunnels, which left the house and headed north, south and west. At times they swung slightly to left or right but, on the whole, kept pretty much to the straight line. Mr Bird's pencil lead advanced through the forests and fields at quite a rate and when it reached the end of each tunnel I distinctly heard a sticky sound as it was plucked from the map. The mark it left was nothing more than a full stop at the close of a sentence, but in that tiny speck I saw quite clearly the tunnel entrance, as craggy as a cave.

A small gatehouse stood where each underground thoroughfare emerged, each with the word *Lodge* as a foundation. The map informed me how these lodges are currently occupied by Digby, Harris, Stoodle and Pyke, whose job it will be to lock and unlock the gates as necessary, to light the gaslights down their tunnel if word is received that they are to be used after dark and to ensure that no children get in.

The chart now consisted of four simple pencil-paths, of roughly equal length. A house with four roots sprouting from it, perhaps, or something vaguely akin to a compass face. But when Mr Bird had got his breath back and wet his pencil a fifth time the set of tunnels he brought into being caused the image to change most radically. Expertly, he fitted a second cross over the cross already on the map. The pie which had previously been quartered was now divided into eighths, so that when he had done with his pencilling the whole arrangement of tunnels was no longer compass-like and more like the spokes of a rimless wheel. For a second I had trouble swallowing and I felt myself come over quite faint. It had never previously occurred to me – a Wheel, with my house as its hub!

Mr Bird looked down at the map with evident satisfaction,

as if he had just conjured the tunnels into existence with a wave of his modest wand. He rested one hand on the table and pushed his spectacles back up his nose with the other. Out of the corner of my eye I felt him sneak a glance at me. Then for a minute or two we did nothing but gaze down and drink in every last detail, until all my pleasure and gratitude finally welled up inside me and overflowed.

'Sterling work, Mr Bird,' I said.

Mr Bird's Account

I should say His Grace first made contact with me a good year and a half before the work was begun. He had me travel up to Welbeck for a meeting where he told me all about his tunnelling plans. In some shape or form he had already worked out in his head what he wanted – he always had quite firm ideas – though he never mentioned to me what purpose they were to serve. Well, to be honest, tunnels weren't what we were normally about and, when the opportunity arose, I told the Duke as much. Garden landscaping, the occasional lake or ha-ha was much more our line. The previous year we had done a little something at the back of His Grace's London residence which, I was informed at that first meeting, had pleased him very much. As I recall, he was greatly taken with the wrought-iron fancywork on the frame of a sunk glass walkway. And so, right from the start, he was eager to impress on me the notion that my company was right for the job.

I remember how he had with him a small wooden box full of sketches which he emptied out onto the table. All sorts of drawings and diagrams, all jumbled up together. Then there were the plans he had never got around to putting on paper, some of which took a long while coming back to him and even longer to explain. But the basic idea was that there was to be a whole series of tunnels leaving the house and going out under the estate in all directions. Most were to emerge by gatehouses; only two were unattended, as I recall. But it would be fair to say that if you didn't know about these last two you would not easily trip over them.

Of the eight tunnels we eventually built on His Grace's estate – a good twelve miles of them in all – half were twenty foot wide, reaching fifteen foot in height and big enough for two carriages to pass without much difficulty, and the rest about half that size. I can't say that they were very elegant to look at: plain red brick in a horseshoe arch, with vaulted roofs where they met under the house and tiled passageways off to the stables. But they were sound and did the job they were built to do and I've no doubt they'll be standing a hundred years from now.

Once we were clear of the house and out into the gardens and surrounding fields most of the tunnel-laying was done by what is commonly called 'cut and cover', which simply means digging a deep ditch directly into the ground and, when the brickwork is completed, putting the earth back over the roof. Consequently, most of the tunnels on the estate are no more than a couple of feet beneath ground level. They were lit in the daytime by skylights – two foot in diameter and four inches thick – at regular intervals of twenty feet or so and each one requiring its own 'chimney', which is probably what slowed us down the most. Each tunnel had a line of gas jets plumbed in, both left and right, for use at night. I heard there were over five thousand such lamps put in place down there but am glad to say that particular task fell to someone else.

All in all, as you can imagine, this amounted to a great deal of work which took us some time to carry out. We employed, on average, a gang of about two hundred men – each on a shilling a day. The Duke insisted that every two men should have between them the use of a donkey for riding to and from the camp and that each man be given an umbrella. Well, you can picture the scene yourself, I'm sure. In the summer it was as gay as the seaside, but in the rain it was very grim.

On top of the tunnels we had stairwells and passages to put in, which went up into the house itself. He was very fond of trapdoors and suchlike, was the Duke. That was what got him going the most.

While I think about it, one thing does come back to me. On only the second or third meeting, I think it was, when we were still at a very early stage, His Grace came in looking highly vexed and asked me straight out, 'What about tree roots, Mr Bird? What about damage to the roots?' When I was quite sure I had grasped what it was he was asking, I did my best to assure him how the roots of the trees on the estate would be in no danger and that if there were any chance of us coming up against the roots of a great oak, for example, then it was quite within our means to steer a course round the thing. This seemed to put his mind at rest.

Anyhow, I don't mind saying that I think we made a good job of it. It was the largest commission my company undertook. We were up there so long that by the time I left I felt like a proper Nottinghamshire man. I was sad to say goodbye.

There were stories, as you know, regarding the Duke's appearance – how he was said to be deformed and dreadful to look upon. But the people who go about saying such things are nothing but gossip-merchants. Anyone who ever met the man will tell you just the same. I saw him a hundred times if I saw him once and the worst I could say was that on a bad day he could look a little ashen. A touch under the weather, is all.

I'm afraid our tunnel-building did nothing but encourage the wild stories. When a man starts acting eccentrically and hiding himself away, people feel at liberty to give their imaginations some slack. By the time they'd finished they'd made him into a right monster, but it was all in their own minds.

The whole time we worked on the tunnels – and we were

up there five years in all – I don't believe I ever asked His Grace directly just what the tunnels were for. It quickly ceased to matter. In the end I suspect I was just as wrapped up in the project as the old man himself. From time to time some of the lads would quiz me about it or make up a little gossip of their own. People like to let themselves get carried away. It comes, I think, from idleness, or envy, maybe. But then His Grace would come out to the site and have a look around and that would nip it in the bud, right there.

There are times when I wonder if he did not simply suffer from shyness. Shyness in the extreme. But then it's not my place to say. Most of us, at some time, have peculiar ideas we'd like to carry out but have not the money to put them in place. That was not the case with the old Duke.

Yes, I was sorry to see the back of him. He was a most gentle man.

From His Grace's Journal

OCTOBER 14TH

*

Woke with a decidedly sour stomach, after a third consecutive disturbed night's sleep. Had intended, this morning, to pay a visit on my old gardener, Mr Snow, who, I hear, has been very ill, but when I peered out at the day from my window the wind was stripping the leaves right off the trees and the barometer tower on the West wing promised more unsettled stuff to come. Resolved to stay indoors, at least until the rain had cleared. Dug out a clean nainsook handkerchief and dipped it in lavender oil. Blew down the pipe for some news on my Balbriggan socks but got no response from any quarter so, like some slippered nomad, trekked down the stairs to see what was going on.

Finally located Mrs Pledger in a steaming laundry-room, her sleeves rolled up to her elbows as she set about a mound of wet washing. She nodded in my direction but continued to pummel away. Today, it transpired, is the day allocated for the washing of bedsheets and it was a moment or two before I was able to fully take in the industrious scene before me. Stone sinks overflowed with hot water, soapsuds slid and drifted everywhere. The piercing aroma of cleaning agent made a powerful impression on the eyes and nose. Damp sheets hung down from wooden slats which were suspended from the ceiling on a web of pulleys and ropes, and this huge expanse of wet linen and the frantic activity beneath encouraged in me the notion that I had stumbled aboard some many-masted cutter as it weathered some terrible storm.

Four girls helped Mrs Pledger with her laundry and as I am in the habit of constantly forgetting the names of those in her employ (they are always coming and going, it seems, or turning into women overnight) I had her introduce me to them. Thus, I learned that the house staff currently includes at least 'two Annies, an Anne and a Sarah' and while they persevered with their scrubbing and rinsing I leaned against one of the vast sinks and repeated their names under my breath, finding the phrase to have a strangely calming quality to it.

With everyone so thoroughly immersed in their business I was left very much to myself, so to pass the time I stared into some temporarily abandoned sink, where I observed on the water's cooling surface the quiet collapse of soapy-suds. Very interesting indeed. What began life as a gently frying pancake of lather gradually changed its appearance as its tiny bubbles gave out, one by one. By exercising my mind on it I found that, with a little effort, the suds took on a shape not unlike the British Isles (a very frothy fellow he was, as if recently covered by a fall of snow). He wore an angular hat for Scotland, stretched his toes out at Penzance, had Wales for a belly and the Home Counties for a sit-upon. This little discovery rather pleased me, although, in all honesty, I could not say for certain how much was in the beholder's eye and how much was in the suds.

Well, those abandoned bubbles continued popping and my suddy Briton duly stretched and shrank, until I saw that he was, in fact, metamorphosing into – yes! – Italy's high-heeled boot. Britain turning into Italy – what confusion that would cause! What kind of weather would we have, I wonder? And what language? We should all have to speak in Latin. (*Amo, amas, amat . . .*) Excellent!

I was still happily ruminating in this manner when Italy's centre suddenly came apart and what had just now appeared to be solid land split into four or five smaller isles. Well, this came as quite a shock, and I had to fairly pump my imagination to come up with another port of call (my geography has always been very poor). Japan, perhaps, or the Philippines. I had to hurry . . . the islands were shrinking like ice-floes in the sun. I just about managed to bring into focus one final archipelago of froth but it was the briefest vision and in a second it had shimmered and gone, leaving nothing behind but a flat pool of dirty water, as if some aquatic apocalypse had run its course.

The whole process, I found, had quite tired me out. All the same, I offered to roll up my sleeves and lend a hand, thinking I would quite like to stir up some suds of my own. Mrs Pledger, however, was adamant that she and the girls were best left to do the work themselves so I loitered quietly in the corner and did my best to keep myself occupied.

Seeing all the sheets having the dirt drubbed out of them reminded me of a theory I have recently been entertaining. One which, on reflection, I was perhaps rather foolish in presenting to Mrs Pledger. Namely, might it not be possible for a bad night's sleep to somehow leave a trace of itself on one's sheets? A remnant of melancholy, perhaps, which the linen could in some way absorb. Is it not in any way plausible, I continued, that my recent disturbed sleep might be the result of some ill feeling, previously sweated out, which, when rewarmed by my body, is made potent once again?

I could tell straight away that my seeds had been cast on the stoniest of grounds. It is, I admit, an unusual theory and still somewhat underdone. But Mrs Pledger has never had much time for progressive thinking. Her long thin lips became even longer and thinner – became, in fact, little more than a crinkly line. She filled her great chest, emptied it in a single great sigh then went back to wrestling with her heap of washing.

All the same, as I left, I asked her to be sure and have one of the girls strip the linen from my bed and give it an especially ruthless scrub.

Mr Grimshaw's Account

It was getting on towards sunset when I received orders to prepare a carriage for His Grace, in order to take him and his valet, Clement, on a visit to see old Mr Snow. That day is fixed most firmly in my memory, seeing as how our return journey was set to be the first one underground and there being quite some excitement at the prospect. So I brought the carriage around to the front of the house and sat and watched the sun go down with a chew of tobacco in my mouth. And I sat and I chewed and I waited, as I seem to have done half my life.

Now, I'd be dishonest if I didn't come straight out and say how that big house hasn't, on more than the odd occasion, made me most uncomfortable just by looking it over, so that I might find myself shifting in my seat, if you take my meaning, and I'm not usually the fidgety type. It is a many pinnacled affair – to my eyes, very ugly – spires and towers all over the place and a roof needing constant repair. There's no doubt that it is large and impressive. A mountain of stone, with who knows how many windows. But I couldn't call it pretty. No. It never seemed to me a jolly place to live.

In olden days, I am told, it was a monastery where many monks would creep about in sackcloth and eat naught but nuts. It was them who built the first underground tunnels, in fear of ... now, would I be right in saying the boys of Henry the Eighth? Well, whoever's boys they were, they were dreadful enough to scare the monks into having escape tunnels dug. Two or three of them, I believe, and very narrow, which, in emergency, they would run along to come up out of the ground in the woods.

So I imagine I must have sat there the usual quarter-hour before they finally emerged ... His Grace with his famous beaver hat on and Clement close behind. I shall always think of His Grace as a pointy little man, with his trowel of a beard and his sharp blue eyes. To my mind, he was always a collection of angles – all elbows and knuckles and knees. Generally speaking, Clement accompanied His Grace on such trips and together they made a curious pair, what with Clement being so very large and silent and His Grace so small and always chattering on.

I might also just say here, if I may, that while I have always myself been very fond of the horses, it's my opinion His Grace went too far in giving them a graveyard of their own. I was brought up Christian and I have to say it seemed somehow unholy to me. I believe they should have gone to the knacker's yard and been got rid of in the usual way. Not given headstones with their names carved on 'em and poetry quotations and all.

Sometimes, like that evening, when the light was all but gone and we left the estate by Horses' Graveyard, my mind would take it upon itself to dwell most morbidly on all the horse corpses resting there. The thought of those tired old nags all a-mouldering would end up giving me a most sickly feeling inside. Would make me grip the reins extra tightly and get my living horses to gee-up, double quick.

From His Grace's Journal

*

Old Mrs Snow had been staring at me through her spectacles for what seemed like a good long while. She had yet to make any utterance, being so wholly taken up with observing me standing on her doorstep in the dark. Her right hand clung tightly to the door latch, as if I might be a robber and it a tiny pistol, and as the silence deepened I could feel the warmth of the cottage seeping slowly past me and out into the night.

Clement stood close behind me and I heard him take a breath to introduce us a second time when, at last, some connection registered in Mrs Snow's bespectacled eyes and she opened up her neat little mouth.

'It's the Duke,' she said.

'It is,' I replied, and bowed my bare head towards her. She nodded back at me – three or four times, maybe more. Then, just as I feared we might be in for a further period of standing about, she embarked on a series of shuffled backward steps, dragging the heavy door with her, then asked why we did not come in.

With Clement's aid, she managed to hang our coats on a hook behind the door. Then the three of us organized ourselves into a caravan, with Mrs Snow at the head and Clement at the rear, and we all set off at a funereal marching pace towards the parlour's orange light.

I'm afraid I could not help but notice the poor state of Mrs Snow's legs – bandier even than mine – and as we processed through the cottage I saw how her hand took support from, first, a stair banister, then the jamb of a door. At the threshold to the parlour Mrs Snow halted, in order to gather her wits, which gave me ample opportunity to look over her shoulder and take in the tiny room. A great deal of space was given over to a thickly-varnished sideboard, laden with all manner of gaudy crockery and assorted ornaments. Both the proportions and shining timber of the thing called to mind a small steamer on Lake Windermere. A dining table and various sitting chairs took up most of the remaining space.

Having herded all her thoughts together, Mrs Snow announced, 'It's the Duke,' again (this time, I assumed, for her husband's benefit rather than mine) then stooped off towards a stool which allowed me to catch my first glimpse of old Mr Snow, held in place by a great many cushions in an armchair by the fire. He smiled a curious half-smile and tried vainly to raise himself up, so I hurried over, took his hand in mine and Clement brought me over an upright chair.

The John Snow before me, packed all around with cushions, was a very different man to the one I had last come across. For one thing, and I can say this without fear of contradiction, the man had visibly shrunk. Yes, indeed. His body had been emptied like a sack. And though he had never been particularly portly his skull now seemed to push at the flesh of his face. The tuft of hair sticking up at the back of his head, his greatly bewildered air, his elbows pinned to his ribs with cushions all put me in mind of a nest-bound, flightless chick waiting to be fed.

'How are you, my friend?' I asked him, pulling my chair right up close to him.

The room was perfectly quiet but for the middle finger of Mr Snow's left hand, which drummed out a complicated rhythm on the arm of the chair which kept him captive. He nodded his head at me, just as his wife had done, but with Mr Snow it seemed not so much an attempt at communication as a man attempting to balance the weight of his head on his neck. He blinked at me – once, twice, three times – and then he nodded some more.

'Mr Snow has suffered a stroke,' announced Mrs Snow.

'So I hear,' I replied over my shoulder, before returning my attention to her husband, saying, 'We are all at sixes and sevens since you left, you know. Not nearly so many blooms.'

I waited for him to take up the conversation but he simply smiled his half-smile again. I went on, 'You remember your lovely gardens?'

His middle finger continued to tap out its frantic message. It was as if he had found a spot on the chair arm and was desperate to scratch it away.

At long last his dry lips parted. He said, 'I am not quite sure.'

Well, this knocked the wind right out of me. Forgotten the gardens? Impossible. How could a man not remember the place he had spent his every working day? I was hurt – I don't mind admitting it – as if the old fellow had actually landed a blow on me. His failure to retrieve any memory of the gardens seemed almost wilful. But I did my best to hide my disappointment and hung on to his withered hand.

I told him how we now had three men doing his job and how they were not doing half so well. I reminded him of his trip to the parks at Battersea and Kew and Crystal Palace after new combinations of bedding plants. I talked of tulips and crocuses and other spring bulbs, hoping to cast some healing light into the dark corners of his mind. And in the same way, perhaps, that a fly fisherman attempts to lure his catch with brightly coloured twists of feathers, so I attempted to reel in my frail old gardener with talk of blossoms and exotic fruit. 'You remember the black muscat grapes you grew me? The pineapples and the peaches?'

I smiled a full, broad smile for the both of us but felt the ground beneath me crack and part. I had an awful need for anchorage. Felt myself slipping away. And I found that I was soon talking ten to the dozen about any old thing that came to mind, while John Snow wore on his face an expression of utter perplexity, broken only by an apologetic raising of the brows. His eyes were terribly distant and though they once or twice flickered with what I hoped might be some sign of revelation, they remained lost and as cold as a pair of pebbles and revelation refused to come. 'The glasshouses are still there,' I told him.

'The glasshouses ... Yes,' he replied.

This small affirmation reassured me. Gave me some small hope to hang on to. In time, I reasoned, his memory might restore itself; like a damaged muscle which requires gentle exercise before it will properly function again. Then he leaned awkwardly over towards me and whispered in my ear.

'Much of it is gone,' he confided, and gripped me weakly on my arm. 'It's all there,' and here he took another bewildered breath, '. . . but there's no getting at it.'

I stared back at him, quietly horrified. His face had buckled into a scowl. His eyes looked anxiously at me as if over some abyss.

Only two years ago I had trouble getting a word in edgeways with John Snow. Forever marching up and down his garden paths he was, picking at every plant along the way. But some awful event inside him, some tiny blockage or severage or flaw, had caused the man's entire capacity to be irreparably reduced. He had been halved; had been more than halved. A lifetime's memory all but gone. Great expanses now underwater, whole continents washed away.

'Mr Snow has suffered a stroke,' said Mrs Snow, and this

time I turned and properly took her in. Two small flames shone in her spectacle lenses – reflections of the lamp's yellow light – but the face itself was as blank as a sheet. The only vitality about the poor woman was her tiny chest which pumped laboriously in and out and trawled the room for air. And in that single moment I became aware how both the Snows had suffered the stroke. How, one way or another, they had both been swept away.

*

We returned home in silence, save for my asking Clement to be sure the Snows' supply of food and fuel be kept in order and to ask Dr Cox to pay them a visit and give me a full report. I was so upset by the whole affair I was obliged to postpone the tunnels' christening and had Grimshaw take us home down the Eastern avenue, though from what little I could make out through the carriage window and with my state of mind being so black we might as well have been travelling a mile or two beneath the ground.

*

OCTOBER 16TH

*

To the north of the house and clearly visible from my bedroom is a row of lime trees, each about fifty feet tall, which hum and fizz right through the summer with their own colony of bees. In June and July and August when the sun is at its peak they fairly work themselves up into a frenzy and the trees become lost in a blur. I suppose they are simply making honey. One cannot blame them for that. All the same, one has trouble thinking straight above their interminable noise.

The bees are perfectly silent now. All dead or deeply asleep. Their eggs secreted in the branches until the world grows warm again. Somewhere in those limes there must be the makings of an entire bee population. Locked away till spring.

The leaves are deserting those lime trees just as they desert every tree across the estate and this stirs in me a most dismal disposition. The walnuts and chestnuts, the ashes and oaks – all now close to naked in the cold and damp autumn air.

As the fall of leaves gradually reveals each tree's wooden skeleton I can sometimes detect how it has been marginally altered since it last stood bare. One tree in particular – an unrecognizable variety on the other side of the lake – looks even more peculiar this year than it did last wintertime. Some folk on the estate reckon it was once struck by lightning – a theory which makes a good deal of sense – yet, though some parts of the tree are certainly stunted, each year it just about manages to force out the odd flourish of sickly leaves. I recall how, several years ago, it looked to me very much like the hanging carcass of a pig. Last autumn it was no more than a monster, a great mass of carbuncles and sores. But this morning, as I strolled past it, I felt sure I saw a horse through its thinning veil of leaves. A wild horse raised right up on its hind legs, with its head and neck thrown back.

*

All day I kept myself busy. Before lunch, Clement helped me shift my bed around so that the headboard now faces due north. I have heard that positioning a bed in this manner encourages a body to sleep more soundly, so I dug out my old brass compass and we aligned the bed right along the old north–south. Inevitably, Clement did the lion's share of the work while I fussed about and contributed nothing but the odd grunt or two. But when we were done and I lay down on the bed to recover I thought I registered a distinct improvement. A greater calmness of the mind.

Rearranged the tunnels' christening for nine o'clock tomorrow; returned a dozen shirts to Batt and Sons (they are three ounces overweight and the collars much too wide); had luncheon – a spicy celery soup – with young Mr Bowen, the stonemason, who is finishing the tunnel entrances and such-like, then inspected the stables and the riding school. In this way I managed to plough an idle furrow right through the day and did not once give myself the opportunity to dwell on my recent visit to the Snows. From the moment I woke I kept myself occupied with the most trivial of tasks, but at the very back of my mind, I have no doubt, some part of me meditated wholeheartedly on the devastation I had seen.

By four o'clock – always my most miserable part of the day – I had run right out of steam and found myself in the upstairs study. Just me and the old tick-tock.

I sat there in the emptiness. I became aware of a slow wave of horror, all set to crash over me. I waited. I listened. And, in time, the wave came crashing down.

It raced to fill every corner of me. An awful boiling and thrashing in my head which, now I have had time to make some sense of it, I can articulate in the following way . . .

Our life experience is kept safe and sound in the strongroom of our Memory. It is here that we store our pasts. We keep no other record, save the odd souvenir, of life's small successes, its staggering failures, of those whom we have loved and (if we are fortunate) the ones who have loved us in return. The only assurance we have that our life has been well spent – or, for that matter, spent at all – is the proof delicately held in our Memory, in those great ledgers of the mind.

But what if the door to that room is broken? What if the rain and the wind get in? If they do, then we are in grave danger of becoming hopelessly and eternally lost.

33

And if such a havoc-wreaking illness should befall us our only solace would be that we might at least remain ignorant of what we had lost, and be left to live out our feeble days in a childlike ignorance. Yet, from what John Snow said, it seems he has been denied even that crumb of comfort. 'It's all there,' I distinctly recall him whispering to me, 'but there's no getting at it.'

Deprived of our memories we are deprived of our very selves. Without our histories we are vacated. We may walk and talk and eat and sleep but, in truth, we are nobody.

I sat here at my bureau for close on an hour with my hot head in my hands. Felt the darkness moving about me. A fearful inner darkness, it was.

※

OCTOBER 17TH

※

The sun was up and out this morning and the whole world looked as sharp as a pin which, one way or another, encouraged a little brightness in myself. Wore my thick beige shirt, poplin waistcoat and Cossack trousers and had a fine breakfast of smoked haddock and eggs, lightly poached. But while cheered by the prospect of the tunnels' christening, found my body still very much at odds with itself and several thundering cups of strong Assam failed to set in motion my morning evacuation.

Asked Clement to round up Grimshaw, a coach and horses and a couple of stable lads then tracked down my new carriage coat and deerstalker. Picked out a yellow scarf along the way.

I now have a choice of four routes to the basement – by which I mean the tunnels – and two dumb waiters besides.

There's the original stone stairwell, via a small doorway beneath the staircase in the Great Hall, then what used to be known as the 'service stairs' which I have had fitted out with new flags and banisters. I have also added a wrought-iron spiral stairwell which leads from a door by my bedroom fireplace directly down to the tunnels (and may be picked up by a tidy little door set into the panelling of the dining room) and, finally, a narrow passageway which wanders all about the house before descending by several flights of stone steps (and whose construction, I might add, caused a great number of complaints from all quarters of the house, to do with dust and general disturbance).

This morning I chose the spiral stairs, so my descent was accompanied by the clanking of my boots on the steps, their echo ringing eerily back at me from high above and far below. The coldness of the tunnels first introduced itself at my ankles then crept slowly up me, in the same way a bather's body is coldly embraced by the sea. As requested, the gas jets in the lower reaches of the house had all been lit. I passed the entrance to the original monastery passages (all gated and bolted now), the underground chapel and the family vaults and came out, at last, behind the landing stage where Clement and two stable lads waited, with their shadows splashing on the walls behind them like great inky cloaks.

I am proud to say that, broadly speaking, the design for the new tunnels was very much my own but put in place, of course, by the ingenuity of Mr Bird and his men. An inner circle, roughly two hundred yards in circumference, links the entrances to all eight tunnels and the passages which lead off to the stables and so forth. The stairways come out at a grotto by the staging platform and it was here that the four of us gathered, to wait for Mr Grimshaw and his carriage.

Standing around on that stone landing stage was a rather chilly affair, due in part to the cold earth all around us but also from the stiff breezes which came sweeping down the tunnels – a problem I admit I had not foreseen. But, looking down one of them, I was pleased to see how the skylights lit the way admirably and made it appear altogether quite inviting. I reckoned that only on the most overcast days would it be necessary to light the gas jets much before dusk. To my eye, the tunnel nearest us looked like the inside of a flute, with the skylights representing the finger holes where columns of daylight streamed through. So it was quite fitting that as we stood there in our quiet little gang, different-pitched whistles slowly made themselves known. Very weird to hear them washing in from the tunnels and stairwells and have them mingle around our feet.

Asked Clement if he would mind fetching me an extra frock coat and my Inverness cape as the carriage coat would clearly not suffice, and suggested he perhaps go up in one of the dumb waiters, to give it a try-out. He was most reluctant, worrying I think that his being so large might cause the lift to fall, but I assured him that it was built with a mind to taking a load many times his weight and, after some concerted cajoling from myself and the stable lads, he rather timidly squeezed himself into its compact little compartment. What an excellent sport! The lads took turns pulling on the rope and the wooden box in which he huddled slowly ascended into the belly of the house. I stuck my head out into the shaft and kept up a reassuring conversation with him which bounced all about the place. 'I shall keep my head in the shaft, so that if you fall we shall both of us be killed. How's that, Clement?' I called.

The lifts were originally installed to save lugging baggage up and down the stairs, but I see now how they might prove to be a source of entertainment in themselves.

Clement had returned (by the stairs, I might add) and we

were all beginning to wonder what was up with Grimshaw when a distant rumble came at us down the inner circle which started up reverberations down all the other passageways. Seconds later, the horses and carriage came crashing round the corner with Grimshaw, very flustered, clinging to the reins. It was a long while after the carriage had ground to a halt that its clattering quit swimming up and down the place and the dust settled to reveal Grimshaw, who was apologizing most profusely, saying how he had got himself first a little confused and then hopelessly lost. He promised to properly acquaint himself with all the turnings and linking passages at the soonest opportunity. Then Clement and I clambered in and made ourselves comfortable and I tied my deerstalker firmly under my chin.

Grimshaw, high up on his driver's seat, pulled back his little hatch and presented his head to us upside-down and framed by his boots, saying, 'First off, Your Grace. You're quite sure there's no danger of me banging my head on owt?'

I told him there was not. He nodded gravely at us, obviously not the least bit convinced. He then asked, 'Which tunnel is it I am to take, Your Grace?'

I gave it a little thought. 'North,' I announced. 'North towards the Pole ... And with a little spice, if you don't mind.'

Grimshaw nodded again, still grim and upside-down, then closed his little hatch. I heard him let out a sigh as he settled himself in his seat. Then, with a crack of the whip and a call of, 'Gee-up, there ... I say, gee-up,' we moved off, past the stable lads who were waving their caps in the air. They appeared to be heartily cheering us – I can only assume so for I could not hear a thing above the wheels and the hoofs. I had no inkling there would be such an intense din and might have considered plugging my ears with my handkerchief had I not been so busy shouting up at Grimshaw, who had missed the North tunnel entrance, forcing us to take an extra run of the inner circle and pick it out next time round.

When we raced past the stable lads again they looked mightily confused but, to their credit, raised their caps a second time and set up another bout of muted cheering. Then, at last, Grimshaw found the right entrance (I made a mental note to have each one clearly signposted) and we went haring down the North tunnel with the horses champing at the bit.

All morning we raced up and down the tunnels – first North, then North-east and so on. The noise was unimaginable; like shouting down a well. The skylights flew by at regular intervals, which had the effect of a constantly flashing light. This initially proved a little sickening, along with the almighty noise, but, in time, became quite exhilarating with the smell of the heaving horses and Grimshaw's exhortations adding to the drama.

With my precious pocket watch I timed the duration of each journey (both away from the house and returning, as some of the tunnels are on a gradient). I had brought with me a notebook and recorded all my findings, at both *trot* and *full gallop*.

By midmorning we were in need of a change of horses and the lads took the first two off to give them a brushing down and soon after I sent a message to Mrs Pledger asking her to put together some refreshment, which we picked up when we next went by the landing stage and ate as we went along.

I was disturbed to hear from Grimshaw how as we emerged from the tunnels into the light the horses were sometimes dazzled, but it was his opinion that blinkers would remedy the problem. I made a note of this in my book.

Both Mr Pyke and Mr Harris stood to attention by their

respective lodges and were plainly most intrigued, so I invited them to join us for a trip to the house and back. Mr Harris (one of our best dog men) seemed to enjoy himself but Mr Pyke needed more encouragement to come along and looked decidedly shaky when we dropped him off.

From the expression on the faces of the stable lads I saw that they had lost a good deal of their punch and each time we passed them I noted how it had waned a little more. So, as a treat, I allowed them a ride on the luggage shelf which cheered them up no end and by the time we were done they were grinning at each other like a pair of gormless fools.

It was close to two o'clock when I finally drew proceedings to a close. A sticky heat filled the tunnels. We had exhausted three sets of horses and Mr Grimshaw needed some help getting down from his seat. Gave him the rest of the day off and had the young lads lead the carriage away. My coats were powdered all over with dust and my ears rang like church bells.

As Clement and I made our way towards the spiral stairwell and passed the door to the underground chapel my eyes lit upon a rather unusual carving. One I felt sure I had not seen before. The design could not have been simpler: on a circle of stone, six inches wide, an infant's face stared out through a screen of grasses or reeds. I stared back at him. Something about his gaze deeply disturbed me, though I couldn't say just what.

I quizzed Clement about it but he claimed to have no more knowledge of it than I did myself. Wondered if Bowen might have knocked it up, though I must say it did not look new, just unfamiliar. I found myself coming over a little sick.

This behaviour, this constant vacillation of mood, is becoming something of a habit with me. One minute I am triumphing over a depressive fit and feeling positively tip-top.

The next, for no good reason, I feel myself start to sink again and spend the rest of the day mooning all about the place.

*

I have nothing but admiration for the engineers of this world. Scientists, mechanics, inventors ... I take my hat off to them all. How I envy their ability to comprehend how a thing is put together without their head getting in the way. To be able to fix that which was broken, to make the apparently irreparable sound again. I should very much like to have that knack.

But I'm afraid such a faculty is something one is blessed with either at birth or not at all and however one might try quantifying it there is no doubt I have always been short on the stuff. At age ten I was still having difficulty tying my bootlaces, and even now the whole fiddly business can get me in a state. Anything remotely technical, such as distinguishing right from left, has, for me, always necessitated a great deal of mental stress and strain, so that my first tutor, a Mr Cocker, perhaps misinterpreting these inadequacies as slovenliness and, worse, something of a challenge, took it upon himself to set me straight. Every day for a whole month a piece of paper was tied with string to each of my wrists – one with the letter R on it for right, the other with L for left. But if he had asked me I could have told him how they were helping me not a jot and at the end of each day when they were taken off I was as lost as when I'd begun. They only made me feel very foolish and tended to get in my soup until, at last, Mr Cocker threw his hands in the air, made a strange sound through his nose and admitted defeat. I remember very well my holding my hands out like a chained prisoner about to be granted his liberty. It was a relief of no small magnitude for I was still spending half an hour every morning guessing which piece of paper went on which wrist.

But I am not happy in my ignorance. Far from it. I like to

think I have the same curiosity as the chemist or the architect; it is simply their talent I lack. Believe me when I say that my backwardness has never stopped me taking things apart, merely putting them back together again.

*

Since I was a boy I have periodically suffered from the irrational fear that I am on the verge of fatal collapse. I think I am right in saying it is my mind which is chiefly to blame. Left to its own devices my body appears to function reasonably well, requiring feeding and watering and a good deal of rest but being for the most part a quite contented and smooth-running apparatus. Yet the moment I begin considering some particular pump or piston – the lungs being a prime example – an alarum goes off inside me and suddenly all hell is let loose.

My mind panics, tries to wrest from my body the breathing controls and before long I am in a fit of difficulty, not knowing whether to breathe out or in. And once I am started I find there is no way back. All that's left is to try and get me to think of something else. So, to distract myself, I might have to recite poetry or skip madly around the room.

But are we not all of us ignoramuses when it comes to our own bodyworks? I somehow doubt that even those who claim to understand every fleshy connection – every last valve and gland – actually regard themselves with such sophistication as they go about their day. For it is my opinion that we all tend to rely upon the simplest mind-pictures which represent for us the functions of our body's various parts. For example, I have one for my lungs, which is as follows . . .

Each lung is in fact a tiny inverted tree with the base of the trunk coming out at my throat. When I breathe in, leaves appear on the branches. When I exhale, the leaves disappear.

41

Thus, the seasons are constantly shifting in my ribcage. They come around every second or two. If I am to stay alive it is vitally important that these little trees do not stay barren for long.

I believe I first conjured up this image when I was still quite small but must have since spent several hundred hours of my life (including a good many as an adult) endeavouring to keep my lung-trees sufficiently leafy. As an infant I would often lie in bed too terrified to fall asleep lest my body forget to keep me breathing through the long dark night ahead.

I would claim that, in fact, the majority of us know next to nothing about our bodies and how they really work. Yet surely such information is essential; should be available to us without having to read it in books. When we are delivered into this world the very least we might expect is to come complete with a comprehensive manual to ourselves.

'Why no manual?'

That is my plea.

'Why no instructions?'

Mr Bowen's Account

My work for His Grace was my first proper job after finishing my apprenticeship so, as you can imagine, I was altogether very pleased with myself and walked about the place with a few inches added to my stride. I was on the estate about six months in all. Was paid and treated very well. I had a room in the servants' quarters and it was left to me to get myself up and out first thing. I would take with me a little bread and cheese wrapped in linen, which I would eat while I was on the job, and my dinner would be keeping warm for me in the kitchens when I came in around seven or eight.

After meeting with His Grace a time or two I was left very much to myself. I'd go to him with my designs and he might sometimes slip me one or two sketches of his own. Odd little drawings, they were, on bits of paper. I would pin them on my workshop wall. But His Grace was not much of a draughtsman, so I would take care to listen to his ideas and work from what he said. Once in a while he might drop by to see how I was faring but on the whole he left me alone.

I was given some of the finishing touches to do on the tunnels, such as the gateposts and so forth. Well, I assumed that what would be required would be an obelisk or a Grecian urn. The usual sort of thing. But when I was ready to get on with them and went to ask His Grace what he had in mind, he asked me how I felt about onions. Onions about a foot and a half wide.

Well, it took me a while to come up with an onion we both

felt happy about. They caused me a bit of a headache. To be honest, I was worried I might become something of a laughing-stock. What I eventually came up with was something quite similar to a traditional stone orb, but fatter in the middle and with a stalk coming out the top. But there was no mistaking it for anything else – it was an onion from top to toe. His Grace told me that he thought it was just the job. Once it was erected folk would come up and ask me about it. Most of them thought it first rate. It was my own design, so of course I was very pleased to be asked if I was the onion-man. Quite proud, I was. So we had onions by the lodge at Norton and cauliflowers on the gateposts out at Belph.

My largest undertaking was what the Duke always referred to as 'the Grotto', which was down where all Mr Bird's tunnels came in above the landing platform. Well, I was instructed to cover the ceiling with plaster – easily thirty feet high – then carve out of it the likenesses of various 'natural' things. His Grace gave me a list of suitable subjects for me to bear in mind, such as pineapples, grapes and fish-heads. I remember he asked if I could do a seashell and maybe some barleycorn.

Well, just like the onion and the cauliflower before it, I had no training in such things and I was a little hesitant at the start. But His Grace asked me if I had an imagination and when I replied that I believed I had, he told me I had better get on and make some use of it. I was told I could include more or less anything which took my fancy, just as long as they were 'natural'.

Well, I gave it a go. Did some fruit to start off and then some creatures . . . snakes and snails and so forth . . . and soon found I'd fairly got the hang of it. After a day or two I didn't worry at all. A bird's head here, an acorn there. Perhaps a fern leaf alongside a feather.

In the evenings I would occasionally nip out for a drink –

the Vault in Whitwell or the old Bird's Nest – and, of course, I would come across all the stories about the Duke which were doing the rounds at the time. As a stranger to the area and with my being a good bit younger than the other drinking men, I sometimes found it hard to go against what they said. If I am honest, I will say that after a couple of jars I found I could spin a tale or two myself. I am most ashamed of that now.

In my last week on the estate I was called in to see His Grace and the first thought I had was that I must have done something wrong. I thought perhaps something I'd said in the pub had got back to him and that I was going to get a dressing down or even dismissed. But he only asked me about a roundel he'd seen by the underground chapel. Wondered if it was anything to do with me. He took me down there and I had a look at it. Very simple it was – just a face peering through a bush. At a guess I'd say fourteenth century, though I'm no historian. Probably put in when the chapel was first built. The stonemasons, of course, wouldn't have shared the beliefs of the monks who paid them so it was maybe just a little pagan symbol which they tucked away. I've heard that they would often do that. At a guess I'd say it was just old Jack in the Green.

From His Grace's Journal

*

What a treat! This morning, as I stared out of the dining room window and wondered what to do with the day, Clement came in with a large tube-like package, bound together with string.

I immediately took control of the situation, saying, 'We are going to need scissors, Clement. Scissors, as quick as you can.'

In a minute we had cut the twine away, removed several square yards of brown paper and were unrolling onto the table the most exquisitely coloured map. Tears welled up in my blinking eyes – such a baby! – so that I worried they might spill onto the map and spoil it. I took out a handkerchief, gave my nose a good blow and tried to pull myself together.

Clement handed me an accompanying note, which read,

My Lord Duke,

Here is the map I once spoke about, rendered by a local surveyor, Mr George Sanderson. Please accept it as a small token of my company's thanks for work so generously commissioned and as a personal gift to mark the end of a most pleasurable stay.

I remain Your Grace's Obedient Servant,
Gordon S. Bird
P.S. I believe it is meant to be hung.

'Mr Bird says it is meant to be hung,' I announced, between gulps. 'We shall need help to hold it up.'

So while Clement went off to drum up some support I took the opportunity of examining the map alone.

Mr Bird and I discovered very early on we shared a passion for cartography. I showed him my modest collection of maps of the North of England and I remember well him mentioning to me a large-scale local map, executed in the shape of a disk. In my usual vague way I promised to make enquiries after it, but never got around to the task. But here I was, years later, standing before the very thing and I was quite overcome with joy. Like most of life's more potent pleasures, it came strangely tinged with melancholy.

I had barely begun taking in all the pinks and greens and blues when Clement returned with a couple of maids who, under his careful instruction, held the thing up so that it could be properly viewed.

Well, the effect was quite staggering. The map is so big that the girls had to stand on chairs. It is easily six foot in diameter. Maybe more.

It is the shape of the map which makes the biggest impression – an apparently perfect circle – so that one is inclined to imagine one stands before a map of the entire world. Here are oranges and purples and yellows, all come together in a beautifully bruised fruit. Yet it is only when one looks a good deal closer and reads the names of the principalities these colours so delicately adorn that one realizes what a very small world this is, with Mansfield as its capital, as if the rest of England has been trimmed away with a palette knife like so much overhanging pastry on an uncooked pie.

Roadways and rivers are clearly visible: the prominent veins of an exerted man. They creep up and down and all about the place, tying the whole peculiar ball together. Every township, village and ox pasture is given its rightful name, every church represented in miniature form, each wood by a caricature plane or oak perching in its own neat pool of shade. The names of each district and county sweep across the map in sizeable script, so that one's heart goes out to those unfortunate enough to live in the shadows of the huge A or O of WARSOP PARISH.

Every gradation is delineated by the bunched scratches of Mr Sanderson's pen. Indeed, the cross-hatching of a sudden incline looks like the grubby thumbprint of the artist himself. It is as if Mr Sanderson has had the pleasure to sit up at God's right hand. To take in the view from our Creator's perspective and sketch it for us mortal men.

But all is not well! On closer inspection, one notes that where many roads come together and many buildings stand the effect is most unwelcoming – like a tumour or a spill of ink. A city of Sheffield's proportions, for example, appears very dark and people-congested; an ugly blockage in the circulation of this little world.

Looking closer still, one sees that, in order to squeeze some peripheral town on to the edge of his map, Mr Sanderson has occasionally lost the circumference's lovely line. Rotherham protrudes from the planet like a boil fit to burst. Bakewell hangs off it like a scab.

So I drew my eyes away from the cankerous towns and cities, to go in search of my own bucolic abode. Whitwell is found easily enough, therefore I must be just a little to the *East*. There is Clumber, so I must have gone too far. I go back – slowly, slowly now. Then, of a sudden – hurrah! – there we are! My house, my lake, my own front drive! Even the ice house is named, and *Greendale* and *The Seven Sisters* – my grand old oaks. This gives me no end of the most profound pleasure. I am located. Verified.

I put my nose right up to my own house, as if I might see me waving from a window. And, no doubt to the great amusement of my young housemaids, I gently plant my forefinger on the map at that very spot.

'I am here,' I say.

*

OCTOBER 27TH

*

Yet another disturbed night's sleep. Woke not knowing where on earth I was. It was as if I had been plucked from sleep's great ocean and flung on some unfamiliar shore.

There is no shortage of fanciful notions which seek to explain the mysteries of sleep. Personally I have always favoured that which proposes that the souls of the sleeping ascend to another plane, so that while our bodies sleep under worldly sheets our spirits play among the stars.

It is my opinion that the finest of threads connects the spirit with the vacated body, the latter acting as an anchor, and that down this line come the vibrations of the spirit's starry gallivanting, which the dormant body perceives as dreams. Thus when we sleep we go kite-flying, yet we are both flyer and the kite.

But if all the world flies kites at night it follows that the sky must be filled with threads. Very dangerous. Question— What happens when two lines become tangled? – for it must be easily done. Might a soul not return down the wrong string by accident and wake to find itself inhabiting a stranger's body? This has concerned me, on and off, for quite a while and was more or less how I felt this morning. It was getting on for lunchtime before I had properly straightened myself out.

This afternoon we took the West tunnel out to Creswell to inspect the damage done by a fire to the cottage of a Mr Kendal, who wandered aimlessly up and down the place in floods of tears, despite my many assurances that everything would be taken care of. I am told he has something to do with the infant school, or the kennels – either way he is lucky to be alive. A dreadful acrid stench still filled the house; every wall and ceiling was blackened by smoke. After five minutes I decided I had seen enough and told Clement to return in the carriage so I might walk back through Tile Kiln and Cow-close Wood.

When a man falls asleep in his armchair with his pipe still lit, the transformation by fire to his surroundings is truly something to behold. Every surface changes texture. Familiar objects – a kettle, a stool, a mirror – are made unrecognizable. But all this is nothing when put alongside the carnage wrought upon woodland by the seasons' change and as I strolled through the estate today I was confronted with destruction of the most comprehensive kind.

The entire scene was drained of colour; every tree and bush quivered leaflessly. The slimmest fraction of the spectrum had been left to them – from an ash-grey to the faintest brown. The rest had been sucked back into the hardening ground or washed away by the rain. The smaller trees stretched out their branches like young beggars, but I could not do a thing for them.

The only life on show was a single rabbit which, sensing my approach, made a mad dash for its burrow. My footsteps produced a painful racket as they came down on the dried leaves and twigs and this crashing was cast back at me by the dumb timber all around. Every tree seemed ... *humiliated*. Hushed and resentful, like a struck child. The only other sound I heard all afternoon was a gun's report (one of my own men, I trust) which twice came up from the Wilderness with the grim finality of a slammed door.

I reckon I am very much like the leafless trees. Autumn scares the life right out of me. Every year I worry I will not survive it, that this may be my last. Sometimes I fear a malevolent hand has cut spring and summer from the calendar and, for a cruel joke, stitched winter straight onto the following autumn. There is never much rest from autumn. Always autumn, it seems.

I must have stopped to catch my breath. I cannot walk as far as I might like these days without the occasional breather which, in company, I attempt to conceal by making a show of taking in the view. Certainly it did not seem to me that I fell asleep but I must have somehow slipped from consciousness for when I came to, slumped on a boulder, the sky had grown quite dark. At first, I felt only a modicum of concern, but when I looked about and found myself deep in the woods with no recollection of how I had got there I suffered the most profound shock. It was as if I had become utterly dislocated from time.

Like my father before me I have suffered from occasional 'absences' – seconds, even minutes when my mind seems to completely switch itself off. In my youth, without the slightest warning, I would become entirely detached from everything going on around me. Friends who witnessed these episodes said only that I seemed to go into a brown study of the deepest introspection. (My father, incidentally, claimed they were the result of a diet lacking iron, which is why he ate so much liver.) So whilst finding myself in such confusion is not entirely new to me I cannot honestly recall being so thoroughly absent and for so long a time. When I came to my throat was dreadfully dry and my whole body was icy-cold.

Getting to my feet cost me a tremendous amount of pain. The blood which had slowed to a near standstill now took to raging round my limbs. A thoroughly unpleasant sensation, which only served to exhaust me more. My feet felt as if they had been filled with twice their proper capacity of blood and might burst at any moment and fill my boots.

The wood was no longer silent. Nearby, an owl hooted in a plaintive tone – perhaps he had stirred me? – and a stiff breeze was intent on rattling the branches of the trees. I had the idea they now crawled with all manner of tiny insects. Night had brought the whole wood to life.

I set off without being at all sure of my bearings. After a few strides a whey-faced moon popped out from behind a tree and followed me along. For a minute or two I was glad of the company – his brightness lit my way. But after turning and watching him keeping up with me a time or two I soon thought I would very much like to be rid of him. The moon is very knowing and he looked down at me as if he understood exactly what I was about. I picked up some speed, but the faster I went the faster he swept through the branches and when I slowed my pace a little he followed suit. 'Damn him!' I thought, 'he will not let me go.' Then, 'If he is going to follow me all the way home I may as well get it over with,' and I broke into a ferocious trot. At some point I think a cloud must have blocked him out and I was able to return at a more civilized pace.

Clement met me on the drive, a lamp illuminating his anxious face. He said nothing, simply wrapped a blanket around my shoulders and escorted me back to the house.

*

Fanny Adelaide had a voice like an angel. When she left the stage after the final curtain she could barely walk for all the bouquets. But when I think of her – and I still think of her all too frequently – it is not her voice that leaps into my mind uninvited, but the neck which gave it life.

She had come up from London on one of her visits and the journey had evidently worn her out for when I returned to the Swan Drawing Room after calling down for tea I found her fast asleep on the chaise. Her gloved hand was tucked under her tilted head, a shoe had slipped from a foot. Her dress swam out around her. Beautifully capsized, she was. Her hair, I recall, was a great labyrinth of stacked curls held together in a manner which was a mystery to me. I watched as she lay there, dozing, breathing through a minutely-opened mouth.

I interpreted her falling asleep as somehow flattering, thinking it showed how safe she felt in my company. So I perched myself on a leather footstool and quietly drank her in. Would have continued to do so had not the jangle of tea things in the hall sent me hurrying out to head off the maid.

But as I gently set the tray down she came to, and in an instant had decided she had no stomach for tea after all, but wished to take a turn around the gardens and breathe in some country air. So I led her out through the French windows and we did a tour of the flower beds and the lawns. And though she contributed very little to the conversation I was pleased just to have her at my side with her hand resting on my arm.

I wanted to show off every corner of the gardens. I started talking spiritedly about a dozen different things – a gabbling fool, I was. But under a cherry blossom she stopped, turned and raised a finger to my lips. Cocked her head as if she had picked out some exotic birdsong, when all I heard were my own foolish words still rushing round my head. Then she looked me in the eyes and said she had given proper consideration to my proposal and that now it was her turn to speak.

O, I would have given anything. Anything. I would have died for her.

When she had finished, she slipped a hand inside her purse, removed a fancy box and held it out to me. I was not to open it until she had gone, she said. She caught the next train back to London. Left me standing there in the gardens, all tangled up and undone.

The following year she married her agent, Peter Nicolson,

and retired from the stage for good. They had two children, George and Charles, who, by all accounts, were as beautiful and intelligent as one could wish for and very well behaved. Every morning the whole family climbed up Parliament Hill. Then, a week after her thirtieth birthday, she ate a piece of fish which she thought did not agree with her and by the following day she was dead. She was buried in Highgate Cemetery. It was in the newspapers, but I did not attend.

The case she presented to me under the cherry blossom contained a gold timepiece. An old-fashioned Hobson and Burroughs fob watch. In its lid a delicately scrolled inscription declared her lasting affection for me.

I have opened up that watch ten thousand times. On its face I have seen countless New Years come about; each one, it seems, in less company and to fewer whistles and cheers. Even now I must open it up twenty or thirty times each day, to count the hours until the next meal or fresh pot of tea. Ten days ago I used it to time our carriage as Clement and I raced up and down my tunnels. But what that watch has measured most precisely is the unwinding of the slow decades since Fanny Adelaide refused my hand in marriage and was laid in the ground by a bad piece of fish.

It is a beautiful watch, and perhaps ironic that such a fine example of craftsmanship should sit in my waistcoat pocket and be a neighbour to my heart which, being merely human, has functioned so poorly since the two were introduced.

*

OCTOBER 28TH

*

Last night I had my first sound night's sleep in a fortnight. I drifted happily in the ether until I was woke by the crackle of the fire. Clement is a wizard with a few twists of paper and the odd dry stick and his broad back was still bent over the hearth when I opened up my eyes. The firelight gave the room a rosy glow which helped chase off some of the chill I acquired from my spell in the woods. Clement strolled purposefully from the room and while I coaxed myself closer towards consciousness the fire's crackle was joined by the gush and splutter of hot water from my bathroom next door. Then Clement re-entered very grandly in his own small cloud of steam, which slowly evaporated about him as he swept over towards my wardrobe. (He's as big as a bear, is Clement, but his step is as light as a kitten's.)

My dressing gown was held open for me and as I snaked my arms into the sleeves' deep recesses I became aware of the extent to which my body ached. Those lost hours spent crouched on the boulder last night appear to have left their mark.

I followed Clement into the bathroom like a faithful old dog. Picked up a hand mirror from a dressing table and found a wicker chair while I waited for my bath.

I should know better than rest a mirror in my lap. It makes the bags under my eyes look like pastries and my face-flesh hang down all over the show. But it is quite likely that this morning a mirror from any angle would have returned an equally awful aspect. So, doing my best to ignore the general prospect of collapse and decay, I concentrated my efforts on those corners of my head where a little repairwork might still do some good.

With nail scissors I carefully clipped at my nostril hairs. Ditto, eyebrows. Then hacked back the bracken sprouting from my ears – my ears, for pity's sake! – and which make them look more like the verdant openings to forgotten caves than the ears of a civilized man. The hairs from all three regions of my head look surprisingly similar – all are dark and disturbingly thick. All grow in a most anarchic manner and at a tremendous rate. I am sure if I did not keep at them with the scissors I should one day look in the mirror and see a wildman staring back.

Just as there is an art to starting a fire, so there is an art to running a bath, and it would perhaps be too much to hope that everyone could master it. Some years ago, when Clement's sister was poorly and he took a week's leave to look after her, Mrs Pledger had one of her girls take over the running of my baths. To be fair, her first effort was not so bad – a little too quickly run and not properly stirred up but, all in all, a not altogether unpleasant experience. Her second attempt, however, was a disaster. An insult to bath and bather alike. It seemed she'd put the hot and cold in back to front and at completely the wrong speed. The whole thing was utterly ruined and had to be thrown away. I sent her back to the kitchens, post-haste, to spoil the potatoes no doubt, and for the rest of the week had to wrestle with the damned taps myself.

Clement cleared his throat. My bath was ready. I blew the trimmings off the mirror and, with my hand clamped on Clement's forearm for support, got first one foot then the other up and into the bath, with my gown and nightshirt still on. Stood there until I was sure I had my footing, then let Clement carefully lift my clothes over my head (which he did with his usual politely-averted gaze, as if he had just that moment noticed a speck of dust on the shoulder of his jacket and was considering how best to get shut of it). Then I gingerly lowered my old bones into the water.

Something is certainly up inside of me. I am in no doubt about that. Organs which, only a month ago, pushed and pulled in a businesslike manner seem to have slowed their undulations to a near halt. But as the hot water crept over my goosepimpled flesh and searched out armpits and frozen toes

I felt that at least some vital heat was being restored. I let myself slide slowly down into the bath until the tip of my beard dipped into the water like some riverside bush, wondering how on earth mankind ever managed to properly relax before hot water was invented. (Apparently, in his declining years, Napoleon rarely left his bath. And the Minoans, I have heard, were so fond of theirs they would often be buried in them.)

As I say, Clement is a Master Bath-Runner and likes to give every bath its own unique character – usually a combination of depth and temperature along with other, less easily identifiable qualities – in order to satisfy what he reckons to be my most pressing needs. I am never consulted on the matter; I leave it entirely up to him. But when a bath is in the offing I sometimes feel his big brown eyes looking me over as he makes his calculations.

This one was hot and deep and soapy. My head lay in a high collar of suds. My kneecaps remained an inch or two clear of the water and were soon the only part of me not turned an impressive lobster-red. My ribcage is like a scrubbing board and as it rose and fell the bathwater crept up and down it like the ebb and flow of rapid tides. As I lay there I wondered if the great to-ing and fro-ing of the world's oceans might not, in fact, be the result of the swelling and shrinking of continents instead of some weird relationship between the sea and a distant moon. It was very much an idle theory, weakly held, and in a minute had drifted off, along with all other coherent thoughts.

This was one of Clement's deeper varieties and the water came right up to the overflow beneath the bold brass taps. As I sank deeper into the suds I set in motion a small wave of water which momentarily covered the overflow's circled sieve before returning up the bath. Then, as the water level gradually resettled, I could clearly hear the gargle of the released water as it went racing down the pipe.

Somewhere above me I heard the distant creaks and wheezes of the hot-water tank restoring itself. A minute later, the turning of a tap somewhere else in the house – the kitchen, perhaps – sent a new chorus of whines and screeches juddering up and down the pipes. I listened most intently, picking out ever-more subtle sounds, until at last I began to see myself as a conductor in charge of an orchestra whose concerts consisted of nothing but watery whistles and groans. I lay there quietly contemplating all the pipes in the house – hidden beneath the floorboards, winding in the walls – and found myself strangely cheered by them. I thought of the fountains out in the gardens and their own small water systems. I thought of all the guttering and the miles of drainpipes. The water closet's violent flush. And for a moment I felt that by simply lying there in my warm bathwater I was part of the house's complex circulation which, despite its whole range of rattles and shudders, continued to function in a most admirable way.

I was still lying in this happy stupor when I heard a tap-tap-tapping come down the corridor. I recognized it straight away as the footfalls of some long-lost loved one – of some errant friend. Emotions which had lain dormant for many years rose up in me, filled me and I was altogether very glad. The footsteps came closer and closer and with each one I became gladder still. Then they were right outside the bathroom door and on the verge of entering. With a full heart I waited, breathless, but they simply would not come in. They fell insistently – tap . . . tap . . . tap . . .

'Open the door,' I think I said.

I opened my eyes and watched as the footsteps slowly transformed themselves into the sound of a dripping tap. As each drop hit the water it rang out, and sent a series of ripples sweeping across the surface. I clambered from the bath, still groggy, and all but threw myself at the door, but before my

hand had even reached the handle I knew I would find
nobody there.

Returned to my bath and sat stewing in it for quite a
while, tearful at my failure to be reunited with the owner of
the footsteps, yet curious to know whose they might have
been.

*

November 2nd

*

All morning we rolled up and down the tunnels, checking no
birds had got in. Went down one after another until I was
absolutely sure. Had a fine jugged hare for lunch.

Following my recent disappearance, Clement insists I do
not wander too far from the house, so this afternoon I took a
gentle stroll out to Norton village and had a scout around.
Called in on Miss Whittle at the Post Office and told her all
about the jugged hare. We exchanged our views on various
broths and sauces until another customer interrupted us and
I set off home again.

The climate of late has been not the least bit kind so I was
all wrapped around with scarves. Had on my famous beaver,
two frock coats and carried a third one over my arm, so I was
a little put out when I came across two infants playing on the
common in nothing but their shorts and vests.

I stood at a discreet distance, trying to make sense of their
game, which appeared to involve a great deal of running and
shouting and the occasional violent shove, but after two
minutes' intense observation any rule or clear objective had
still to make itself known to me. The whole thing seemed
utterly lawless, but the two boys kept relentlessly at it and

would have probably gone on all day had one of them not spotted me as I attempted to sneak by.

The other lad continued running and shouting until he became aware that the game had been held up. Then both the boys simply stood and stared at me, their mouths hanging slightly ajar. Their play, with all its tupping and skipping, had made me think of mountain goats, so I greeted them with a hearty,

'Hallo, young goats,' which was met with a stony silence. The young goats continued to stare.

One was much larger than the other but it was his little friend who finally spoke up. He had recognized me, apparently, and bade me a very good day, so I bade him a very good day in return. He then asked me what it was I had on my head and when I introduced it as my beaver their eyes fairly lit up. The larger and quieter of the two asked me how I had caught it and I explained that I had not been present and therefore could not say for sure, but supposed that most likely it was caught with a trap.

The three of us then proceeded to have the most stimulating conversation, in which I was quizzed with disarming ingenuousness on my appearance, wealth and newly completed tunnels. The smaller boy earnestly informed me how it was his intention to one day own a beaver very much like mine and we soon found ourselves agreeing on the many virtues of tunnels and beaver hats.

As we chatted the boys became a good deal more relaxed and did not stand so rigidly. The quieter of the two showed me a trick with a piece of string and the other tried to teach me how to whistle by inserting my forefingers in my mouth. At last I got round to the game I had just seen them playing and asked what the rules of it were. Well, they looked at one another, quite baffled, standing there in their tatty vests and shorts, and the small boy looked up at me and said, 'It wasn't the kind of game which has rules, sir.'

Feeling altogether old and foolish, I thanked them for a most pleasant conversation and said that I must be getting along, else my valet would start worrying. They both nodded, as if they too had trouble with worried valets, and I gave them each a penny and a pat on the head.

I was a hundred yards down the road when I thought to myself, 'How hot their little heads were.' If an adult's head were half as hot, he'd be put to bed and a doctor called for straight away. I turned to find them already fully re-immersed in their unruly game and for a second I stood there and thought how like little furnaces children are. Little engines – that's how one might see them – with their own enviable reservoirs of power.

This got me thinking about how, sometime last year, as I was walking along the Cow-close path I found a dead sparrow lying on the ground. It appeared not to have a mark on it, so there was no knowing how it might have died. I picked up the motionless creature and held it in my hand, half expecting it to suddenly revive itself and fly off in a flurry. 'How little a sparrow weighs,' I remarked to myself at the time, and, 'How unconvincingly dead it seems.'

But I knew in my heart that it was indeed dead, for it felt cold in the palm of my hand. Its tiny feathers were finely frosted and its colour was all gone. I thought at the time how all creatures are just vessels of heat and how this one's small quota had been used up or had somehow leaked away.

So, perhaps every creature carries inside it a living flame – a modest candlepower. If, for some reason, the flame falters the creature's existence is put at risk. But if our inner flame flares up and engulfs us, madness is the result. I think that makes some sense.

But there are so many different creatures in the world –

from flitting insects to great lumbering beasts: it is inconceivable they all possess the same candlepower. It stands to reason that the twitching sparrow lives at a speed wholly different to the worm it drags from the ground, and that the inner flame of the cat which slowly stalks the bird must burn at a rate wholly different again.

Perhaps the variety in speed-of-life from one creature to another is common knowledge and recorded in the great science books. But do they also record the difference in candlepower between the young and old of a single species? For who would deny that a child lives at a rate nothing like that of an old fellow like myself? In a child's eye each day lasts for ever; to an old man the years fly by.

Time's back is bent on the candle flame. For each one of us the sun arcs through the sky at a different speed. For some creatures life must be but a series of shooting suns. Others must have but the one sun which takes a lifetime to rise and fall.

*

November 6th

*

First thing this morning I had a boy run into town with a message for Dr Cox, telling him to come at once. I had woken with an uncomfortable nagging sensation in the small of my back and pain all about my waist. Needed Clement's help just to sit me up in bed.

My belly is quite distended – a most distressing sight. If I were any more distracted I might imagine I was in the latter stages of some unnatural pregnancy.

It was well past lunchtime when Mrs Pledger knocked on my bedroom door. Dr Cox came marching in. He had his 'I am a very busy man' written all over his face. That was clearly what was on his tongue's mind, so I swiftly countered with, 'And I am very sick.'

This knocked the cocky beggar off his perch and before he had hoisted himself back onto it, I followed up with, 'So what are you to do about it?'

He stuffed his hands deep into his trouser pockets and puffed out his waistcoat, as if I might like to admire its buttons. He held his breath for a couple of seconds, then let the air out noisily through his nose.

'Clement tells me you've been getting yourself lost in the woods,' he said.

Clement was noticeable by his absence.

'Something's up with my stomach,' I replied. 'Now get your stethoscope on the job.'

He turned away and trundled over to his little black bag. Opened it up, gazed inside it for a second or two before removing a large, soiled handkerchief and snapping it shut again. He sauntered back over to my bedside, blowing his nose in a series of short blasts, and deposited his vast, tightly-trousered behind on the edge of my bed so that its springs creaked and groaned with the strain.

'Did the scrofula clear up all right?' he asked, a coy little smile playing on his lips.

'Thankfully, it passed of its own accord,' I replied. 'Must have been a mild attack.'

He made a wide-eyed face at me and nodded. 'Very good,' he said, unbuttoning my nightshirt and slipping a freezing hand inside. 'And the lockjaw?'

'I found it eventually eased with time,' I was obliged to concede.

'And the meningitis?'

'That too.'

'I see,' he announced. Then, having warmed his hand on

my chest, he retrieved it and heaved himself off my mattress to leave me bouncing in his wake. He gestured for me to button up my nightshirt, then threw an arm round Mrs Pledger and marched her off to a corner of the room, where the two of them stood in secret conference with their backs towards me – Dr Cox doing a good deal of whispering while Mrs Pledger nodded her head along. At last, Dr Cox sprang out of their little knot. He seemed to be making for the door.

'Is that it?' I shouted at him, exasperated.

'It is, Your Grace,' he said, and was gone.

I was left staring at Mrs Pledger who remembered some soup she had to take care of and scuttled away herself, pulling the door to behind her.

'He didn't even take his hat off!' I cried.

*

Later, when I asked Mrs Pledger about her tête-à-tête with Cox, she said he had offered her no diagnosis and when I asked her what in the world all their muttering and nodding had been about she said he had been telling her how best to stew fruit.

'Stew fruit!' I yelled at the woman. 'A man lies on his death-bed and the doctor gives his cook tips on stewing fruit!'

Unfortunately, Mrs Pledger is not the least bit afraid of me. I only wish she was. She squared up her ample shoulders as if contemplating charging at me and knocking me out of my bed.

'He said it will do you good,' she trumpeted and made a grand exit, which involved her slamming the door as she went.

What is the matter with everybody? They keep slamming my bedroom door.

Information is being kept from me. I am being left to die like a dog.

*

Clement poked his head round the door; rather sheepishly, I thought. He had with him some soup in a small tureen. It smelt fair enough but when I'd taken a mouthful of the stuff it was all I could do not to spit it back into the bowl.

'Is there fruit in this soup?' I asked him but he just shrugged his shoulders and spooned up some more.

*

All afternoon I lounged uncomfortably in my bed, bedraggled, like a shipwrecked sailor on his raft. Memories of childhood illnesses came back to me – those unending days of feverish tedium. I remember a stuffed bear which I clung to throughout one particular sickly bout. When, at last, I began to improve a little he was taken from me and put on the fire. Mother reckoned he was full of germs. Quite naturally I assumed that he had caught these germs from me and I was riddled with guilt for weeks afterwards. How many days of my childhood did I spend in a bedroom with the curtains closed, I wonder? *Poorly* ... the very word fills the room with its sickly-sweet smell.

The sheets made me sweat which made me restless. They got all tied up in my feet. A crumb somehow found its way in to me and I simply had to get it out. It was trying to penetrate my very skin. Neither properly awake nor properly asleep I lumbered through the day in an irritable stupor. Once in a while I would stir, sit up and glance under my nightshirt but the sight of my swollen belly did nothing but make me feel worse.

*

I don't mind admitting that after this morning's fiasco with that blasted Cox I feel some essential trust between doctor and patient has been broken beyond repair. Traditionally, when one feels ill one consults a doctor who identifies what is wrong. Isn't that the way it goes? When the doctor gives a name to one's previously nameless malaise is that not the first step towards recovery? The doctor informs the patient that he is right to say he is sick. The problem is located, some term or title dispensed (*You have a chill, sir*, for instance or, *I believe you have broke your toe*), then one has something to hold on to and can set about being ill in earnest. The doctor gives permission to act out a specific sick-man's role. It is a small but integral part of the drama of being ill.

But if a fellow's complaints are simply dismissed with a wave of the hand, if he is not even properly consulted, then the whole relationship is in danger of completely falling apart.

I mean to say the man didn't even get out his stethoscope! His bowler stayed on his head like it had been glued there. The only thing he took out of his bag the whole time he was here was a damned handkerchief! How is one supposed to have faith in a man like that?

Well, there's an end to it right there. I am done with the medical world!

*

The only thing to cast some light on an otherwise dismal day was the return of the Sanderson map from Watson and Blakelock, the framers. They've done a first-rate job and I had them hang it on the wall right beside my bed. Now, *there* is order, *there* is sense, *there* is reason. There is observation put to use.

*

I've been blowing down the tube like an elephant. I want some food which tastes of something other than stewed fruit.

*

*

By six o'clock this morning I was wide awake, my stomach filled to bursting with the most incredible ache. It has hardly let up the whole day, like a steel plate strapped tight around me – a cummerbund of pain.

Words fail me. I *hurt*. That is established easily enough. And I can immediately locate the discomfort all around my waist. But in no time at all, it seems, words disappoint me. I may endeavour to dream up more cummerbunds, more steel plate – and knives and spears, come to that – but none conveys the sensation sufficiently to diminish it in any way. Words, evidently, aren't up to sharing pain out. They fall well short of the mark.

Dozed off again and slept fitfully until around midday. Blew down to Mrs Pledger for some tea with honey and asked her to bring up a quantity of hot towels. These I placed across my distended belly and they gave me some small relief.

For my distraction and entertainment this afternoon kind Clement rounded up various members of staff to play a game of Association football. He has heard that Worksop have started up a team and thinks it might be an idea for the estate to do the same. The lawns were nowhere near long enough so they were obliged to use the cricket pitch. Unfortunately, it is several hundred yards from the house and as I had no intention of venturing out in my present state it was through the cold lens of a telescope that I watched my cooks and keepers and stable lads congregating for the match.

They were quite a collection of shapes and sizes, I must say, and practised kicking the leather ball between them with tremendous apathy, managing to waste a further five minutes arguing over how they were to divide themselves into two teams. But once these shenanigans were finally settled and the ball had been passed around for inspection they began stretching and warming up a little more earnestly. Makeshift goals were marked out on the ground with piles of discarded jackets and one forlorn chap from each team delegated to stand in between them as last defence. Then, when Clement, who was umpiring the match, peeped on his whistle and the football was finally placed and kicked, every man – about sixteen in all – set upon it like a pack of wolves.

They ran from one end of the pitch to the other. They ran in one great screaming and kicking mob, while I surveyed the whole bloody battle through my telescope, like a general up on a hill.

After ten minutes or so the older men had grown tired of running around and tried to compensate by resting strategically about the field, so that if a colleague happened to win possession of the ball they shouted that they should kick it over into their acre of space. Thus the game was gradually transformed from a scene of outright pandemonium to one involving at least a modicum of skill, as members of each team attempted to pass the ball without the intervention of their counterparts. As time went by and weariness took a firmer hold it became apparent which of the men had some talent and which of the men had none. Once or twice some unspoken manoeuvre would develop between fellow players and a pleasing piece of kick-about would result. Lobbed balls and passes wove cat's cradles. Angles slowly unfolded and were a minor joy to behold.

Keeping my telescope firmly on the action, I began to anticipate possible feints and runs from my vantage point. Several times I was obliged to shout out some advice, little minding that none of the footballers were likely to hear. At some point, the leather ball was kicked high into the air and the game slipped briefly into limbo as one brave young gardener positioned himself right under it so that his head would interrupt its descent. But with the ball having gone so far up in the first place it picked up a good deal of velocity on its way back down and when it finally made contact with the gardener's head he was knocked to the ground in a crumpled heap. He seemed about to change his mind at the very last moment. But by then it was too late. The other players all flinched in horror and a great chorus of 'Oh' went up as he was felled. Needless to say, the lad's foolishness was well heeded and after he had been carted off the field there were no more acrobatics of that sort.

All in all, though, the ball was given a sound kicking and by the time the last man had run himself into the ground and a truce had been agreed, everyone looked very proud of the fact that they had covered themselves from head to foot in mud. Even as a spectator I found it a pleasant way to waste an hour, although I can't say I remember the score.

When they had all trooped off to wash and have their lunch I took to wondering about the young boy who was hit on the head with the ball. I wondered what particular pain he suffered, what sensations currently addled his mind. But, try as I might, I was forced to acknowledge that I could not summon them up. A ball on the head, that's a nasty thing. I had no trouble picturing him but whichever way I came at it could not quite manage to climb into his boots. Perhaps I had enough on my plate with my own discomfort – mine is certainly much more vivid and real to me. His fellow-gardeners had probably dumped the chap in some darkened room to recuperate. That is usually the way. It was with a certain glumness that I concluded that all pain-sufferers are doomed to be shut away in quiet, shadowy places and that each one of us must suffer our pain alone.

*

Spent the rest of the day in near agony, rifling through an old medical dictionary after a label for my malady. At first I had suspected appendicitis and spleen trouble later on, but under closer examination both hypotheses proved somewhat unsustainable. Then, around five o'clock when I was deep into the dictionary and the sun had all but given up on the day, my finger came to rest by some odd-looking entry and the next moment I was exclaiming a small 'Eureka!' to myself.

Under *Stones* I found a whole range of fascinating information. It appears that given half a chance, these stones will make a home for themselves in just about any organ in the body of the unsuspecting man. And when I came down to *Stones, of the kidney* I saw at once what Dr Cox had chosen to ignore. My symptoms correspond exactly with those in the medical book. 'A band of pain extending from the base of the spinal column, towards the groin' . . . and so forth. Well, that is me all over. My symptoms were tailor-made for 'kidney stones'.

But my joy very soon grew muted, after a moment's reflection made me realize that these stones would likely require surgery of some sort. For once a stone gets itself inside a man, one cannot imagine it being easily shaken out. Presumably big knives would be necessary and my belly would need completely opening up.

Question – How did these stones get inside of me to begin with? In my bread? In my soup?

Whichever way they got in, the dictionary seemed to suggest that, by now, they had most likely set off on a journey through my insides, which is apparently what causes the pain. I pictured great boulders . . . stationary at first . . . then slowly starting to roll . . . and gathering some unstoppable speed as they went along.

They made a terrible rumbling. I lay there listening for a full hour, not knowing what to do.

✳

When I woke I was all in a lather, having dreamed how a tiny carriage had got inside me and how its progress through my personal tunnels was making my stomach ache. I was, if I remember rightly, the man in the carriage as well as the man whose innards I journeyed through.

It was seven o'clock when Clement brought me some fruity-tasting game pie. I insisted he check no carriages were missing and that none of the tunnels were in use.

Tomorrow I will get me another doctor. Not some ape in a waistcoat, but one who really knows his stuff. I will get me a qualified surgeon and tell him about the stones.

✳

NOVEMBER 9TH

✳

My head is a barometer. Has been all my life. And though blood, not mercury, creeps through my veins and my face lacks a needle to point at *Fair* or *Change* the anticipation of the shifts in climate are registered there just the same. So when I was woken last night in the pitch-dark by a sickening pressure behind the eyes and my scalp a nest of shooting pains I knew before I was properly conscious that some tempest was on its way. If there had been a hint of daylight I could have looked out of the window, consulted the barometer tower and had my findings verified. But I was marooned in the depths of night-time and everything was as black as could be.

Pains in my head I am used to – I have twinges every week

or two – but these were not the familiar forebodings of a downpour or the premonition of a blustery day. A storm of colossal proportions was coming, for my head felt completely pumped full of air and my skull was about ready to crack. Yet the discomforts up top were nothing compared with the stresses and strains I was experiencing down below. My belly was so bloated I was having trouble breathing. I was ridden with pain. It had rendered me awake.

I leant out of bed and lit a candle to try and calm me down, but its flame barely dented the dark. It merely slunk back a foot or two and continued to study me. I sat myself up, blinking, in my big four-poster. Looked out from my small corner of candlelight, still reeling from dreams. The shadows swung lazily to and fro as if the whole house pitched in the night, while the pains in my head and stomach squeezed me like a vice.

The bedsheets had fallen from me to reveal a stomach straining at my nightshirt's seams. I stared down at it – at my own unrecognizable stomach. What, in God's name, was I full of? If it were indeed a stone then it was growing at an incredible speed, must now be a good ten inches wide. Fearfully, I slipped my fingers under my nightshirt and peeled it back over my spherical belly. The flesh, usually slack, was now tight as a drum. My belly button, an aperture normally capable of swallowing half my thumb, had been forced out into a tight, bulging knot – a wildly staring eye. Some little monster had picked me as its place of refuge. Some evil had made me its home.

The storm kept on advancing. 'God help me,' I heard me say.

The thick curtains at the windows danced a little, twitching in the gusts from the cracks. Outside, a gate rattled madly on its latch, as if the wind shook it with its very own hands.

I thought I heard the creaking of an ancient ship: ropes and timbers straining to hold it all together. An awful chorus of discordant screeching and scraping, it was, before some final coming-apart. But the sound came not from beyond the windows, nor even the bed where I failed to sleep. I was sickened to discover that the sound came from me, and that I was that creaking ship.

Something heavy lurched inside of me. Turned and slid to one side. Whatever creature had recently taken up in me stirred. What was in me had come alive.

A tear crept out from the corner of my eye and hurried down my cheek. Such *pain*! I had never known such pain. The monster inside me forced my legs apart and began to burrow its way out. I grabbed the candle from the bedside table. Held it between my legs and peered into the light. One hand gripped a bedpost behind me while the other tried to keep the candle in place. And the next moment I was seized by the most incredible agony, as if I was being ripped in two. A mountain moved inside me; the first raindrop dashed itself against the window-pane.

A high-pitched rasping noise came out of me, like the tearing of a sail. It caught the candle and transformed itself into a blinding, billowing flame. Purple-blue, it was, and six foot long, lighting up the entire room. The flash came back from the mirrors and bounced from wall to wall and that dreadful noise continued to launch itself from me as I clung to the bedposts with both hands. But just as my own great flame began to dwindle and the pain had begun to abate I became aware of other, new flames in the room. The netting round my bed had been caught up in it and my sheets were all alight.

I leapt from the bed, dancing madly. Tripped and fell. Got to my feet. Tripped again. The flames swept up the muslin with an evil crackle and multiplied themselves.

'Fire!' I shouted, as if to wake me. 'Fire!'

I continued running frantically around the room and caught sight of me in a mirror. A small flame clung to the tail of my nightshirt, like some evil party game. I leapt back, aghast, and when I looked again, saw how the flame had spread; now crept around me in a cruel embrace.

'Fire!' I yelled, louder this time. 'Fire!'

I hopped from one foot to the other, slapping my flaming nightshirt with bare hands. I was like some demented person, like some injured bird. One second the flame went out – O, blessed relief! – the next it had returned. I patted it out at my shoulder only to see it reappear at my waist. I must have put that same flame out a dozen times – I was beating myself like an African drum – until at long last the blasted thing went down and did not come back up and, with a sudden inexplicable charge in my blood, I set about extinguishing those larger, wilder flames which were consuming my aged bed. 'Off my bed!' I shouted at them. It was as if a different part of me took over – a brighter and much braver man. I looked around the room. I could not say what for. Then, in a flash, I had dived under the flaming four-poster and come out with my china pot. Almost full. Excellent. I took aim and threw its contents in an ever-widening arc.

There was a moment when the chaos seemed to hang in the air and wait for instruction. The next moment, all the flames were out.

The room was pitch-black again and suddenly silent. I stood listening, gulping in the smoky air. The door swung open and there was Clement, with his lamp held high. The room slid back into the light. The bedsheets were wet and blackened, the muslin hung in tatters everywhere. A thick pall of smoke crowded the ceiling and huddled over the whole sorry scene. I opened a window to let the smoke out, but the rain and the wind came in instead. A handful of leaves entered, formed themselves into a whirlpool, then skipped like infants around an invisible maypole.

In the long mirror, I caught sight of somebody. An old beggar of a man, he was – all singed and smudged. The charred remains of a nightshirt hung from him and his pale body showed through here and there. I tried to stand a little straighter, but it did no good. Did not improve my opinion of him at all.

Clement looked on from the doorway in his leather slippers and freshly-laundered robe. He had a puzzled expression on his face.

'Gas,' I explained.

*

NOVEMBER 10TH

*

The hairs on my legs are all singed away but my stomach is flat as a pancake. All that talk of stones and my being opened-up like an oyster is done with. I shall sleep in one of the guest rooms until my own is redecorated.

*

The sky had been lardy all day long – or, at least, since I first set eyes on it around eleven o'clock. I had resolved to get out for my constitutional at some point and charge my lungs but kept putting it off in the vain hope of a little sun and by late afternoon the same grey veil hung over the world so I settled on a swift twenty-minute circular, then getting myself back indoors. I took with me one of the stable dogs – a whippet called Julius, who is blind in one eye – and, all things considered, we were having a quite agreeable time, with Julius nearly catching a rabbit and me finding a handsome stick. But as we were heading over towards the Deer Park a mist came up around us with all the opacity of a Turkish bath.

It was thickest on the ground, up to a height of about three feet, so that we were able to wade through it like a shallow milky lake. Very strange and quite intriguing at first, but when the great oak towards which we were headed was swallowed up in the fog I began to find myself somewhat at sea. Poor Julius, with only his one good eye, was in right over his head, so I quickly put a leash on him, for he had got into the habit of standing stock-still and I am quite sure I would have lost him if he hadn't been making such a row with all his whimpering.

We had wandered around the meadows long enough for me to go beyond being merely irritated and to start to feel a little troubled, so I thought it best to stop and make some firm decision about which way to go. In the mist the world had lost all its edges; had become vague and unreliable. I searched for some familiar landmark – a copse or fence or stream – without success. Dusk was beginning to slip in all around us and we were neither of us dressed to spend much time out in the cold, but were in no immediate danger, when the most peculiar thing came to pass. Without warning, I recoiled – quite violently – as if I had been stung by a wasp. It was as if some crumb of a dream stirred in me – the smallest fragment, from long ago. Some nightmare, which had haunted my earliest years; no more than an itch to begin with, but I scratched at it and there developed in me the most convincing scene . . .

I am in a carriage with my mother and father. I am in my travelling clothes. It is an old-style carriage with the hard bench seats. I am very small, I am in my travelling clothes and I can smell the sea.

I can see no others in the carriage. There is no one, I think,

*except Mother, Father and myself. The wheels make a sort of
'whishing' sound; the horses' hoofs are somehow dampened
down. We trundle along quite slowly, and out of the window I
see sand thrown up by the wheels.*

*We are on a beach somewhere. That is it. The wheels are
making a 'whishing' sound for we are travelling across a beach.*

A shout.

I hear a shout . . .

Then I have lost it. I lose the carriage at the shout. I think
too hard on that particular shout and the carriage disappears.

So I try a different sort of remembering. I dwell on the
travelling clothes I wore with such pride. Encourage myself
to recall the smell of the sea and look for the sand as it is
thrown up by the wheels.

And the carriage gradually re-emerges. Comes up slowly
out of the sand. Then . . .

*I am in my travelling clothes. Mother . . . Father . . . the whole
family is here. A shout. The driver shouts a 'Whoa!' to the
horses, and the sand is no longer thrown up by the wheels. The
carriage has come to a standstill, which grieves me, for I was
enjoying watching the sand fly.*

*I hear the driver put the brake on. I become frightened. We
do not move and this frightens me.*

*Father opens a window and leans out. The cold smell of the
sea sweeps in. He has words with the driver, the two of them
conversing in a way which is incomprehensible to me. I am
very young and hear nothing but an exchange between grown
men, so I get to my feet and look out of my own window,
where the sand is no longer thrown up.*

*A thick mist has come up all around us. The mist has
brought us to a halt.*

But here I lose it again. The thing slips from me. It is very
hard to hold. When the mist came up it escaped me. So I tell
myself to think of the voices. Think of Father's voice . . .

78

*And I am back among the voices. There are three of them. My
father's, the driver's and another one. I do not understand
what they are saying but understand that something is wrong.
My father does not get angry. He is quiet and smokes a pipe.
But I hear anger ringing in my father's voice and see anxiety
on my mother's face. These elements . . . along with the mist
and the halting . . . have stirred all the fear up in me.*

  I can feel it brimming.

  In a minute it will fill the whole carriage up . . .

Then the dream stops in its tracks and collapses, and I find
myself back in the Deer Park with Julius, in a lake of mist.

I set off at quite a pace, dragging the half-blind dog behind
me. I worry I may be cut off from the house.

How strange. Not five minutes' walk from my own front
door and I am frightened that it is out of reach.

✳

NOVEMBER 11TH

✳

As a boy I had great difficulty sleeping; was often troubled
by dreams of abandonment. Time and again I would wake
sobbing deep in the night and have to wrench my fearful
body from the bedclothes to go barefoot down the hallways
of the house. For an age, it seemed, I would run the gauntlet
of my own ghouls and demons towards the sanctuary of my
parents' room.

I remember heaving against their heavy door and standing
trembling in my nightshirt on the cold stone floor, only
vaguely able to make them out in the half light, sleeping on
the altar of their bed. Yet something would hold me back
from calling out. Perhaps the fear of stirring up more mon-
sters in the dark. I only know that in those endless moments

79

before I finally summoned up the courage to call I would look upon the bodies of Mother and Father and think to myself, 'Far from me ... far from me ... They are far, far away.'

And it was true, they were indeed far from me; their bodies vacant, minds drifting on a distant plane. Together they had slipped away and lay wrapped in the winding sheets of dreams. Side by side they quietly drifted. Mother and Father at sea in sleep.

And though, in time, they would always groggily return to me, for those moments while I shivered in their doorway I would convince myself that this time they were gone for good. I listened for their breathing, watched to see if their bodies rose and fell, until finally fear itself squeezed out of me a squeak loud enough to bring them home. Then one or the other would turn momentarily from their dreams to say, 'What? ... What is it, son?'

It was a question, of course, I could not properly answer. I might have said I had a stomach-ache or was in need of a glass of water. But now that I am older and wiser and understand myself a little more, I can answer truthfully. 'I woke from a bad dream and ran here for safety,' I should have said, or even, 'I feared the two of you had slipped away.'

*

This morning, as I made my way down to the mausoleum, I remembered a song my father used to sing to me, which was entitled (if my memory serves me right) 'Every Wingèd Thing', or something similar. A curious little piece it is, with each verse given over to a different bird. No real chorus to speak of, but a few bars where one whistles in the manner of each verse's bird. So as I descended the back stairs and felt the temperature around me fall I filled the whole well with echoes of all sort of birdsong and made believe I was the keeper of some underground aviary.

I tend not to visit my parents' tomb more than two or three times a year, but have lately felt a growing need to impart a small prayer in their presence. To make some attempt at communion.

The mausoleum was the first thing I commissioned. I was twenty-two at the time. I see now how I was still too tender in years to properly run a house, but I had no option. Both parents were gone and I was the only child. So I took charge and did my best to run things in a manner worthy of their memory. Got up bright and early, ate my breakfast and spent the day marching manfully about the estate. First thing I did was have a resting place built for them, on the grandest scale. In other words, I jumped right in.

One enters through a huge wooden portal, where two dozen musicians reside – each in his own small compartment. A great gang of frozen troubadours ... pipers piping, harpists plucking and so forth. In the mausoleum proper, six carved pillars support the ceiling, with a stone figure brooding at the base of each one. Beneath one pillar an aged scholar reads from an open book, beneath another a naked boy blows on a conch shell. At first they quite enchanted me, these stone inhabitants of my own small underworld, but when I now go down to lay a wreath or reflect awhile I find myself saddened by the old man studying the same blank page or the melancholy boy still failing to produce a sound from his shell.

The roof is crowded with cherubs and angels. Once, they looked down on my parents' tomb with a benign attitude and generally cast their love around. But no one warned me that the air down there is very damp and that in time it would eat away at the stone. So the cherubs now seem to contemplate only their own disfigurement and the angels are more kin to the gargoyles who gape from the house's guttering.

The trimmings up and down all the archways, so lovingly fashioned by the mason's chisel, were pocked and perforated within the year. A braided maiden's torso remains miraculously untouched, unaged by the atmosphere, but where her slender arms once offered grapes and flowers she now offers nothing but her breasts, has only chipped stumps jutting out below both shoulders. I came down one day to find her stone fruit lying shattered on the ground, as if she had had enough of holding them year in, year out and had cast them down.

Only last year, one of the gryphons which had perched on a ledge by the ceiling with never a murmur of complaint decided to try and leap across the vault to spend some time with his crusty twin. No doubt he had squatted for so long with his pounce all tightly-sprung that he felt he could clear the distance in a single bound but discovered, no doubt, that he was stiff from all that sitting and as things turned out covered hardly any space at all. He simply fell, hit the floor and exploded, trimming the nose from a woman with babe-in-arms on his way down.

It is as if the entire population of that vast damp room has returned from the same strange battlefield. It is like some hospital for fractured statues. Every month I have the floor swept from one end to the other but there is always the crunch of fresh grit underfoot.

This morning I bowed my head by the effigies of Mother and Father, who lie side by side just as they did in their sleep all those years ago. The stone angels continue to crumble all around them, but the figures of my parents remain pristine, carved as they are from Carrara marble and wiped clear of debris by a housemaid every second week. Their features, though beautifully shone, are in fact poor representations. My father looks more concerned in death than he did alive. My mother is almost softened by the stone. The marble has given them a sallow glow, as if they had been cut from candlewax, though there is no denying that my parents' flames went out long ago.

Strange that their faces are now younger than mine. In their absence their only son has grown old. When I think of them I am always a bright young boy. Not the bald and bent old man I have become.

After I had said a prayer for my mother and father, I said a prayer for myself. I find I am troubled by that half-remembered memory, that fragment of some distant dream. Something very far back demands my attention.

I asked my parents, 'What is it I cannot remember?' but received no reply.

They are not telling. Their lips are firmly closed. In the end, of course, they did indeed slip away from me.

*

NOVEMBER 12TH

*

A day spent around the house, recuperating. Still a little pain in my stomach region. I think the skin must have become stretched while accommodating all that mysteriously-accumulated wind. Otherwise I am feeling much improved, if a trifle tired.

Took a mint bath first thing and dressed in velvet trousers and smoking jacket. Wrote a letter of thanks to Miss Whittle at the Norton Post Office from whom I received today a package containing one tin of 'Essence of Beef'. An accompanying note explains how she has heard I have been suffering from 'difficulties with stomach' and that 'the enclosed beef essence', which is entirely new to me, 'is a guaranteed remedy for the unsteady gut'. She goes on to say how it is frequently employed in her household as a pick-me-up and comes with her heartiest recommendation.

An odd little tin, I must say. No more than four-inch square, but quite a weight. On the underside a printed label, announcing...

> This essence consists solely of the juice of the finest beef, extracted by a gentle heat, without the addition of water or of any other substance whatever, by a process first discovered by ourselves in conjunction with a celebrated physician ... best taken cold.

It seems not a single item finds its way onto the chemist's shelf these days without some physician, celebrated or otherwise, putting his name to it (and for a tidy remuneration, no doubt). Every razor blade, bunion cream or hair-restoring device now carries the enthusiastic personal approval of some much-respected Expert. Yet I note how a good many of these revolutionary remedies, hailed on the inside page of magazines one month, are seldom there the next. It would be too much to hope that their manufacturers had gone bankrupt and been hauled up before some humourless judge, so I must assume instead that these fellows are constantly transferring their energies on to other, ever more miraculous cures.

Which is not intended as any slight towards dear Miss Whittle and her tin of essence of beef. She concluded her note by suggesting I take half the tin at lunchtime with a brandy and water, and as I put such store in the woman's opinions I resolved to do just that. The odd whine and whinny still came up from my stomach and it seemed that beef essence might be just the stuff to quieten them down.

Noontime found me in my dining room, looking nervously down at the tin which I had placed on the tablecloth. Its case had moulded on it a strange bas-relief and I mused awhile on how the lid's lovely rounded lip and exotic design might lead one to suppose it contained not beef but some flavoursome Turkish tobacco. In this way I managed to dally for several minutes before getting around to removing the box's lid with my penknife. It was quite a struggle to get the blade into the nick between the lid and base and, having got some purchase, even more of an effort to prise the two apart. The knife seemed to push in vain against a vacuum until at last the lid sprung off with a mighty 'pop'. Beneath was a muslin cover, very sticky to the touch, and, having peeled back its corners, I found beneath a solid leathery block, like a shrunken pocket Bible, set in a thick film of gelatine.

The knife went through the stiff jelly and into the beef substance with no trouble at all, but as soon as the skin of the latter had been punctured the most rancorous smell leapt out. My whole body reeled back as if I had been struck on the chest and it was all I could do to hold the tin away from me while trying to keep my balance and shake some sense back into my head. So pungent and pervasive was the odour, it was as though a living beast had appeared right there in my dining room. I had to wipe my eyes with a handkerchief until I recovered myself sufficiently to open some windows and let some breathable air in.

I was amazed and, quite frankly, more than a little impressed that such a potent odour could be contained in such a tiny tin. I edged my way back up to it and tentatively peeked inside. 'Who on earth would actually eat the stuff?' I thought to myself, giving the beef a little prod with a fork. It had the same texture as the dirt packed around a horse's shoe.

About then I saw me put my head round the door at the Post Office and Miss Whittle asking how her medication had gone down. I have never been much good at lying. She would see right through me at a glance. I would simply have to bypass the Post Office for six months – or a year, maybe. The last thing I would wish to do is hurt Miss W.'s feelings but only a fool of the highest order would insert into his body something which smelt so convincingly of living cow.

It was a good five or ten minutes before I finally lunged at the tin with my little fork and wolfed down a chunk without a single chew. I then grabbed the brandy decanter by its delicate neck and took a couple of swigs, paused, then took a couple more.

I must have sat in the chair for quite a while, waiting to see what happened next. When Mrs Pledger came in to announce lunch I doubt if I had moved a muscle; was not sure if the essence of beef was happy where it was or might suddenly reappear. She stepped into the room, filled her lungs to speak, then paused, with her mouth hanging open. A look of consternation quickly spread across her face, causing both eyebrows to bunch up together above the bridge of her nose. She took a second, more discriminatory sniff of the air, her eyes flashed left and right before settling on me in her most withering glare. Then she span her great weight around and exited, without having uttered a single word.

It is now a good eight hours later. Thankfully I am still alive. And though my stomach is a little queasy and my breath much beefier than before I comfort myself by thinking how I can at least now face Miss Whittle with my conscience clear.

*

NOVEMBER 18TH

*

Afternoon spent catching up on accounts and correspondence. Wrote a note to Dr Cox expressly refusing to pay his bill and telling him, in plain English, how I want nothing more to do with the fellow. Blew down to Clement and had a boy take it round to him straight away.

I learn from his letter this morning that the Reverend Mellor has been excavating the caves at Creswell – something I apparently gave my consent to several years ago – and now seeks my permission to stage a lecture there. Yesterday I received a tearful epistle from one Sarah Swales, appealing for the continued use of a cottage, following her mother's recent death. Gave the Reverend Mellor permission for his lecture (he can stage a circus there if he can fit all the animals in) and dear Sarah, who I am told works out at Norton, appears to have wrongly assumed I am about to throw her out. This is, of course, absolute nonsense and I wrote to assure her of the fact.

Sitting quietly at my bureau, fiddling with papers and pens, brings me no end of pleasure. It is here I fancy some order is restored into my cock-eyed life. I am told it is a Dutch 'cylinder-front' bureau – by now well over a hundred years old – previously belonging to my father and his father before him. In a house packed with ancient furniture which long ago set to sagging and spewing their stuffing all over the floor my bureau is one of the few remaining upright pieces in the place.

Inlays and veneers cover about every inch of it: a kaleido-scope of fine marquetry. Weird birds and butterflies flutter up and down its sides, leafy vines creep across its drawers and dangle down its belly. The whole thing glows warmly from a thousand French polishes – ten thousand! – so that an idle caress evokes an exquisite squeal.

Three solid drawers make up the bulk of it, curving most seductively, as if it they may have melted in the sun. And when the ribbed lid is rolled back, to disappear into its own slim cavity, a heady aroma is released – not just of lovely woods and varnishes but also inks and pencil shavings, old manuscripts and book-binding glues. A neat little row of sentry boxes stands at the back, housing tilted notebooks, ragged letters, miniature ledgers and suchlike. In the middle of them sits a small stack of drawers, six inches wide, where odd bits of wax and blotting paper, nibs and pens are tucked away. These worthless but oft-sought odds and ends are what my paper-sentries so nonchalantly guard.

Golden hinges and handles and brackets are cold to the touch the whole year round. Every corner and moulding and edging is hewn from the finest woods. One chap said he had never seen so much amboyna lavished on a single piece. But when one's eyes have done feasting on the bureau's beauty and one's nose has drawn in the many elements of its complex bouquet, when one's fingers are sure they have found out and fiddled in every last nook and cranny, a dozen secret drawers and compartments will still have eluded one's eager grasp.

For the whole cabinet is riddled with hidey-holes which only give themselves up to the most intimate acquaintance. Pick the right panel to press or the right latch to twist and some swivelling chamber will reveal itself. Pull the top drawer out altogether and another drawer comes into view. A whole series of springs and levers are sunk deep in the carpentry so that a handle tugged here releases a catch over there and what appeared just now to be solid becomes a tiny sliding door. The whole thing is a great hive of recesses which rarely see the light of day. I only wish I had more valuables which needed hiding, with so many little places they could be hid. Some old coins, a few private letters and documents are tucked away here and there, but more for the clandestine fun of it than necessity truly demands.

*

Whilst making this entry I have paused several times to look out on the day. The grounds seem utterly deserted, as if humanity has been erased from the face of the earth. Now that the trees are bare I can see in every direction, but whichever way I look there seems not to be a single soul about. Contrary to popular wisdom, I believe winter actually greases the world's wheels. When the weather is kind we are more inclined to stop and have a chat, for in the summer it is pleasant to let the sun warm us, so we take our time between one thing and the next. But when the weather turns cold and the frost comes we want to be back indoors as quick as we can so we hurry through the landscape, leaving it altogether barren and sad.

*

NOVEMBER 21ST

*

The frequency of my evacuations is returning to normal, though the stools are quite painful to expel. I have heard (or perhaps just imagined) that consumption of eggs may impede one's movements and have a tendency to generally clog up the works. So, no eggs – at least for a fortnight – to see if this does any good. After a breakfast of kippers, toast and marmalade, washed down with a tablespoon of cod-liver oil, I felt nothing if not lubricated. So much so that as I sat there letting it all settle I felt as if I might slip right off my chair.

Though every tree on the estate looks haggard and wretched, the sun shone all around and as the morning unfolded I found myself tempted out of doors. Dressed myself in a lime double-breasted frock coat with fur collar and a knee-length burgundy cape. At the door I picked out a grey, wide-brimmed top hat, a pair of goatskin gloves, cream lambswool scarf and a cane.

I had planned to go as far as Creswell but was not a hundred yards from the house when I felt some sort of fearful shudder pass through me, as if someone had stepped over my grave. For that fraction of a second I felt utterly vulnerable – was almost quaking in my boots. An awful, anxious moment which came from I know not where. Then it was gone. The sky was clear, a slight breeze blew. Most perplexing. Perhaps I have been holed up in the house for too long.

Creswell suddenly seemed a long way away so I changed course and aimed for the lake, thinking I might go on after toward Wallingbrook and march some circulation back into my frame. I reached the lake in a matter of minutes and stood on the old landing bay, looking out over the water which was perfectly solid and still. At that corner of the water's edge stand plenty of horse chestnuts and sweet chestnuts and I bent down to pick up one or two of their rotting leaves. I might have derived some pleasure from their splendid colours if I had not so wished that they were still up in the trees. I held one sad specimen up to the cold sun. 'Did you jump?' I asked him.

His thin veins seemed to map a river's tributaries. I thought to myself, 'You have fingers like me. You are just a flat hand.'

And then, 'A tree is a many-handed man.'

I was dwelling on the precise impracticabilities of one year sticking all the fallen leaves back into the trees when a noise, close by, broke the silence and caused me to look up.

A fish had leapt out of the water. Its silver back caught the sun. But before I had begun to properly grasp the situation it was back in the water and gone. How shockingly odd. The lake, which but a minute before had seemed so dull and lifeless, had thrown a fish up into the air, then swallowed it again. I looked about me, stupidly – as if needing confirmation from someone else. But I was the only witness. The fish had jumped only for me.

From the spot where it had re-entered the water – and a fair-sized fish it was, too – a dozen ripples gently spread across the lake's oily skin. And like those circles rolling over the water and now delicately reaching the shore, the picture of the fish – the sheer surprise of it – kept recurring in my head.

It was a few minutes before I recovered myself and, even then, the splash and glint of the creature would suddenly leap back into my mind. I found myself looking out at the water, half expecting it to jump a second time. But nothing stirred. The lake was flat and solid again.

Several minutes passed, full of the lake's silence and punctuated by my memory of the jumping fish, before I slowly began to make sense of what I had seen. In my pocket I found a scrap of paper and a pencil and noted down my thoughts . . .

> When considered against the backdrop of eternity the period between our birth and death is the shortest of trajectories. From the moment we first feel the smack of life to that moment when we re-enter the deep, black pool is but one breath. We are no sooner aloft than we begin to feel gravity's inevitable pull. We hang there but for a second in all our twisting glory. We feel the air on our bodies, our cold eye snatches at the light. We turn a little, as if on a spit. Then we start to fall.

I concluded with a thick full stop. Listened to my thoughts a second and found myself apparently not the least bit alarmed by what I had just jotted down. On the contrary, I felt quite exhilarated. I returned the paper and pencil to my pocket and set off back home.

*

*

After lunch I became increasingly listless, which is by no means exceptional for me this time of year. I do sometimes wonder if we human beings are not meant to hibernate in the dark months, along with the squirrels.

My stomach is not yet sorted out and my lower back has been uncomfortable the whole day and I thought a good walk this afternoon might do me the power of good.

It occurred to me, not for the first time, that perhaps the autumn air is bad for me. So I decided to walk to Creswell, as I had originally planned to yesterday, but to do so underground. I forwent the lime frock coat for a light-coloured paletot and took a fur muff instead of gloves. Otherwise I was dressed much the same as yesterday when, around two o'clock, I set off down the Western tunnel. The coach rode twenty yards behind me, with both Grimshaw and Clement aboard. Clement insisted he come along, bringing with him blankets, sweet biscuits and a pot of cold rice pudding in case I required sustenance on the way.

A grand walk it was, too. I had not examined the tunnels so closely since they were finished and I must say I was very pleased with what I saw. The brickwork is quite magnificent and the Western tunnel in particular runs about as straight as an arrow. One problem which neither Mr Bird nor I had reckoned on was that the tops of some of the skylights have got covered over with fallen leaves. I made a mental note to have some lads sent out and sweep them clean as soon as we returned.

Felt altogether quite bright and cheery as I headed underground towards Creswell village, so I set up a little singing session, starting off with 'Johnnie Sands' – an old favourite of mine – then on to a few rounds of 'I Am Ninety-Nine'. The many echoes at first interfered with my performance and made me lose my place but in time I managed to gauge their duration and incorporate them into the song, so that I was able, after a fashion, to duet with myself. I broke the song up, line by line – one harmony placed carefully upon another – until at last the whole tunnel rang with a chorus of my voices. I sang the lead and I sang the alto, had a stab at treble and a breathy 'profundo' bass. Like a military man I marched along and opened my lungs right up, once or twice even managing to knock together some semblance of a descant on the top.

Reached Creswell in next to no time. As I emerged from the tunnel the sun did indeed dazzle me and a light breeze goosepimpled my flesh. Mrs Digby was hanging out her washing so I raised my hat to her and asked after her cats. But by the time the carriage had come out of the tunnel and pulled up alongside of me, our chit-chat was drawing to a close and I was having trouble remembering why Creswell had seemed such an attractive prospect. Came up with no good answers so I cancelled the rest of the expedition on the spot. Turned, waved goodbye to Mrs Digby and set up another singing session as I passed through the tunnel gates.

Sang mainly ballads returning home – my father's bird song and an old sea shanty. Most of the shanty's verses had slipped my mind, which rather obliged me to fill in with some of my own. Amused myself with the thought of the cows above, lazily munching in an empty field, and the sound of some old fellow coming up from the ground, roaring on about the rolling waves and the hunt for the great white whale.

All in all, a most satisfactory day. I am sure tonight I will sleep like a top. But something has been troubling me. As I looked back just now on the day's events and saw me striding down the Western tunnel, I saw not a man who strode along on his own. I had the impression that ... how can I put it ... that I had *company* with me. Not entirely visible, perhaps, but company just the same.

A very young fellow – that is all I can come up with. A young fellow who generally hangs about.

I have often wondered if the chap I engage in conversation when I debate some issue with myself is within me or without. Maybe this is my man? What's more, now that I turn my attention to it I rather think he has been there for a very long time.

*

NOVEMBER 24TH

*

Not quite right yet, by any means. The discomfort comes and goes. Gave myself a dry-rub with a bath towel to invigorate me (what my father used to call an 'Aberdeen bath') but succeeded only in adding exhaustion to my list of ills. What was last week most definitely a twinge has developed into more of a throb. Very strange – the damned thing appears to move about. I feel sure it is deeper inside me today and further up toward the ribs.

At lunch I had just drunk the last of an excellent oxtail soup and was chewing on a piece of bread when my teeth clamped down onto something which they had difficulty getting through. 'A bit of gristle?' I thought, and fished about with my tongue. The matter had lodged itself between my teeth. Then, with finger and thumb, I picked out what proved to be, on closer examination, a tightly-packed papery wad.

'Paper in my bread,' I said.

With a good deal of effort I managed to unravel the scrap

which, when flattened out on the table, measured some two inches by half an inch. I could just about make out on it a message of some sort, written in pencil. The paper was damp from its short stay in my mouth but, in time, I was able to decipher the following words:

'... *for the bread we there eat is one bread, and the wine we drink* ...'

Well, this meant absolutely nothing to me – rang no bells at all – and I soon concluded that it must be but a fragment of a longer piece. Quite frankly, I found the whole thing more than a little disturbing, partly due to the text's declamatory tone. Someone is sending me messages, I thought. Messages to do with bread and wine. And if I was in possession of only a fragment of what I took to be a much longer tract, then who was to say I had not swallowed the rest, which would be sure to upset my digestion even more? I called Mrs Pledger in.

'Mrs Pledger,' I explained, calmly, 'I have found some words in my bread.'

After the situation had been laid out before her she asked to see the scrap of paper. Her eyes swept over the handwriting and she gave a knowing nod. 'Ignatius Peak,' she said.

The name was completely new to me. It conjured up some craggy mountain-top. But, as Mrs Pledger informed me, Ignatius Peak is an employee in our bakery. Then, lowering her voice to a whisper, said she believed him to be '... an overly-religious man'.

Twenty minutes later he stood before me in my study, still dressed in his apron and white cap and dusted all over with flour, as if he had been put up in a cellar and forgotten about. The robustness evoked by the fellow's name was decidedly lacking in the man himself. He stood there and did not say a word. I had, I think, expected an apology without his needing a prompt. He was a small man, with well-trimmed whiskers, but when he spoke he fairly brimmed with God.

'I believe you put some words in my bread, Mr Peak.'

'Not just words, Your Grace, but religious words. They are from the Bible, which means they are sacred. They are holy words, Your Grace.'

As he spoke his short arms waved all about the place, causing a gentle avalanche of flour to fall down his jacket and settle on the floor.

'And why were these holy words put in my bread, Mr Peak?' I asked.

'Well now,' he said, staring in to the distance, 'I believe that this morning, while I was about my baking, I got the sudden inspiration to do so, sir. It happens on occasion ... the inspiration to spread God's Word.'

This confounded me somewhat. He smiled most beatifically, which did not help at all.

'Just *my* bread, Mr Peak, or everybody's bread?'

'O, everybody's, Your Grace. Every loaf in sight.'

He stretched out both arms as far as they would go, so that his tiny wrists protruded from his jacket cuffs and he swept his hands backwards and forwards to draw my attention to acre upon acre of holy bread. Throughout our conversation he had a tendency to gesticulate, as if he were preaching from some lofty pulpit. Once or twice he went so far as to clench his fists and raise them above his head, as if summoning his own thunderbolts and lightning. There appeared, however, to be little correlation between these grand gestures and the actual words as they came hurtling from his mouth.

'What is the quotation I found in my mouth just now?' I asked, and handed him the scrap of paper.

He barely glanced at it before rolling his head back on his shoulders, screwing up his eyes and addressing the ceiling in such a calamitous tone I nearly jumped right out of my skin.

'"*We are joined together into one mystical body, and declare ourselves to be so, by our fellowship together in the ordinance of the Lord's supper; for the bread we there eat is one bread, and the wine we drink is one wine; though the one be composed of many grains of corn, and the other made up of many particular grapes . . .*" One Corinthians, ten, seventeen.'

His eyes stayed tightly shut the whole time but his arms flapped wildly about, continuing to flap for several seconds after his recital had reached an end. Then, quite suddenly, they foundered, as if they had been shot out of the sky, and fell dramatically to his side, where they knocked two new clouds of flour down his trouser legs

'And what does it mean?' I asked him.

'Fellowship through the Lord, Your Grace,' he replied.

I considered this for a moment, watched keenly by my baker-man. Then I asked if his bits of paper did not burn in the ovens, but was informed that the quotations were, in fact, inserted after the loaves had been baked.

'I just makes a little cut with a palette knife and slides the fellows right in.'

I nodded at him, finding myself in something of a quandary. I had originally called Mr Peak in to see me in order to reprimand the man but I was having difficulty finding suitable grounds on which to do such a thing. 'You don't worry you might choke someone?' I asked, rather hopefully, thinking that if I could locate somewhere in him the smallest kernel of guilt I would at least have made a start.

'None have choked so far, sir,' he said, smiling. 'They are only short quotations, after all.'

'And do you always use quotations that are to do with bread?'

'In the main, sir. Yes, I do, sir . . . It seems appropriate somehow.'

I agreed that it did. I was completely at a loss as to what to do with the fellow. Clearly he had done nothing gravely wrong (or, more to the point, nothing which *he* thought was wrong). A heavy sigh rose up in me. The pain in my ribcage gnawed away. On a whim, I asked, 'I don't suppose you happen to heal, do you, Mr Peak?'

He looked at me for a moment, before launching into, 'The *Lord* heals, sir. "*Lest they see, and convert and be healed.*"'

'Yes, I'm sure. But it is healing of the body I'm after, Mr Peak, not healing of the soul.'

'He heals the body too, Your Grace. "*I will heal thee of thy wounds, saith the Lord.*"'

He was quiet for a second and I felt a deep despondency creeping through my bones. Here was a man who was utterly and happily immersed in his faith. He knew his way around it (or at least its vocabulary) like the back of his hand; seemed to have no doubts at all about the world and his place in it. This depressed me mightily. I think perhaps I envied him more than any other man I have ever come across. He stood before me with bowed head – busy, I felt sure, digging ever deeper into his memory for other, more impressive passages from the Good Book. At last he looked up and asked,

'Have you ever seen the Oakleys, sir?'

Now, if the name of the man before me had conjured up a craggy mountain-top, the Oakleys put me in mind of a range of low hills, such as the Malverns, or some other lush terrain. But, as Ignatius Peak informed me, the Oakleys are in fact two sisters living out at Whitwell who are said to have the rare ability 'to look deep inside a man'.

'Are you poorly, Your Grace?' he asked me. I told him I thought perhaps I was. 'Well, they're the women you're after. They are the best diagnosers in the county, those two. They'll diagnose where all others fail.'

So I thanked him and wished him well with his quotations. Then, as an afterthought, suggested he might consider attaching them to the loaves with string. That way they would tend to remain intact, would not risk being eaten and could be read by the recipient at their leisure.

'O, no, sir. That would be no good. You see, the surprise of the discovery is what makes the sinner stop and think. That is how we win him over.'

'I see,' I said.

He smiled broadly, gave me a brisk little bow and marched off towards the door.

It was a second or two after his departure, while I was wondering if I should chase these two weird sisters up, that I noticed on the rug where Mr Peak had stood two perfect footprints in a small heap of flour.

*

NOVEMBER 25TH

*

Straight after breakfast I had Clement go out to the Oakleys' and by ten o'clock he was back with news that they would be happy to receive me this afternoon. A price, agreeable to both parties, had been arranged and by two o'clock we were clear of the North-west tunnel and making our way through the village of Whitwell. We had especially taken the fly to tackle the steep hill but Grimshaw soon found it difficult to keep the horse moving and it became necessary for Clement and me to alight and walk the last few hundred yards.

The dull throb in my ribcage had rather been keeping its head low and I was worried I might reach the Oakleys' with no discomfort to speak of at all, but as we reached the crown of the hill and stopped to admire the cold corner of Notting-hamshire spread out below, the throbbing suddenly returned and I drank in the view before me, strangely relieved to have relocated my malaise.

What little I knew of the Oakleys I had picked up from Mr Peak – namely that they were middle-aged sisters with a reputation for possessing some peculiar spiritual power which enables them to see right inside a man. It was said they could observe a functioning organ as if it sat before them twitching on a plate. As we stood there, looking out over the fields and woods, I asked Clement what he reckoned to such claims of visionary powers, but he politely declined to comment. I don't mind saying that there are times when his unflagging diplomacy can be more than a little irritating.

Five minutes later we had reached the Oakleys' and Clement went off to take tea with Grimshaw, whose cousin lives nearby, and I found myself before a modest stone cottage on the top of the hill, with an overgrown garden and a marvellous view all round. As I rapped on the knocker I noticed how all the curtains were drawn and wondered if perhaps the sisters were taking an afternoon nap. Then I heard the clatter of the latch and the door swung back to reveal two splendid women – in their late forties, I should say – with jet-black hair down to their shoulders and both dressed in starched white pinafore. Mr Peak had failed to mention that they were, in fact, twins and made a most striking combination. Not quite identical-looking, but plainly cut from the same stone.

One of the two raised her eyebrows and smiled at me. The other whispered, 'Won't you please come in?'

I was shown into the front parlour, the room which had all the curtains pulled to. It was very sparse, the ceiling so low it almost grazed the ladies' heads. The only ornamentation was two framed pictures on the mantelpiece – one of a Russet apple in cross-section, the other of the same fruit hanging on the bough. I accepted their offer of tea and, a few minutes later, all three of us sat round the table with only the squeak and rattle of our cups and saucers to disturb the growing silence. I eventually felt obliged to venture a little polite conversation. 'I'm an apple-grower myself,' I announced gaily, nodding towards the pictures. But the sisters simply smiled their tiny smiles and continued to sip at their tea.

After another lengthy silence I expressed some enthusiasm for their brew of tea, saying how it was 'very fine indeed'. But my words hardly seemed to register with the women, who kept their gaze firmly fixed on the table top, both apparently wrapped up in some profound and unspoken exchange.

I was wondering what other trifles I might be obliged to bring to their attention (the weather perhaps, or the table-cloth) when they rose simultaneously from their chairs without the slightest warning.

One said, 'Would you care to follow us, Your Grace?'

I rather hurriedly returned my cup to its saucer, catching the teaspoon in the process and causing quite a fuss, by which time both sisters were over by the door and gently beckoning me towards the neighbouring room.

Like the parlour, heavy curtains shut out the daylight. The whole place was lit by a pair of ceiling lamps which between them effused a good deal of warm and amber light. Two long-case clocks faced each other across the floor and knocked the seconds between one another like a tennis ball. Both sisters waited patiently by the door for me, standing so still and silent that as I entered the only movement in that warm, velvety room seemed to be the pendulums in the bellies of the clocks. The atmosphere was so altogether slow and syrupy that I found myself becoming quite alarmed. It was as if I was being invited to jump into a very deep pool. My breathing quickened, my head began to spin.

One of the sisters took me by the hand. The other said, 'It is all right, you know?'

And with that, I have to say, all my fear evaporated and I

felt only embarrassment at the beads of sweat on my brow. I can only imagine that some animal instinct had momentarily surfaced, prompting in me the irrational urge to run right from the place. But the sisters had recognized my anxiety and, in an instant, had soothed it away. They had said, 'It is all right, you know,' and, just like a child, I was assured that it was.

One sister helped me off with my jacket, the other asked me to lift my shirt. And there I stood, in the middle of that honey-warm room with my shirt pulled up around my chest.

The sisters began to slowly circle me. The clocks ticked and tocked in counterpoint. Every pendulum swing sliced away another moment of time. One called, the other replied.

'What a strange little world,' I thought to myself, feeling buoyed-up and beginning to float. I felt increasingly calmed as, one by one, the years of my life slipped away and from deep, deep inside a child's voice whispered to me, 'I have a tummy ache.'

'Where is the ache, Your Grace?' asked a sister.

I touched my stomach, just below my ribs. I pressed, to show how deep it was. Then one of the sisters took my hand, moved it aside and positioned herself in front of me. She settled herself there and proceeded to stare at me. The other positioned herself behind. And as the seconds slowly unfolded and the twins dwelt on me I felt myself sway a fraction of an inch from side to side. But I never feared I might take a tumble, for I was pinned securely in place by the sisters' powerful gaze.

And the room had become perfectly quiet now. One sister nodded her head before me, the other hummed in agreement behind. The whole place was awash with the most unusual atmosphere. Unseen currents shifted everywhere. And it dawned on me, in the most agreeable way, that the sisters were, in fact, observing the tea inside of me. Were following it as it steadily made its way. They had given me a cup of tea to sip at and now watched to see how my organs dealt with it.

I felt not the least bit troubled by their penetrating eyes. In fact, for the first time in my life, became quietly conscious of the independent existence of each organ as they worked away. The sisters' nods and gentle 'ums' and 'ahs' flew back and forth and I nodded forward and looked into the lovely redness of my lids. And, gradually, I came to picture, in quite vivid detail . . . my liver, my heart, my lungs. I had no idea of their size or their colour, or the tubes which connected them up. Had no idea what stopped them slipping from their separate shelves. But they were no longer raw, anonymous entities but individual beings with their own characters and important duties to perform. *Fishes* . . . that is how they seemed to me. Fish, nestling at different levels of my pool. Like the trout I had once seen just beneath the water, sleeping by a stone, their whole bodies gently swelling and contracting inside of me.

'Finished, Your Grace,' one of the sisters whispered.

The clocks' tick-tock suddenly returned to fill the room.

Both sisters now stood before me. It was a while before I recovered myself. And by the time my feet felt the earth beneath them one of the sisters was indicating towards the door. The other was smiling.

'Shall we?' she said.

As I followed along behind them, tucking my shirt back in, I noticed how my gums ached, as they do when I have dozed off in the afternoon. We each took our place around the table and both sisters looked across at me.

'If you don't mind me coming straight to the point,' I said, '. . . what exactly did you see?'

They looked at one other while they decided which one was to speak.

'You have been eating beef,' she said. It was more of a statement than a question.

I thought for a second, before spluttering out, 'Yes. Essence of beef, I ate ... and very foul stuff it was too.'

'Beef does not agree with you,' said the sister.

'Good Lord, and oxtail, too,' I went on, excited. 'I had an oxtail soup just yesterday.'

'Beef does not agree with you,' she repeated.

This time I heard her and conceded, 'Very well. I'll steer clear of beef from now on.'

Then the two of them exchanged further meaningful glances before the other sister said, in an even quieter voice, 'When you first came in ... we noticed ...'

I nodded at her, to help her along.

'We noticed that your aura is not right.'

Well, I must say, this rather stumped me. I had not the first idea what my aura was. Had been ignorant of the fact I even owned one until that very moment.

'It is the light which emanates from a person,' the other sister said. 'Yours is incomplete.'

Well, as you can imagine, this was highly distressing news. Who would want an aura which is incomplete?

'Then how do I make it whole again?' I asked.

'Perhaps you are lacking something,' the quieter sister said, and gave me a second to digest this. 'You must make it your business to find the gap and fill it in.'

*

I handed them their fee in the hallway, shook their hands and thanked them for their time. When they opened the door the daylight flooded into the hall. I paused on the doorstep for a moment or two.

'I'm sorry,' I said, 'but if you don't mind my asking ... what exactly do you see when you look at a man?'

'We see inside him,' said one.

The other added, 'We see how he is put together.'

*

Clement met me at the garden gate and escorted me back to the carriage. 'They're not fakers, Clement. Honestly,' I told him. 'They saw the essence of beef.'

Clement nodded appreciatively as we carried on down the hill. At some point I turned and looked back at the sisters' cottage and thought I glimpsed a white face peering out between the velvet curtains, but when I looked again a second later the face was gone.

*

NOVEMBER 26TH

*

A long while ago, when I was still a socializing man and drank brandy and smoked cigars, I heard the most curious anecdote from my friend, the good Lord Galway.

While we sat gazing into the coals of a roaring fire, coming to terms with the enormous dinner we had just packed away, he told me about an old friend of his who had come bounding up to him at a function the previous spring with 'the most wonderful news'. And indeed it was good news for, after many a barren year, his wife had just been told she was pregnant and, not surprisingly, Lord Galway's friend was as pleased as Punch, not least because he might finally father a son who would one day take over his affairs.

Well, for several months after these glad tidings Lord Galway was kept very busy and when the two of them next met up he straight away detected the most solemn attitude about his friend. Fearing his wife had perhaps lost the child, he decided, as he put it, to 'act the diplomat' and kept up his end of the conversation until his friend got around to saying what was on his mind. Apparently, he was very worried about his wife's mental state; indeed feared she had already gone some way down the road towards insanity. Lord Galway trod ever more carefully – the grave look on his friend's face told him this was wise – but, bit by bit, managed to draw the fellow out.

It transpired that the man's wife was a coal-eater ... was always at the stuff. He first discovered her sucking a small chunk of it crouched under the desk in his study. Then, at lunch a few days later, he noticed a piece which she had hid in her napkin and was crumbling into her soup. As the weeks went by he found coal all over the house: tucked in her muffler, wrapped in silk handkerchiefs, even a piece in her very best bonnet. At night-time, after the light went out, he could hear her munching under the bedclothes, for she even kept a piece in her pillowcase to suck on till she fell asleep. In the morning, apparently, the sheets were filthy and her lips and teeth jet-black.

Well, all this upset her husband no end. He shouted at her and stamped about the place and confiscated every bit he could find. He forbade her from going near the stuff and made his staff act like prison guards but, of course, there was no way he could keep an eye on her all day long, and he knew full well that as soon as his back was turned she would sneak down to the cellar to get herself a fresh supply.

Now it was unfortunate for Galway's old friend that he had kept to himself for so long what he felt sure were the first signs of his wife's creeping lunacy, for if he had earlier shared out the information he might have been earlier put at ease. For Galway is very worldly-wise and had heard tell how a woman who is carrying a child becomes susceptible to a whole dynasty of inner-change which, in some instances, may result in cravings of the most irrational kind. It has been suggested that the craving of coal – in fact, not at all uncommon – may be nothing more than the mother-to-be's need for iron.

Anyhow, Lord Galway swiftly passed all this information on to his friend, who went on his way with a terrific lightening of his load. A few months later his wife gave birth to a beautiful son, her passion for coal having passed just as quickly as it came about, and as the years went by her husband was relieved to note that it was a habit not inherited by their child.

I think this tale must have been lingering somewhere at the back of my mind as I walked around the grounds some months ago. It was a beautiful morning in June or July and the sun was pouring down. Mr Bird directed a gang of men in the construction of the new bridge across the lake and with the weather being so warm and humid some of the lads had stripped to the waist. I had already raised my hat to Mr Bird and was intent on quietly passing by when one of his men turned away to mop his brow and I noticed that he had on his back a huge tattoo of Ireland.

It was livid-red in colour and reached from his shoulders right down to his waist. Of course, the amateur-cartographer in me became most excited and I hurried over to get a better look. As I drew near I saw that the map-tattoo had been somehow effected in relief form, which really rather baffled me, and it was only when I was a couple of yards from the fellow that I realized that what I had taken to be the work of a tattooist was, in fact, a huge expanse of scab.

He must have seen me recoil a little for, without my having uttered a word, he announced, in a matter-of-fact way, 'Psoriasis, sir.'

'Psoriasis,' I echoed dumbly.

Fortunately, he was a bright chap and, seeing that I was in the dark, added, 'It is a skin complaint, Your Grace.'

'Aha,' I said and moved back in on him.

Well, I have to say, he was most accommodating and let me scrutinize the magnificent scab without seeming to mind a bit. It was all very much of a solid piece, with a surface like burnt jam. The shape of the scab, to my mind still very much like Ireland, was a little flaky round the coastline and had, here and there, come away from the skin. It occurred to me, I remember, that I should very much like to slide my fingernails under it and rip the whole thing up. Luckily, it was an urge I managed to keep reined in, for he was a broad fellow, used to heaving a pick and would, I'm sure, have been greatly upset by any interference with his scab.

I asked him if the scab always took the shape of Ireland or if it ever resembled other countries of the world and he replied that while the scab was constantly on the move – sometimes shrinking, sometimes spreading – the similarity between it and a map of any country had, frankly, never crossed his mind.

Still, I found our encounter most fascinating. I gave the good fellow sixpence and thanked him for his time and was in the process of taking my leave when another question popped into my head.

'I was wondering . . .' I said, 'how you treat it.'

And, again without the least inhibition, he told me how a physician had recently recommended exposing the scab to the sun's rays whenever possible, which is why he had his shirt off today.

I was still absorbing this information, when he added, 'And coal tar, sir.'

Now, as I have already mentioned, I must have still had drifting at the back of my mind the wife of Lord Galway's acquaintance gorging herself on coal for, before I had properly got my thoughts in order, the words

'You drink *coal tar*, man?' had popped out of me, in a voice so loud and clear that the fellows who had recently returned to their digging immediately stopped again and stared.

The big chap looked me over very coolly, his eyes narrowing to two tiny slits. When he spoke it was as if he was addressing a backward child.

'Not *drinks* it, sir. Wipes it on.'

In the circumstances it seemed like an easy mistake to make, but would have been impossible to explain.

'Of course, of course,' I said. Then I bade him good day and left the scene just as fast as my legs would carry me away.

It is one of those awful moments that I know will haunt me for many years to come. (When I was a child I used the seeds of dried rose-hip as 'itching powder' and, for want of some other child to 'itch', would put them down my own back. I mention this because it seems to me that the two sensations are somehow similar.)

No doubt while I sit here recording the embarrassing event that same labourer holds court in some nearby alehouse, telling anyone who cares to listen all about the mad old Duke who suggested drinking coal tar to cure his psoriatic scabs.

*

November 27th

*

Taking to heart the advice of the Oakley sisters I have ordered that, henceforth, no beef be included in my meals. Mrs Pledger has risen to the occasion and presented me this lunchtime with a delicious croquette of Stilton and asparagus which fairly sent my tongue into raptures. The croquette – about six inches in length and beautifully breadcrumbed –

was accompanied by honeyed carrots and a light, spicy gravy. Tonight, I am told, we are to have devilled lobster. At this rate I think it will be no great effort to forgo the dreaded beef. I only hope the benefits will soon make themselves felt.

The repairwork required by my damaged 'aura', however, may not be so easily carried out. The sisters' description left me with the impression of something like a warm glow around a lamp. That picture, I think, is a good one. A warm glow will do very well. But when I try to imagine this glow as 'incomplete' or broken, I run immediately into problems. If I had been asked to imagine the aura as a cloak, for example, I would be as right as rain. The cloak – let us say, a large tweed redingote – has a small rip in it somewhere. Perhaps I snagged it on a nail. Clearly then, what is needed is for me to lay my hands on a needle and thread and stitch it up where it has been rent. But a *glow* – how does one go about mending a hole in a glow?

I repeatedly put my mind to the problem but end up neither here nor there, wavering constantly between a warm glow in the one hand and a redingote in the other.

※

I am certain the little fist of malevolence last located below my ribcage is on the move again. It is higher up in me than it has been and seems inclined towards my spine. As my lungs are always susceptible to infection I worry it might get at them and give me a nasty cough, so last night I had Clement light a camphor candle to keep the blasted thing at bay and when I woke I felt sure it had smelt the camphor and promptly doubled back. I conclude that it is shrewd and conniving but also cowardly; still heading in a northerly direction, but by some different route.

※

Received another remedy this afternoon – this one from the Reverend Mellor. Convinced that I suffer from 'rheumatics', his note contained a recipe which he insists I should have made up. It came to him from a sister-in-law in Whitby where, apparently, the trawlermen take it right through the winter months. The recipe is as follows . . .

Stone brimstone
turkey rhubarb
powdered guaiacum
powdered nitre
. . . of each a quatre of an oz.,
made into pills of 6 grains each
. . . take two every night at bed time.

Well, I must say the ingredients put me more in mind of gunpowder than any medicine, but I duly sent a boy off to mix the concoction up. When he returned, proudly showing the pills off on a plate, they looked very much like tiny cannonballs – all pocked and dangerous. I had him put them on my bedside table. If I am feeling especially brave tonight I might fire a couple into me.

I might admit to being old and creaky, my body racked with innumerable twitches and unnameable pains, but I feel sure it is not plain rheumatism that I suffer from. The word simply doesn't fit.

As I sat at my bureau this afternoon, keeping warm by a well-stacked fire, I came around to wondering how the news of my ill health had reached the Reverend Mellor. Certainly, I did not mention it in my letter and, as far as I know, he hasn't called round to the house.

It is fascinating to speculate, is it not, on how the word generally gets about. Miss Whittle at the Post Office may, on occasion, dispense a little more than postage stamps but one would never seriously accuse her of being the village gossip.

And yet between Miss Whittle and the Reverend Mellor I'll wager there exists an intricate web, along which the news of my unstable health has merrily worked its way. Perhaps I am mistaken. Could be that the Reverend was in the Post Office and happened to mention me. Then Miss Whittle might have countered by saying how she sent a tin of beef essence up to the house, upon hearing I was unwell. But then I turn up another question. How was it Miss Whittle first came by that information? How did word get to her?

Well now, I have dozens of employees spread all over the estate. On a slow day I suppose it not inconceivable for two of them to exchange news which, at a pinch, might include their master's health. There need be no malice in it; just the common verbal barter of one man with the next. And if the result of that chain is that one or two acquaintances show their concern by sending me remedies, then I'm sure I should be nothing but flattered and pleased. But once or twice I have overheard men talking, where the exchange of information has been driven not by benevolence but the profoundest spite. Nothing in the world moves at half the speed as a rumour with the scent of scandal to it. Have we not all been guilty, at one time or another, of repeating the words a better man would have kept to himself? Yet, to some people news of another's misfortune – whether true or purely speculative – is their bread and butter, and they like nothing more than to squander their days whipping that wheel on its way.

Just now I attempted to draw a map on which the journey of some item of interest might be laid out. Using my illness as an example, I began by writing the name of Miss Whittle on one side and the Reverend Mellor's on the other. I estimated that between these two people it might have taken perhaps two or three others to unwittingly act as the stepping stones for the news. But, just when I was feeling very pleased with my little diagram and thinking how easy it was proving to be, it occurred to me that those two or three nameless individuals between dear Miss Whittle and Mellor would hardly be likely to tell a story just the once. No, if a tale is remotely worth telling then one might tell it a dozen times. So suddenly every line on my simple map is multiplied by twelve and they go shooting off all over the place. And, of course, each of the twelve who are told the story may pass it on to a dozen more. This process continues and in no time one winds up with nothing but a ball of twine.

I quickly saw how I was about to give myself a headache so I thought about something else for a while (a flowering bud, a pot of jam). Then I wondered if perhaps a better way of setting it out might be in the form of a family tree. At the top of the page would be the name of the pair who first exchanged the story (or *conceived* it, as it were) while below, in an ever-expanding fan, would be the many generations which followed on. As in any family, one might expect the features of the later generations of the story to have some, but by no means all, the characteristics of the first. Yes, very good.

Encouraged by this, I tried to dream-up other unusual journey-maps and recalled one I have often thought I would like to commission, which is the route taken by an ordinary postal letter. How many pairs of hands must the envelope pass through between the moment it is first dropped in the post box and the moment it lands on the mat? No doubt along the way the letter must spend many tedious hours waiting in various bags and piles. Perhaps not so interesting, after all. But how wonderful to at last be sorted and carried down the lane in the postman's sack. How wonderful to be plucked open and read!

A Local Woman's Account

It is well known round here how the Duke was deformed very bad as a result of the syphilis. His old body was riddled with it, right from top to toe. This is what led him to have all those miles of tunnels made, so he could hide his terrible face from view and pop up out of the ground at will.

My husband knows a man who saw the old Duke face to face, just as close as I stand here next to you. He says his left eye was a good two inches higher than the right one and that he dribbled from the corner of his mouth the whole time. A terrible sight to behold, he was. The children would run a mile from him or be struck dumb on the spot. And there's plenty others round here that'll back me up on that score. You knock on any door. Shocking, that's the old Duke for you. A shocking sight all round.

From His Grace's Journal

*

Annoyed with myself all day, today. Could not get anything done.

By all accounts my aura is in tatters and I have not the first idea how to put it right. I feel as if I have sprung a leak somewhere. Look for signs of me listing to port.

The pain which has been travelling up my body has emerged between my shoulder blades, which now clench together like pincers to try to squeeze the life out of it (an action over which I have not the slightest control). Last night I took a couple of the Reverend Mellor's rheumatism pills. They looked and smelt like rabbit pellets and I imagine they did me about as much good.

What with the concern for the state of my aura and the twisting dagger in my back, I have felt highly agitated right through the day and just about ready to snap. Hardly the best condition for introspection, but that was just what Fate had in store. There are few enough days when one's resilience is up to taking a cold hard look at oneself, to ask 'What have I made of my life?', but it seems the days we undertake such assessments are often the days we are least likely to be satisfied.

I have never composed a work of art. I have invented nothing, discovered nothing. The land and wealth which were left to me, though hardly squandered, were not employed as fruitfully as they might. And while I may have built the odd row of almshouses and a cottage hospital out near Belph, there will be no statues unveiled in homage to my benefaction, no great weeping when I go. I did not even manage to marry the woman I loved – a feat most men manage to carry off. No, all I've done with my life is take countless melancholy constitutionals and grow apples by the ton. Even the credit for the apple-growing belongs elsewhere. As things stand I will be remembered as the Duke who built the tunnels and kept himself to himself. Otherwise I am eminently forgettable – but half a man.

If Fanny had married me instead of Nicolson she would not have been poisoned by a bad piece of fish. She would still be alive today. I would have fed her on the finest titbits, would have tested every spoonful myself. She would have come up to live with me in the country and brought this sad old house to life. Her bright dresses and her songs and laughter would have chased misery from every last corner. I can see her now in her great sweeping dresses going from one darkened room to another, pulling back the shutters and letting the sunlight in. She throws the dustcovers off the divans and armchairs, orders windows to be opened wide. The fresh air rushes in and every room in the house is brightened by her good cheer.

By now we would have grown-up children. Grandchildren most likely, too. I would teach them how to whistle and let them climb all over me as if I were a tree. If I had been loved by her I would be a stronger man and my flame would not now be going out. But there are no children, there are no grandchildren. There are covers on the divans. I live in three or four rooms in total and leave the others empty and unused and when a maid comes in to open a window I scuttle away like a crab.

No doubt I should count myself lucky to have such a fine staff waiting on me. Indeed I should. When the sun shines I can have a horse saddled up in a minute and spend the whole day trotting round my estate. If I wished, I could waste my worthless time in one of a thousand different ways. But every happy moment has the brake put on it, for I know it will be recalled alone.

There are men who in years to come will explore the world's furthest corners, who will think up great philosophies. But when it comes to real creation men are of little use. We are not gifted in that way, have not the machinery. All we can do is stand by and wonder – and perhaps offer to lend a hand. For, in reality, there is but one set of true makers and the men are not among them. At best, men are the midwives of this world.

*

All day I have been in this stupor, like a dog which has forgotten where it buried its bone. So agitated and uneasy with myself that I simply had to get up and move around.

When I am restless, I find I have a proclivity for going in search of the past. A territory which is, I suppose, more familiar – more solid and safe. Which is probably how I came to find myself on the tiny flight of steps leading up to the attic. The door was firmly locked up and I had to blow down for some help. It was only when Clement finally came puffing up the stairs with his big bunch of keys that I was able to make my way in.

As a boy I imagined that heaven would be something like an attic – for no other reason, I suspect, than it was right at the top of the house and full of discarded things. I assumed that when a man died and became redundant he would be taken up to the attic of the world.

But if memory served me right my previous trips had been

to a warm, even humid place, whereas today it was frightfully cold. My breath was visible before me and a lamp was required to illuminate the rooms. Clement was anxious to stay with me in case I set the place afire but my spirits were so low that even his benign company was too much for me to bear and I shooed him down the stairs.

Spent over an hour rifling through the chests and trunks – mostly rubbish, of course. The debris of five generations washed up on the bare floor, each forming its own musty little isle. Folded clothes – ancient and reeking of mothballs. Once-fashionable furniture. Trinkets, hatstands, framed paintings and broken bits and pieces whose purpose I could not ascertain. Then box upon box of decaying papers – many of them rotted right through, my fingers gradually growing so utterly numb that I was unable to continue picking through them and gladly returned to the civilized world.

If I had been unknowingly searching for some lost treasure I am sure I did not turn it up. The only trophy I came away with was a wind-up monkey which now perches on my bureau (originally purchased, I believe, from Hamley's toy-shop in Regent Street, back in God-knows-when). Not so much a toy as a conversation-piece but I'm sure a child would like it just the same. There is a key in its back to wind it up. The monkey nods its head and lifts its little top hat. Most dignified. But it is tatty now from sitting in the attic and its wheels and cogs are all clogged with dust. In the middle of lifting its hat for me just now it paused, as if distracted. That is all I have to show for the day . . . a wind-up monkey whose thoughts, like mine, are elsewhere.

*

*

Woke with a shout of 'Information!' which quite shook poor Clement up. He was standing right by my bed at the time and very nearly dropped his tray.

The stiffness in my neck was incredible. I had never known the like. It was as if six-inch nails had been driven between my skull and my collarbone. Clement had to carry me to the bathroom and lower me into one of his specially-prepareds. The night had been bitter-cold, which might have contributed to my freezing up, but I now had not the slightest doubt that some evil little fist was at work in me. It had dug its fingernails right in.

The heat of the bathwater gradually found its way through to me and began to thaw me out. I tried to nod my head up and down a little, then slowly side to side until, in time, it was just about moving independently of my shoulders. Even so, the merest twist beyond these axes brought about a blinding pain, which was accompanied by a most disconcerting noise and put me in mind of the rubbing-together of many small stones. 'My body is at war with itself!' I announced from my bathtub. 'Civil war is what it is!'

I have tried to be calm, tried to be steadfast, have even tried to befriend that craven pain. I have run the whole mad gamut of emotion while it took a merry jaunt around my shaky frame. But this morning I was just plain angry. I had had enough and resolved to take it on. As I lay hunched and twisted in my steaming tub I swore I would locate it and put a stick right through it. I would crack its miserable skull.

Took breakfast in my bedroom. Tomatoes and mushrooms sprinkled with ground peppercorn. The accompanying rasher of bacon looked not the least bit appetizing as it lounged in its shallow lake of grease, but I am nothing if not resourceful, so I unbuttoned my shirt and placed it flat against my neck. The fat was still warm and I found that rubbing it against the affected area afforded me some small relief.

When I had done with breakfast I searched for some paper – where is the paper in this house! – and having at last tracked down a notepad wrote myself out a plan, while my spare hand held the cooling bacon in place.

I made a heading . . .

Information

which I expanded to . . .

Information Required

and composed a short list beneath it . . .

Drawings;
Photographs;
Maps;
Writing of any sort – regarding bodies, necks in particular.

Blew down to Mrs Pledger, Clement and Mr Grimshaw, announcing, 'Information required.'

'What information, Your Grace?' said Mrs Pledger.

'Body information,' I told her. 'Information on neck-bones.'

By lunchtime no information had surfaced and I found myself dozing off before the fire.

When I woke the fist had its grip on me again. My upper body was completely seized, so that I could not turn my head without the rest of me coming along. I felt like an automaton.

'Damn you!' I yelled at my body.

Called down to Mrs Pledger, asking for more bacon – as hot and greasy as it would come.

When Clement arrived with the bacon I grabbed the plate and slid the rashers straight under my shirt. Buttoned it back up to keep the fellows in place. Told Clement to round up reinforcements as I intended to carry out a daylight attack on the library, and in no time I was joined by a clutch of housemaids and a couple of lads from the plumbery. Once briefed, we all set off down the corridor: Clement silent and cautious, the boys and girls falling in behind while I marched at the front, proud and barefoot, my bacon-epaulettes now showing through my shirt.

We made the library in no time. The door was open. If it had been locked I would have broken it down. 'Books on bodies is what we want,' I announced to my company, and ran through the list again.

We spread out, taking a dozen or so shelves apiece. Only one ladder between us so I ordered the rest to pair up and help one another to climb the shelves. The room was much bigger than I remembered. A chap could get lost in there. Many of the books brought down a thick layer of dust with them and we were soon enveloped in great clouds of the stuff. We had to cover our mouths and noses with handkerchiefs to stop us choking. Could barely see my hand before my face.

By the time we pulled back we each had our own small booty – medical books, atlases, sketches, daguerreotype collections and so on, which included . . .

Anatomy, Descriptive and Surgical by Henry Gray;
Chambers Journal of Sciences (1860–65);
The Anatomy of Melancholy by Robert Burton;
and several collections of sketches by Leonardo da Vinci.

Had the whole lot dropped off in my bedroom beneath Mr Sanderson's map. Thanked my comrades and shooed them away. Searched out my medical dictionary and added it to the heap. Sat my wind-up monkey on top. Remembered Mr Peak's short quotation. Located it in a jacket pocket and pinned it to the wall.

In a book called *Ancient Chinese Healing* I found a peculiar diagram. A man whose body was fairly coursing with a complex system of interconnecting streams. They ran up and down his arms and legs and filled his torso, as if he had consumed a great deal of string. I ripped the map right out of the book and pinned that to the wall as well.

I have created in a corner of my bedroom a kind of shrine. I am quite sure that somewhere within it is the key to my current distress.

✻

I became tired. Sat by the fire, dozing and stirring, right through the afternoon.

At some point I wrote on my notepad . . .

Add to previous entry on gossip, postal letter, etc. . . .

Coins – circulation of. A penny, for instance. Might well be in circulation for many years. How many miles does an average coin travel in its lifetime? How would map of same look? All the purses it resides in. Number of palms.

Consider – is it likely a man would be in possession of same coin twice? How would he know? Would have to make a recognizable mark on it.

Consider – when I have a penny in my purse, do I not think of it always as the same penny?

Also – consider heat in coin. Miss Whittle's habit of holding change in her hand while she is talking, so that when she eventually hands them over, the coins are very warm. How might this connect with previous ideas on heat, etc.?

✻

When I woke again it was dark. Clement brought me some soup, but I could do nothing with it. Woke again to find him stoking up the fire.

The next time I came around the house was perfectly still and the fire was almost out.

Clement helped me change into my nightshirt and put me to bed. I slept but there was no rest in it. It was an exhausting sleep. Had a dream . . .

I am at the reins of a two-horse brougham, endlessly circling a leafy wood – desperate to find a way into its secret world of bramble and brush. All night I wrestle with the reins and steer that carriage around. I shout 'Ho!' and 'Come up there!' at the horses until my throat is raw. I circle and recircle for hour upon hour, longing to land and lie down and close my eyes. But the wood keeps me locked out, forcing me to go around again, until at last I am delirious from the torments of sleeplessness.

It was early morning when I next opened my eyes. I knew straight away there was something wrong. There was no newness to the day. That was the problem.

I stumbled over to the mirror above the mantelpiece. My hair stuck out in the usual places but my eyes were wild. My head looked as if someone had removed it and glued it back on. An absolutely shoddy job. My neck had twisted right round and got lodged there. I had to turn my body sideways to get a proper look at me. My mouth was all agape with pain.

I remember Clement coming in. And me collapsing. This happened very slowly. Seemed to take an age.

I have the vaguest memory of Clement carrying me down the back stairs to the tunnels. I remember the sound of his huge feet on the old stone steps.

When I next came to my head was in the crook of his

elbow. He cradled me as we went along. Out of the carriage window I saw a blur of red brick as we sped down the tunnels.

'I am in pain,' I told him.

He looked down at me and gave me a grave nod.

'Where are we going, Clement?' I asked him.

'We have found you a neck-man, Your Grace,' he replied.

*

DECEMBER 2ND

*

When I next opened my eyes we were pulling up outside an unfamiliar row of cottages, with me propped up in the carriage like a broken doll and still swimming in a dream. I saw Clement stroll up one of the garden paths and knock at a low gabled door. Saw him turn and walk back towards me. I recall the carriage door opening, him leaning over me and the cold morning air coming in. Then I was heft up into his arms again and gently carried towards the tiny house.

I leaned my head against Clement's shoulder and gazed up at his large round face as he marched me up the narrow path and ducked his head under the lintel. Then I found myself in a plain white room, warmed by a modest coal fire. My shirt was unbuttoned for me and pulled over my spinning head and I recall being eased back onto a trestle table, which was covered with a single sheet. Being naked amongst so much whiteness made me feel like a corpse on a mortuary slab.

'Good morning, Your Grace,' said a kind voice above me. 'My name is Conner.'

'Good morning, Conner,' I croaked back at him. 'And what is it you do?'

'I'm a bone-setter,' he said.

'A neck-man?'

'In a manner of speaking, yes. So tell me, Your Grace, how are your bones this morning?'

'O, they are old bones, Conner, and in very poor shape. My back is all locked-up.'

'Well, then,' said Conner, 'I shall do my best to unlock you.'

'O, I wish you would,' I said.

I was in such discomfort I had hardly opened my eyes, but as he turned me onto my stomach I caught a glimpse of the chap. He was youngish, stout and florid, with dark brown curly hair and a neat moustache. He wore a clean white apron over his daily clothes and had his shirt sleeves rolled up past his elbows, revealing an impressive pair of forearms.

As I lay my cheek on a lavender-scented pillow, I felt a large warm hand rest on my shoulder. 'A little oil,' he whispered, '. . . for lubrication.'

And in the gully between my shoulder blades I felt a sudden liquid heat. My mind, at first, was thrown into terrible confusion, not sure if the sensation was pleasurable or adding to my distress. Meanwhile, tiny harbingers of ecstasy shot out in every direction beneath my back's cold flesh, as the warm oil crept confidently along the shallow valley of my spine.

'You have had breakfast, Your Grace?' he asked me, easing the oil into my shoulders with neat circular movements of fingers and thumbs.

'I have not, Conner – no,' I wheezed from under his mighty hands. 'Clement brought me straight from my bed.'

'I thought I smelt bacon,' said Conner.

'That would be yesterday's bacon,' I replied.

'Ah,' he said, his thumb-circles now expanding. 'Strange how a smell can linger.'

And he kept up this gentle banter as his hands encouraged the oil into my flesh. Most of our conversation was of little significance and evaporated as soon as it was out, but I found an underlying kindness to it which gradually put me at my ease so that in a few minutes I was able to admit, 'I think I have been a little agitated this last day or two.'

To which Conner replied, 'That is understandable, Your Grace. A body does not like to be tied up in knots.'

And now his fingertips pressed deeper into me, tracing precise symmetrical eddies down either side of my spine. 'And how does a body come to have so many knots in it?' I enquired.

'O, a hundred different ways, Your Grace. I should say accumulation of tenseness is most common. Or a sudden twist of the head, perhaps. Sleeping badly is another ... too many pillows, too few ...'

And blow me down if, as he spoke, he wasn't working his magic on me. His fingers seemed to draw the pain right out of me, like a spell. And looking back I see how, unlike the ignorant Dr Cox, Conner actually encouraged me to voice my anxieties, dealing with each one of them there and then – smoothing them away with his fingertips and the soothing flow of his voice.

'Tell me, Conner,' I said, 'do you not worry that some of the bad feeling you draw from a patient might come to rest in you?'

He bent down and whispered in my ear, 'What I do, Your Grace, is think of myself as a chimney ... that way, any ill feeling just passes right through.'

'A chimney,' I said. 'Yes. Very good.'

Then he turned me onto my back and moved round to the head of the table, taking care to keep a hand on me all the while. I must say, having my chest exposed to the room made me feel decidedly vulnerable, but I was quickly reassured by Conner's trusty fingers as they gently slid under my neck. He raised my head an inch or two off the table and held it there in the cradle of his hands and for the first time I felt able to open my eyes and briefly survey the scene. Like an infant I looked all about me. In a far corner of the ceiling I spotted a cobweb, slowly waving above an otherwise spotless room. And now Conner had my head in the palm of one hand while the other slowly worked its way down my neck, his fingers checking the condition of each vertebra before moving on to the next. I noticed that the walls of the surgery were completely bare. Not a picture or a chart in sight.

'Give me the full weight of your head, Your Grace,' he told me. 'I will not let you drop.'

Then, by almost imperceptible degrees, he began to rotate my head – a most peculiar sensation, which initially induced in me near-vertigo, so that it was all I could do to resist an urge to lock my muscles up and bring the whole process to a halt. I felt like someone's puppet, not to say a little foolish. The room shifted around me mechanically. But after a minute or two of having my head eased this way and that, I felt myself becoming, first, unspeakably comfortable, then mercifully heavy-lidded. I recall drowsily dwelling on the complexity of the joints which could accommodate such a complicated manoeuvre and wondered at the many muscles being called into play as my skull swung slowly through space.

Conner's voice came to me from a great distance, saying, 'I think I might make a small manipulation, Your Grace.'

From the cradle of his huge hands I dreamily concurred.

I was asked to take a deep breath and to slowly let it out. So I filled my old lungs right to the top and began exhaling into that small white room and began to feel for the first time in many weeks that I had located a quiet corner in which to meditate. The world was slowing-up most pleasingly.

Then Conner suddenly yanked my head eastward with such incredible power and violence that an almighty *crack* went bouncing between the room's bare walls.

I was absolutely horrified, not least because I feared my head had just been pulled clean off my neck. I feared also that some small but important bones had just been rendered useless. I pictured me lying in my own cottage hospital, in a bed with all manner of devices strapped around my head. My anxiety must have been evident, for Conner said wistfully, 'It is a dramatic sound, sir, is it not.'

I agreed that it was and asked, rather sheepishly, 'Are there more?'

'There are,' he replied.

After checking the whereabouts of another vertebra or two (which were, by now, most definitely on the move) he calmly asked me to fill my lungs up and to let the air out, as before. Well, I did as I was told and was exhaling (more self-consciously this time round) when my head was suddenly jerked over to the west, emitting another great bony crack.

'Now take a minute or two to recover yourself, Your Grace,' said Conner. 'And when you are ready, I would like you on your front.'

Well, to be quite honest, I was worried that when I rolled over my head might stay behind on the pillow. The sound produced by Conner's manipulations was like a full tray of crockery being dropped on a stone floor and continued to ring in my ears. So when I finally dared to lift myself off the table I was much relieved to find my head was still attached to the rest of me – if not quite as surely as before.

Now my cheek was back on the lavender-scented pillow, with Conner's fingers inching methodically up and down my spine, searching for clues. When they came across something suspicious they halted and, while one hand crept out along a rib to the left, the other went off to the right. On the odd occasion when the fingers came upon some nexus of painful muscle they would rub, quite firmly, for half a minute then gently check over the surrounding terrain and, when they were satisfied that all was in order, would return to the trail. My back felt as if it was a human puzzle which Conner was intent on solving, joint by aching joint. 'I'm all over the place,' I confided.

'O, you're going back together just fine,' he replied.

'How on earth does a man's back become so higgledy-piggledy?' I asked.

'When one bone goes astray,' Conner informed me, 'others will tend to follow. The body tries to restore some balance but sometimes can do more damage than good.'

'So one might end up a little like ... a Chinese puzzle,' I suggested.

'Exactly, Your Grace,' he replied.

Then he rolled me onto my side so that I faced away from him, tucked one of my arms right under me and brought my left leg up to my chest, all accomplished with such facility I was inclined to congratulate the man. He simply tapped me gently behind a kneecap and the leg folded obediently into place. Seemed intimately acquainted with every spring and joint inside me; to have as much command over my body as I had myself. Not since I was a young lad playing with my father had I been so ably thrown around.

He pulled my raised hip gently towards him with one hand, while his other eased my shoulder toward the table top. He held me there a second, leaned closer and asked, 'Are you ready, Your Grace?'

I must have whispered some sort of tentative assent; in truth, I had not the first idea what terrible contract had just been agreed.

My shoulder went down into the table. My pelvis went the other way. Between these two opposing forces my spine had no choice but to surrender. Every vertebra in my back made a popping sound – one after the other – like the rasp of a fresh pack of playing cards. Who would have thought one's body could be made an instrument to produce such exotic sounds? I was grateful I had on my baggy trousers for a tighter pair might not have come through the experience intact. This occurred to me as I was rolled over onto my other side and my head buried deep in Conner's apron (which had about it a faint whiff of carbolic), whereupon the whole noisy business was repeated, my spine now arching in the opposite direction but producing the same startling sound.

Then I was left to lie on my back to recover, and consider how, when I eventually came to take my leave of Conner, I should anticipate doing so a much taller man. I took a deep breath to reassure myself that it would not always be followed by the crunching of my spine. My bone-setter, meanwhile, had gone over to a bowl of water and was now busy soaping his hands. 'Tell me, Conner,' I called over to him, 'do you believe in auras?'

A moment's silence. Then, 'Well, I would have to know what such a thing was before I could say if I believed in it.'

'It is a light or a heat which emanates from a man.'

'Well, I wouldn't know about light, Your Grace, but there is certainly heat. That I know for sure.'

I chewed this over. 'Do you believe in spirits, Conner?' I went on.

'Why do you ask?' he replied.

And so I explained about my general state of mind and the moon in the woods and the boy who has been following me around. 'Do you see the boy?' was his only question.

'I suppose I must do, yes.'

'Then surely you believe in him, Your Grace?'

'Well, that may be true ... but I cannot tell if he belongs in the real world or in my imagination.'

'With respect, Your Grace, how much does it matter which world he inhabits, if he is real enough to be seen?'

'I take your point,' I said.

Conner swung my legs off the table and helped me get to my feet. Told me to let both my hands hang loose by my sides. He stood behind me and, when I had found my balance, moved his fingers slowly up and down my spine.

'That's a little less higgledy-piggledy, Your Grace. In fact, not a bad arrangement at all.'

Then he came round and stood before me, placed a hand on either shoulder and generally took me in.

'Shoulders roughly the same altitude,' he said.

And for the first time I looked him full in the face. He was as kind and handsome as I had imagined, but while his voice was full of purpose I thought I detected about him some remoteness ... an almost unanchored air. As he spoke his eyes seemed to wander, as if they could not concentrate and preferred to cast about for cobwebs up above. Perhaps he is just a trifle shy, I thought to myself, and has difficulty looking another man in the eye – that is sometimes the case. It was another moment or two before I realized that Conner was, in fact, blind.

'How is that now?' he asked me.

'That is much better, Conner. Thank you,' I replied.

He nodded and smiled so that his moustache extended another inch or so at either end. 'In case you wondered,' he told me, 'I have been blind since the day I was born.'

I was flabbergasted. 'How in the world did you know what was on my mind?' I asked.

'Well, to be fair, I should think this must be your first chance to have a good look at me. But, just now, you paused a moment before answering my question. And when you did answer there was a hint of hesitancy there.'

'You're quite right, Conner,' I told him, ashamed of myself. 'Please accept my apologies.'

'Not at all, Your Grace.' He shook his head. 'No need. No, not at all.'

I studied him for a second, as if the man had just appeared before me in a puff of smoke – how peculiar and intriguing he was – before realizing I was staring at him as if he was some sort of circus freak. I had allowed a silence to grow between us, so I spoke up and brought it down.

'Forgive me saying this, Conner, but you must notice all manner of sounds and noises which pass most people by.'

'I may well do, Your Grace,' he replied. Then added, 'But they're there for everyone to hear.'

'Quite so,' I said. 'Quite so.'

And I looked around that tiny room as if it too had just been brought into being. The door and the shelves and the spartan walls all came to me anew. I considered the contents, hidden in darkness and found by measured steps. The jars of oil, the water jug, the coal tongs – all had transformed themselves into a blind man's things. Had become suddenly weightier. More palpable somehow.

Conner helped me get my shirt back over my head and I watched as he reached my jacket off a hook. He returned and held it open for me, then led me gracefully through the cottage towards the door.

'You must excuse my sudden silence, Conner. I have not come across a man such as yourself before.'

'Well, I should say we all have our little qualities which are not apparent at first. But I assure you, Your Grace, I'm the same man as the one you met an hour ago.'

When he opened the front door Clement was already waiting there, ready to escort me back to the carriage. As I shook Conner's hand it seemed my own palm was newly-charged, and for the briefest moment I sensed something of a whole other world which was lost to me.

'You have set me straight, Conner,' I said, 'and I very much appreciate it.'

He smiled, then leaned towards me and whispered, 'If this spirit of yours keeps pestering you you might do well to have words with him.'

'I will, Conner,' I said. 'Goodbye. And thanks again.'

'Goodbye, Your Grace,' said Conner. Then, 'Goodbye Clement,' though Clement had not said a word.

✻

DECEMBER 4TH

✻

Since Conner's recent treatment I have had not the least inclination to eat, my body perhaps regarding a reconstituted backbone as quite enough on its plate without being troubled with digestion's stresses and strains. Around lunchtime yesterday I managed a sliver of toast spread with a mushroom pâté, but that has been about the only solid food to pass my lips.

Mrs Pledger, however, is adamant I should at least maintain my consumption of liquids and boiled up for me a big pot of camomile and lemon-balm tea. This, I was assured, would calm me down after the recent hectic days and encourage in me a more tranquil frame of mind. I must admit that, while the aroma (and indeed flavour) are reminiscent of some damp corner of the garden, I found I had soon developed quite a taste for it. A fondness which rapidly developed into a fierce, almost unquenchable thirst. It seemed the more I drank of the strange yellow brew the more desiccated I became. Perhaps I have recently misplaced some vital inner juice. Perhaps my body recognized in the tea some mineral which I currently lack. What ever, my original request for Mrs Pledger to boil up a second pot was swiftly followed by ever more frequent and desperate appeals. I felt thoroughly parched, like some poor wretch lost on a desert's sands and, like a human sponge, I soaked up every last sip.

By early evening, however, the prodigious tea-drinking

135

had caught up with me and the constant trips to the water closet were becoming tedious. I was awash with camomile and lemon-balm. If I shifted too quickly in my armchair I could feel pints of the stuff splashing around inside, so that when Mrs Pledger put her head round the door around seven she found me beached in my armchair, utterly (if naturally) intoxicated and having difficulty staying awake. At which point Clement was called to help put me to bed.

To cap it all I slept remarkably well – without interruption or a single bad dream. The most satisfying sleep I have had in many a month. When I woke, a good fourteen hours after my head first hit the pillow, I felt myself thoroughly rested and quite a new man, although when I opened my mouth to let out a yawn found my breath still had about it the faint reek of scented grass.

❧

December 5th

❧

I do not think I have left my rooms all day and I can't say I feel any the worse for it. When Clement had finished drying me after one of his soapier baths, I simply changed into a clean nightshirt and took my breakfast by the fire. Managed some coddled eggs and a cup or two of Assam but resolved to spend the whole day very quiet and give my bones a chance to settle themselves. Had Clement dig out my old satin skullcap and a pair of thick knee-socks, so that with my dressing gown pulled tight around me I was almost completely insulated against the outside world.

My session with blind Conner has given me a new perspective on my body and to consolidate some of the issues raised by it I took my *Gray's Anatomy* down from the shrine and opened the old chap up.

Much of the day spent in my armchair with that weighty tome in my lap, idly picking over the pages and pausing only to heap more coal on the fire. Though I must have spent several hours in the book's learned company I cannot claim to have 'read' it as such. It is much too crammed with technical terms for me to pick up any speed. Rather, I would pore over each pen and ink drawing which took my fancy, then move on to the next.

Many of the illustrations depict some specific visceral valve or bone-corner and, in truth, these are of little interest to me. I prefer the pictures with slightly broader scope, where one can more readily identify the whole locale as part of the human form (such as a sectioned arm or leg). Each time I turned the page to cast my eye over some new junction of muscle and bone I always sought out the hand or toe or eyeball which might help me get my bearings, but if, after half a minute, I could still not tell north from south, I would simply turn to the next page and begin the whole process again.

The 'subject' of the drawings appears to be the same poor fellow throughout and it was not long before I found myself pitying him for having undergone such torture on my behalf – for assenting to be so thoroughly taken apart. His face, where it is visible, wears an attitude of weary resignation, which is commendable to say the least, considering that half his face has been crudely ripped away to show the network of nerves and veins beneath.

On one page the brave chap stands with outstretched arms, his bare back turned toward the reader and not a single scrap of flesh left on him. One looks upon a truly naked man. The only stuff covering his poor bones and organs are the ribbons of muscle, wrapped around him in fibrous swaths ... pulled tautly over the shoulders, under armpits and seeming to glisten on the page.

Amidst this sea of twisting muscle I noticed the bone causeway of the spine – an unhooked necklace of numbered pearls, beautifully bisecting his back. And as I peered at them I found myself moved a little, recognizing them as the same tiny bones which had so recently been checked and shifted by the knowing fingers of kind, blind Conner.

I studied every string of this body's bow and still he refused to flinch. In fact, so convincingly was his skinlessness mapped out for me that I had to suppress an urge to go in search of a blanket to cover up his sticky form.

On one page hand-bones were laid out like rows of flint, every knuckle and joint labelled and given its proper Latin name. How many small bones there are in one hand – as complicated an organization as the bones of a bird! – and so convincingly represented that when I next turned the page I found myself half-listening for their rattle.

The rack of ribs seemed not so much an aspect of the human form and more some butcher's shop window display. Or some bleached-out sheep-relic one stumbles across while walking upon a fell.

Then, at last, the skull! – that constant grinner – a likeness all faces gradually acquire. Each time I confront the mirror I see a little more of him peering through.

Once my cheeks were full of pie but they have slowly become hollowed-out and every year now my forehead has about it a greater determination.

Strange to think that we each carry inside us a functioning skeleton; that buried deep within the meat of me my own bone-tree patiently waits.

*

Not surprisingly, this morbid reading did nothing for my appetite so that when word came up that it was boiled gammon for lunch I called down and asked to skip straight to the pudding.

By the end of the afternoon I was still happily reading and jotting down the odd note, when I felt a dismal and lethargic cloud begin to slowly settle all around. This is not in itself unusual, for when the light first fails on a winter's day I often experience a corresponding dwindling of spirit, which can tend towards melancholy. On this occasion, however, I decided to try and counteract it with a quick bout of standing-on-my-head. As a boy, this was a favourite pastime and could be more or less relied upon to induce an agreeable light-headedness. Fortunately, I took the precaution of locking the bedroom door, for no sooner were my legs up against the wall than my nightshirt fell down around my ears.

With a thick cushion on the floor to protect my head I managed to maintain the position for several minutes, feeling refreshed and then reflective and finally a little faint. When I was upright again I could feel blood cascading through me like so many mountain streams. I was altogether much invigorated and promised myself from now on to spend at least five minutes a day upside-down.

*

Some time ago I found a small briar pipe at the back of a desk drawer which had once belonged to my father. It is carved in the shape of a Dutch clog and fits snugly in the fist of my hand. When I came upon it I saw how it had in the bottom of its bowl a scrap of ancient tobacco and it seemed not unreasonable to suppose that this tiny strand helped make up my father's last smoke.

Sometimes I think I am nothing but a foolish old man, for tonight when it was dark and the fire roared in the grate I took a twist of some new tobacco mixture (which claims to be beneficial for the heart and lungs) and filled up that briar pipe. I took care to keep in place the ancient string of tobacco and, after tamping and tucking the bowl of the pipe in the way I fancied a smoker might, I lit her up.

With an old coat around my shoulders I went out on to the balcony and in the cold night air allowed myself to imagine I inhaled the same smoke my father drew into his lungs all those years ago. I pictured it slowly wafting through my innermost caverns and felt myself much calmed. I stared up at the stars, scattered between the horizons, and added the modest glow of my pipe to their sombre display.

While I stood there in my own small cloud of smoke, thinking all manner of dreamy thoughts, I became aware how, not more than a couple of yards over my shoulder, there floated the mysterious boy. If I had reached out I could have touched him. But he would not have liked that and most likely would have disappeared. So I continued to puff quietly on my father's Dutch clog pipe and gaze up at the stars, while the floating boy kept me company in the vast, near-silent night.

*

December 7th

*

Lassitude continues. Perhaps I have drunk too much of the camomile. The whole day amounted to little more than a series of yawns and stretching of arms. Strange to report that at each yawn's peak I hear the sound of church bells ringing. Have never noticed them before.

Mrs Pledger continues her herbal assault on me. No plant on the estate is safe. Now I am quite happy to drink a little sarsaparilla to purify my blood. But one minute she is bringing me crushed mugwort (to stimulate the appetite) and the next it is elderflower and peppercorn (to clear my cloudy head). I only wish I had it in me to tell her that my head might not be so cloudy in the second place if it hadn't been for the mugwort in the first. But such talk would not go down well with her and I shudder to think how she might react. All the same, I would get along much better with all these concoctions if they didn't taste and smell like so much boiled-up bark and root. There must be a limit to how much folk-medicine a man's constitution can take. At times it is like taking a swig from a stagnant pool.

All day it has been Mrs Pledger's objective to get my appetite up so at midday, in order to show willing, I announced how I quite fancied an apple (something we are never short of in this house) and made a show of smacking my lips. Ten minutes later I was presented with a platter stacked with half a dozen varieties, from which I picked my favourite, a beautiful Russet – coarse, tanned skin; tender, creamy flesh with a rich and smoky flavour.

I rolled its lovely roughness in my palm before cutting it cleanly in half, the knife ringing out as it struck the plate. The two halves separated perfectly, flat and white, and as I took one up and bit into it watched a single pip, which had leapt from the apple's split core, gently spinning on the plate.

Such colossal potential in the humble pip! How pleasing that locked away in the very heart of the fruit there nestles a tight cluster of its eager seed. And that in each dark little teardrop is the makings of a tree.

But we do not like to eat them. They are bitter! We spit the fellows out. Yet, when spilt or planted (or even spat) onto fertile soil, that little pip will set about its ambitions of one day becoming a sapling, one day a tree. In its tough little shell are all the elements required to throw up a tree – bizarre ... a tree from a pip! – which one day, many years hence, may produce pippy apples of its own.

*

Around two o'clock I decided that if I did not make some effort to move about I might expire right there in my chair. So I called down for my long sable coat and beaver and laced up a pair of brown ankle boots. I already had on my moleskin trousers and knitted waistcoat and when I added my coat and hat and stood before the mirror I thought myself very smart indeed. As he picked the odd speck of dust from my shoulders Clement expressed concern at the prospect of my walking out alone, but once he understood I merely intended to take a stroll around the house he was greatly put at ease.

I checked my supplies before departing – compass, handkerchief and a pencil and paper in case I needed to make some notes – and had removed my sable while I limbered up when, out of the corner of my eye, I spotted Clement slipping a large oatmeal biscuit into my coat pocket. Made no mention of it.

Stood at my bedroom doorway, having difficulty recalling whether there was still a stairway at the end of the West wing or if it had been removed after becoming riddled with worm. By and by, however, I satisfied myself that it was the East wing not the West which had suffered the worm and that the stairs had most definitely been replaced ... a good fifteen years ago, most likely. No, twenty. (Or even twenty-five.)

Clement was still most eager to accompany me but I insisted (quite forthrightly I thought) to be allowed to go on my own. We both stood by the door for a minute, rather stuck for something to say. Then I patted him on his shoulder and set off, feeling like a soldier marching off to war. When I looked over my shoulder a few seconds later I found

Clement still standing there, so we waved to one another and I carried on my way.

I was right at the end of the corridor before I realized I was headed eastward instead of west. What an idiot! Thankfully, Clement had surrendered his post at my bedroom door and was busy tending the fire so I was able to retrace my steps and creep past on tiptoe. Cantered quietly down the corridor until I had reached the bend.

I was completely lost within five minutes, but not altogether troubled. It was quite exciting to meander from room to room, taking in some which were quite foreign to me and others which I found I knew quite well. So, here was a study crammed with furniture and a ten-foot marble fireplace that might as well have belonged in a neighbour's house. But here was a room I remembered very fondly, for I had planned to decorate it and name it the Bachelors' Hall, where all the single men in Nottinghamshire could meet and socialize. I had envisaged indoor sport and much singing and manly camaraderie, but the long tables stood bare and dusty, without ever having had a single port or pastry set down on them. It is disturbing sometimes to find one's old dreams half alive and shabby-looking when, in truth, one would prefer them dead and six foot underground.

I strolled down one corridor after another, exploring every new avenue I came upon. One was carpeted with rugs from the Orient, the next had a plain parquet floor. Down one curving hall I ran the gauntlet of my whole glum ancestry, who glared down at me from their portraits. Another was lined with the mounted heads of deer. The walls of one room were covered with oil paintings of horses whose legs were too big for their bodies. And round the next corner I found my mother's old Sewing Room, which I had always thought to be in another part of the house.

When I became hopelessly disorientated I consulted my trusty compass. It was a minute or two before it dawned on me that finding North was not necessarily going to help me out. But by wiping the grime from a pane of glass and squinting out at the cold, damp world I found I could roughly calculate my whereabouts in the house by my relationship to one of the trees.

Eventually found myself down in the kitchens. Two girls were peeling the vegetables and quite taken by surprise. I think they mistook me in my sable coat for a bear which had wandered in from the woods. So I swiftly removed my beaver and introduced myself and their screaming died down in no time at all.

I was pleased to inform them that my walk had stimulated in me a healthy appetite and asked them to pass this news on to Mrs Pledger. As I turned to go I noticed two chickens stretched out on the table, waiting to be plucked. They looked rather pathetic lying there, with their heads dangling off the deck, so I put in a request for a little parsnip soup instead, then scurried away before Mrs Pledger had a chance to show her face.

I was out of the door and halfway down a cream-painted corridor before I realized my predicament. Had to return to the kitchens and ask the girls for directions back to my rooms.

*

Stood on my head for a good ten minutes, which left me seeing stars for about half an hour. After dinner I put on my sable and went out on to the balcony to puff on my father's pipe. The white smoke went down into me and filled me up and soothed me from top to toe. Few men, I think, could manage to fill a pipe and smoke it without becoming more philosophical by several degrees. There is something in the very nature of pipe-smoking which demands it.

As the smoke curled all about me I took in the icy moon through my old telescope. They say it has its own seas, just like ours. So, for a while, I dwelt on those distant waters and wondered what drove their tides. I studied the same stars I have studied a hundred times before and in my own modest way considered my Maker. Think I might have hit upon something, namely . . .

> . . . that perhaps we have a God up in the heavens to give us some perspective on our lives. And that the search we each undertake for a partner in life might work along similar lines, i.e.: that by establishing a point outside of ourselves we seek some much-needed objectivity. In other words, by regarding ourselves through the eyes of another we are momentarily relieved of the burden of inhabiting ourselves.

I am no clearer now, an hour later, if any of this makes sense. It may have just been the tobacco talking. However, of one thing I am certain, which is that as I stood out there on the balcony grappling with such grand and hefty thoughts, I again sensed, very close to me, the presence of the floating boy.

He was silent – just hung there in the near distance, looking down at me. He is a nervous boy, so I took great care not to frighten him off, and managed to find a way of looking up at the moon through the telescope whilst observing him in the periphery of my other eye. In doing so I began to make out something of his form. He is very young. There is a milkiness about him. He is a most blurred and milky young boy.

✳

*

I had just finished breakfast this morning and was admiring Sanderson's map when Mrs Pledger knocked at my door and came striding in, full of bustle, with her mouth firmly set.

'What can I do for you, Mrs Pledger?' I asked.

'I have some bad news, Your Grace,' she replied.

In that case, I told her, she had better come right out with it, double-quick. So she filled her chest and raised her head and, in what sounded suspiciously like a well-rehearsed tone, informed me that Mr Snow, my old gardener, had recently passed away.

Well, this knocked the stuffing right out of me. I must have slumped down in a chair. All sorts of emotion began to bubble up inside me and I was still waiting to see how they might manifest themselves, when Mrs Pledger raised her hand to regain my attention, then proceeded to tell me how Mr Snow had passed away quite peacefully in his sleep but that ... and here she faltered ... but that Mrs Snow had died soon after.

Well, by now I had more than enough to cope with, but Mrs P. had her tap turned full on and words continued to pour from her ... how it was 'a most dreadful thing, to be sure', but how Dr Cox reckoned 'the shock of losing her husband had almost certainly contributed to the death of his wife' until, with her left hand twisting her apron pocket, Mrs Pledger finally drew her speech to a close by saying how Mrs Snow was 'nearly as old and infirm as Mr Snow and how it was hardly any surprise at all'.

By now I was altogether swamped and baffled. I may have nodded my head and murmured, 'Quite so,' once or twice but, in truth, this represented little comprehension on my part. Several conflicting thoughts fought for my attention, like sheep all squeezing through a gate. One was grief at the loss of my old gardener and it whispered in my ear, 'Mr Snow, your old gardener ... gone.' A second was more concerned with that dependency between Mr Snow and his wife which I had witnessed on my recent visit, and it whispered, 'Here is confirmation, as plain as your nose – one flame is extinguished and it takes another one with it when it goes.'

Other thoughts gnawed away at me – all of them murky and half-formed – by far the loudest being a nagging voice of doubt, which wondered at the peculiar manner Mrs Pledger had divulged her story and why, at that very moment, she refused to look me in the eye.

'How long between the death of Mr Snow and his wife?' I asked Mrs Pledger.

Her fingers screwed her apron pocket tighter still. 'Three days, Your Grace,' she said.

And now a new voice leapt into the chorus. 'Three days!' it shouted. 'John Snow dead three days!' And yet another voice, more distant, began ranting, 'All that contemplation last week on the circulation of gossip, yet no one thought to put you in the picture ... Three full days since John Snow died!'

And an anxious, bilious ball rose in me. I was not as strong as I had been a minute before, but I staggered to my feet and, though there was barely room for it, drew in a breath and looked my housekeeper full in the face.

'When is their funeral, Mrs Pledger?' I asked and heard the stitching of her apron pocket coming apart in her hand.

'Their funeral was two days ago, Your Grace.'

I buckled beneath an impossible weight. The whole house folded up around me. My ears had in them a high-pitched ringing, so that I barely heard Mrs Pledger as words continued to fly out of her. 'You have not been well, Your Grace,' was in there somewhere. As was, 'Dr Cox said it would only upset you more.'

And now the growing ball of anxiety pushed right up into my throat. My whole body brimmed with emotional pain. I thought, 'My staff and Dr Cox have decided between them that I am weak. They have kept the Snows' death to themselves.'

I saw the cortège carrying their bodies, laden with wreaths and not a single petal from me. 'Have I not the right to grieve?' I thought to myself. 'I am a grown man – why not let me grieve?' The horses leaned forward into their harnesses and the cortège began to pull away.

'He was my friend,' I told Mrs Pledger. 'I should have liked to have said goodbye to my old friend.'

She nodded at me, then mercifully turned and left me to suffer my distress alone. And as the door closed behind her I felt the bubble finally burst and I fell, as if my legs had been kicked from under me. I fell and continued falling and was at long last engulfed in my own tears.

I wept for my old and much-loved gardener and his faithful wife who had followed him to the grave. I wept for my absence at their funeral; their being seen off without my being there. I wept from the shame of my own staff thinking me weak and mad and not to be trusted with the truth. And I wept because of that damned pain which climbed the ladder of my ribcage and might have strangled me had it not been for kind Conner. And somewhere in my tears I believe I wept for Mrs Pledger – for having picked the shortest straw and having to wend her way up to me, to own up to my staff's deceit.

With one hand I rubbed at my streaming eyes while the other clawed at the rug on which I sprawled. I think my fingers would have liked to unpick the whole carpet, thread by thread. I shook and shuddered, as if some pump had broken free inside me; had to snatch my breath in great wet gulps until my shoulders ached. But when my eyes ran dry and my sobs subsided, I got to my feet and stumbled over to the mirror on the mantelpiece. There was the old man looking back at me, his pink little mouth all twisted and limp. His brows were knitted together above a pair of marbly eyes and his whole visage looked thoroughly beaten and bruised.

But I was in no position to be of any use to him, for I was too busy enjoying the show. How perverse that at such moments I am still fascinated by my every twitch and tremble, by my tear's slow journey down my cheek. That even as I moulder in a pit of misery some part of me still coolly observes my every move.

*

I did no headstands this evening. No pipe-smoking, no gazing at the stars. I did not leave my rooms at all. I simply lay on my bed and stared into space.

I had lost a friend and missed his funeral, and suffered the indignity of not being the master in my own house.

I was tempted to get on the mouthpiece and blow down to every last one of them and ask if they'd prefer me to be the black-hearted tyrant instead of the whimsical old fool that I am.

At last, I took down my wind-up monkey and gave him a turn or two and watched him go through the effort of raising his little hat for me.

*

*

Although the sun had barely risen, enough of it filtered through the skylights for me to make my way along the tunnel without incident. When I emerged near Holbeck village I still had no idea where my destination lay and it was only my seeing a curl of smoke from the Reverend Mellor's chimney which prompted me to pay him a visit.

After a restless night's sleep I had woken early, with just one thought on my mind – that I must get out of the wretched house or risk being suffocated by it. I dressed quickly in a blue cotton morning suit and took the main stairs down into a deserted hall; called in at the cloakroom where I picked up my beaver, a burgundy frock coat and matching cape. Took the door under the Great Stair Way down to the tunnels and, without any particular forethought, set off down the South-west passage to find myself, within the hour, on the doorstep of Reverend Mellor's vicarage.

The Reverend himself opened the door to me looking somewhat muddled and badly organized; shirt and waistcoat were all asunder, as if his seams had finally given out. His neck and cheeks were covered with shaving soap and he clutched a razor, rather menacingly, in one hand. As he stood there blinking at me a bead of blood slowly seeped into the soap.

'You have cut yourself, Reverend,' I told him.

There was another moment or two's squinting, before his face gave way to a smile.

'Your Grace,' he said. 'I am not used to such early callers.' Then, 'Come in, come in, come in.'

I was led into a parlour-cum-study where he turned and squinted at me again. Mellor is a solid, plump sort of fellow who, by some freak of nature, has only a young lad's legs to support his considerable weight, which jut out from under him at acute angles like the legs on a milkmaid's stool. His tiny feet had on a pair of Oriental slippers and were positioned 'ten-to-two' on the rug, as if they were about to launch him into some great balletic leap.

'I must apologize for not recognizing you, Your Grace,' he said, 'but I am without my spectacles.'

He leaned towards me and squinted at full strength, as if assessing what the situation required.

'Cup of tea?' he said, raising his eyebrows.

'A cup of tea would be just the thing,' I replied.

He smiled and nodded towards the hearth. 'Kettle's on,' he said.

Then he waved his razor in the air again. 'Now, if you don't mind, I must complete my ablutions,' and he skipped off up the stairs, leaving me to make myself at home.

Finding a path through the room was no easy matter, for it was packed with so much clutter and stuff. Bookshelves heaved on almost every inch of wall and framed watercolours and sketches and yellowing prints all jostled for the remaining space. There must have been close to a dozen tables, all different sizes, scattered around the room, each one piled with papers and boxes and stacks of threadbare books. Half-naked statuettes thrust their swords into the air and some teetering vase or fancy lamp jangled with my every step. Even the narrow window sills were crowded with glass ornaments and the sunlight took their pinks and turquoises and sent them shimmering on the floor.

I advanced carefully through this jungle of bric-à-brac, nervous of catching some table corner or protruding text and bringing about some dreadful calamity. But at last the fire-place swung into view and I found myself in a clearing before a sagging mantelpiece with a pair of armchairs standing by and so I set about removing my coats. A fresh fire was settling into the day's business and I don't mind admitting I felt a twinge of jealousy for the master of such a hearty little room.

I was idly picking over the shelves of books when the Reverend reappeared. He was now all brushed-down and buttoned-up and his eyes swam happily in his spectacles. As he nodded, gently priming himself for speech, it occurred to me that he had about him not a fraction of Ignatius Peak's zeal. The Reverend Mellor, I decided, keeps his God very much under his hat.

'Now, Your Grace,' he said, eyeing me closely, 'I assume you have had your breakfast?'

When I told him that, in fact, I had not his eyes grew very wide indeed, almost filling his spectacle lenses. A small, incredulous smile played upon his lips.

'Your Grace, I believe you have run away from home,' he said.

Counselling the bereaved and distraught members of his parish has clearly made him an expert in getting quickly to the bottom of things.

'I needed to get out of the house for a while,' I told him and added, 'I left a note for Clement.'

'Well, in that case, he shall not be worrying. Tell me, would you like me to toast your muffin or would you care to toast your own?'

And we soon were leaning forward on our armchairs like boys around a campfire, each holding out a toasting-fork with a muffin skewered to the end. The Reverend brewed up a pot of smoky-flavoured tea and opened a new jar of quince jelly (a gift, I assumed, from some grateful parishioner). The muffins and the tea were excellent and, finding no good reason to call the proceedings to a halt, we continued to stuff ourselves for getting on an hour until at last the sheer volume of bread and tea inside us forced us to sit back in our chairs. As we rested I felt about as round and breathless as Mellor himself and wondered if it wasn't perhaps muffins and quince jelly which had given him his distinctive shape. Sitting side by side I thought the two of us must look like a pair of Toby jugs.

The Reverend said how sorry he was that I had missed the Snows' funeral service and I assured him that there was no man sorrier than myself. I thanked him for his recipe for his rheumatism pills and he asked if they had done me any good.

'In all honesty, I don't think so,' I told him.

He nodded. 'It was the same with me,' he replied.

We were still meditating on this when, quite suddenly, Mellor sat up in his chair, made a weird, muted exclamation and pressed a forefinger to the side of his head. He leapt to his feet and with admirable alacrity picked his way between the heaped tables and dangling plants, reached a bank of drawers, drew a couple of them straight out from their cases and returned with one under each arm and a large magnifying glass clenched in his teeth.

He rolled back into his armchair with the drawers in his lap. His head disappeared into them. There was the sound of much scuffling and rattling about. When he re-emerged he looked much invigorated and held up a curious looking object which he passed to me, saying,

'What do you make of that, Your Grace?'

Well, it was flat and fairly heavy – about eight inches by four. White and smooth, like something which had been washed up on a beach.

'Is it a bone?' I asked.

'Full marks,' announced Mellor. 'Now, Your Grace, any idea what beast?'

I must have stared at that cold old bone for getting on a minute, as if it might whisper me a clue, but at last I was forced to admit that I was completely in the dark.

'It is the jawbone...' said the Reverend, with eyes widening, 'of a hyena. And a big fellow he was, too.'

He held both hands out in front of him, a foot apart.

'Head about so big,' he assured me, raising his eyebrows. Then he gazed down at the space between his hands, so utterly engrossed in his hyena-thoughts that I feared he might suddenly throw back his head and let out a terrible howl.

'Found just over a year ago, in your own caves up at Creswell.'

'Well, well,' I said, noting how he had got me nodding along with him.

Another fragment of bone was tossed over to me, about the same size as the razor Mellor had been waving about. I turned the thing over in my hands. It was considerably lighter than the previous one and smelt, I thought, vaguely of mutton.

'Take a closer look,' said the Reverend, handing me the magnifying glass. So I held it over the narrow bone and through the swell of the lens managed to make out several rows of tiny scratches along the bone's edge, not unlike the fractions of an inch on a ruler, or the cross-hatching on Mr Sanderson's map.

'What are they for?' I asked.

'Decoration, maybe . . . Art of some sort. Who can say?'

I must admit I was a little taken aback by the Reverend's rather dismissive tone and, of course, he picked up on this straight away.

'You'd be surprised, Your Grace, how that which we are in the habit of referring to as "historical fact" is often little more than speculation. A thousand years from now some chap might come across an ornament of our day. He might identify it as such in no time. But when he comes to decide what it is *for*, exactly . . . well, that is going to be guesswork, wouldn't you say?'

I conceded the point while privately vowing to give more thought to it later on. And like a truffling pig the Reverend went back to rooting in his drawers of bone. One specimen after another was turned up and offered to me and while I examined one he was furiously digging out the next, so that my lap was soon heaped with them. All, the Reverend assured me, had once belonged to some creature who stalked the local countryside, many centuries ago. Bison, reindeer, mammoth, wild horse ... they were beginning to weigh me down. As I shifted in my chair they ground against one another and made an eerie scraping noise but the Reverend was much too deeply immersed in the past to notice any discomfort I was presently suffering.

At some point I asked what tools he used to unearth these relics. 'Oh, just a teaspoon and a small brush,' he told me, still foraging. 'The cave floors are nothing but silt, you see? Perfect for preservation. But we would never have had an inkling what was down there if the farmer who used one of the caves to shelter his cattle hadn't tripped over a fossil or two.'

He stopped for a second, raised his head and peered over his drawers at me. 'Have you not seen the caves since they were tidied-up, Your Grace?'

I told him that I had not and admitted being unable to recall ever having been right inside them, though I drive past them often enough.

'And you being such an underground man,' he said. 'Well, we must go. Yes, of course we must,' and he began nodding. 'We must go this very minute.'

He paused for me to nod along with him. 'How splendid. I shall show you round your own caves.'

He was now nodding his head so violently the two drawers in his lap had begun to bounce about. But all of a sudden he stopped and raised a finger, for us both to hold our horses. 'Before we go,' he said gravely, 'one final bone.'

And, with considerable care, he presented me with an almost circular piece of bone. Quite small, but heavy as a rock.

'And who is this?' I asked the Reverend.

'The woolly rhino,' he replied with evident pride. 'Very rare.'

'A rhino in Nottinghamshire?' I asked him.

He gave me his surest, wisest nod.

I was most impressed. 'If you don't mind my asking, Reverend, how do you know it is a woolly rhino?'

He indicated a row of books. 'It's all in there,' he said, and sighed a little, as if recalling every weary hour of reading, the many months spent with his head in a book. 'But, you know, one must also employ a little bit of this,' and he tapped the side of his round head.

'Naturally,' I said, less certain with every second just what it was we were talking about. 'And in your opinion how might a woolly rhino actually look?'

'Well, now . . .' The Reverend took his time chewing over this one. He gazed into the far distance, as if down all the centuries. 'I would say he looks much the same as the modern rhino . . . but with a little more hair.'

I am sorry to admit that at this point my estimation of archaeologists plummeted somewhat. So much so that I wondered if, with the aid of the odd book or two, Mrs Pledger and I might not prove as proficient an archaeologist as Mellor himself.

*

It took us less than half an hour to trek across the fields to the caves, the Reverend setting an impressive pace. A strapped-up five-barred gate was the only thing that caused us any real delay.

The cave entrances are about fifty feet up a huge craggy slab and, from a distance, look like the gaps in an idiot's grin. We paused at the bottom of the sharp incline which leads up to them. The Reverend raised his nose and sniffed the air. 'Chilly . . .' he said.

I was still considering this when he went charging off up the sandy slope, leaving a trail of dust behind. Well, there was little else to do but chase after him, so I set off at my own bow-legged trot. I soon caught him up on the incline and was becoming closely acquainted with his vast behind, having good reason, all of a sudden, to hope that his momentum did not suddenly give out on him.

We were both of us well wrapped-up in overcoats and our brief gallop generated a fair amount of heat, and when we had scrambled up the last of the steep path we sat ourselves down on a rocky ledge by the cave entrance to look down at the river below and try to recompose ourselves.

We were too breathless to make any conversation and the perspiration was still drying on my brow when the Reverend reached into his rucksack and brought out a small oil lamp.

'Let us have a little look-see, shall we?' he said and placed the lamp on the ground between us. Then he produced from his waistcoat pocket a porcelain matchbox, in the shape of a cherub, whose head bent back on a hinge to reveal the matches hidden inside. Mellor took one out and struck it on the underside of the box.

'Show us the way, young fellow,' he said, as the match burst into life.

We advanced down a damp, narrow passage which went straight into the rock. The second we had set foot in it I felt the temperature dramatically drop and every breath was immediately transformed into a shocking blast to the chest.

'No wonder the bones keep so well,' I remarked to Mellor. 'It is like an ice-house in here.'

With his lamp held out before him the Reverend led the way, our footfalls coming right back at us from the cold and stinking rock. We had covered hardly any distance when the tunnel began to shrink around us. A most unpleasant feeling. But we kept on, creeping deeper into the earth, one tentative step after another, until Mellor's breadth prevented all but the faintest flicker coming back to light my way and I was forced to stumble in his dismal wake. In no time my hands were out in front of me, lest I be struck by some protruding rock, my fingers fussing over the stone around me – sometimes dry, sometimes greasy with moss. I was utterly lost in the darkness and bumbling along so clumsily that when Mellor suddenly stopped to catch his breath, I walked straight into him.

Our faltering journey had advanced maybe thirty yards in all when the tunnel's roof dropped by a couple more feet. Originally, it had cleared our heads by several inches but now pressed right down on top of us, so that we were obliged to walk bent-double in order to avoid cracking our heads. I found I kept looking keenly back over my shoulder, towards the entrance's ragged circle of light, each time noticing how it had diminished a little, until it was nothing more than a distant, fading sun.

I could not say I had so far taken much pleasure from our little underground hike, but any hope of such a thing was trounced entirely when I found myself taken over by a quite irrational but profoundly-rooted fear. Without warning, I became utterly convinced that I was about to be cut off from my precious circle of light. In an instant my breath quickened to the pant of an exhausted dog, my heart pounding frantically at the walls of my chest. Some imminent rockfall was about to cut us off. Some faceless adversary was plotting to shut us in. The same awful fear possessed me which I had felt as I entered the Oakleys' front room, but I had not now the sisters' kind words to soothe me, their quiet confidence to calm me down. I was filled up with trepidation; it animated every fibre of me painfully. My own infant's voice pleaded with me to abandon the journey, to dash back down the passage. 'Danger!' the voice insisted. 'Run for the light, before it disappears!'

Well, I did everything in my power to silence that voice. I blocked my ears and clenched my jaw. I did my damnedest to bring my breathing under control, telling myself again and again, 'You are all right, man. You are all right.' It was a desperate and pathetic struggle but I was determined that Reason should win the day. When, at last, I managed to recover myself a little, managed to reach some momentary plateau of near-calm, I found I had lagged several yards behind Mellor and his oil lamp. My mouth and throat were completely parched. I swallowed hard and pushed on into the dark.

I continued to walk with my hands out in front of me (more like the antennae of an insect than appendages of a man). Every half-dozen or so steps I would halt and spread my fingers on the tunnel walls to sense how much space I had around me in which to breathe. It seemed that this futile gesture – of my palms pressing against the rock – was all that kept it from closing in on me and crushing me to death.

Twice the Reverend stumbled. Both times he called out, 'Careful here.' The words skittered down the tunnel, returning first as a single echo, then a second and third and fourth, until they all ganged-up together in a deafening, lunatic roar. When I heard him slip a third time and call out, 'Careful here,' again, I very nearly lost my head. There was little enough room in the tunnel, without his demented voices flying everywhere.

The tunnel roof had now sunk to such a miserable height it was right down on our backs and the two of us all but crawling on our blessed hands and knees. Time and again I told myself, 'I shall turn and get out of here in a second,' while becoming less and less certain there was space enough to execute such a manoeuvre. The pressure in my head was close to bursting and both my shoulders were grazing against the rock when I thought I felt the hint of a cool breeze sweep across my face.

The next minute Mellor and I were clambering free of the tunnel, were standing upright and stretching and stamping our feet. We had come out into some sort of cavern, perhaps thirty foot at its highest point, and when the Reverend lifted the lamp above his head its amber light filled the entire dome. The cave walls hung over us like great ocean waves, frozen at that last moment before crashing down.

I must have stood there, entranced, for several minutes, trying to make some sense of the place. It had about it an ochre glow which seemed to emanate from the very rock. Tiny rivulets had eaten away at the chamber walls and made rocky fingers out of them so that one felt almost as if one was caught in a giant's cupped hands.

The Reverend found himself a boulder on the cave floor and daintily lowered himself onto it. He placed the oil lamp on the ground beside him and folded his arms in a proprietorial way while I proceeded to silently circle him and take in every aspect of this weird subterranean place.

The lamp's flame momentarily flickered and I saw my own shadow shudder on the wall and this had on me a powerful, almost hypnotic effect, as if the shadow was not mine but some distant ancestor's who was feinting this way and that. I thought to myself, 'He is trying to mesmerize me with some ancient dance.'

The light in that cavern was at such a premium and the darkness so eager to return that the shadow which stretched and shrank before me seemed a good deal more at home there and had a presence at least as convincing as my own.

The Reverend clasped his hands round his knees, leaned back on his rock and stared up at the ceiling. 'What do you make of it, Your Grace?' I heard him whisper, before the words were taken up by the cave walls and tossed about the place. My reply lodged itself deep in my throat, fearful of what the cave's acoustics might do with it. A word here too harshly spoken might let loose a whole Bedlam of broken voices. But I was also silent because the peculiar beauty of the cavern had all but robbed me of my speech.

High up, where the Reverend had fixed his gaze, were minerals, embedded in the rock. They crackled silently in the light. The cold air now began to find its way through to me, investigating every cranny of my boots and coats, and I began to feel a little unwelcome among all the smooth formlessness of the cave.

At last I said, 'It is somehow similar to how I imagine the surface of the moon to be.'

The Reverend smiled and nodded back at me from his stone seat. 'I have often thought the same thing myself,' he said.

I asked if all the other caves were as grand and the Reverend told me that this was by far the largest and queerest but that, at one time, all would have offered shelter to some creature or other.

'And was it only animals that used them?' I asked.

'O, no,' said the Reverend. 'Primitive Man once lived here. There's no doubting that.'

I tried to picture Primitive Man, dressed in nothing but a few rags of hide, as he went about his Primitive Life ... creeping out into the valleys of ancient Nottinghamshire to hunt wild bison and reindeer (and the woolly rhino) and spending his nights in the cold, damp dark. For a second I even fancied I saw the carcasses of those beasts laid out on the cave floor and the crude implements which my primitive ancestor might have used to rip their flesh apart.

Well, I could not have chosen a worse time for such a reverie. These gruesome pictures of brute gore were still most vivid in my mind when the Reverend drew me to him with his finger and gave up half his boulder for me. I perched myself down beside him and was still wondering what his enigmatic expression meant when he reached over to his oil lamp and whispered, 'Watch carefully, Your Grace.'

And the flame on the lamp's wick began to hesitate; gave out as it was slowly choked of air. All around us the light slowly drained from the cave and seeped back into the ground. The lamp's tiny flame shrank and spluttered to a single ounce of light and the cave quietly reasserted its awful power over us. Every second of its thousands of years of darkness returned to it. The brief moments of light we had brought in with us were erased. Horrified, I watched the flame dwindle, and with a final flicker, die.

I was alone, deep in the rock. There was no light. No memory of it. Only the darkness pressing down.

'What is this?' I hissed at Mellor and a thousand snaking voices sprang to life.

He said nothing. He was no longer next to me. I could not move for the rock.

'That is enough, Mellor,' I insisted, but my tongue was thick with fear. 'For God's sake, man, strike a match.'

My own voice jabbered back at me in chorus before slowly consuming itself. Then there was nothing but the darkness and the silence. Nothing but the deep, dead rock.

At last, I heard the Reverend say, 'Hold tight. Just one more minute . . . Ah now, look up, Your Grace.'

Well, I did as I was told. At first, nothing. Blindness. No sound, except my own mouth, gasping for air. Then somewhere up above, out of the corner of my eye, I saw the glitter of the very first star. Then it was gone again but as I tried to retrieve it I found another, further over. Then another. All the stars were coming out. They twinkled mercifully up in the heavens, each one its own small message of hope. And, slowly, the faint moon revealed itself, calmly filled itself with ghostly light and took its place among the stars.

'Can you see it now?' Mellor asked me.

'Yes. Yes, I see it,' I said. 'It is beautiful ... Very beautiful indeed.'

From our shared stone seat we continued to look up at the stars until at last I said, 'I'm afraid I don't understand.'

'It is a hole,' he said. 'A natural chimney. Which is why this cave is called the Pin Hole Cave. Only a small hole but big enough to let in the light which picks out the crystal in the rock.'

So was there mercy or was there not? I was still trying to make sense of it and staring up at the moon and the stars when the Reverend struck a match. The brightness was too much for me and I had to cover my eyes against its terrible glare. And when the lamp was relit I found myself back in the cave's strange ochre glow. The heavens above had been turned to stone. The stars had been washed away.

'Time to go?' said the Reverend, nodding. 'Hup. Hup.' And he helped me to my feet.

It was as if the hands on my mind's clock had been frozen, then released by the match's flame. Time suddenly flooded back in and exhausted me.

The Reverend lifted his lamp, smiled and made towards the tunnel and I had no choice but to stagger after him and prepare for the long trek back. But as Mellor squeezed himself into the tunnel and stole the light away I had one last glance at the place.

I felt as if I had come within an inch of Primitive Man. Spent a fraction of a second in his skull.

The journey back down the passage was, thankfully, without incident and as we made our way along it I managed more or less to allay my fears that the Reverend might somehow contrive to get himself wedged between the tunnel walls. In time, the tunnel began to open itself up to us and the light from the entrance formed a gentle halo around the Reverend. And in what seemed like half the time it took us to get in there we were walking out into the day.

The view from the cave entrance, though frosty and wintry, was a marvel to behold – full of colour and distance and depth. I looked up and down the valley and drew in its rich air, wondering how it might look with a huge glacier to fill it up. I imagined that massive slab of ice as a vast silvery ship, sitting on a slipway, calmly awaiting its launch. Slowly, century by century, it inched towards the sea.

I looked at my watch – barely midmorning, though I seemed to have crammed in enough experience to last me the whole of the year. Mellor was busy packing his lamp away and I thought perhaps I should be getting back or Clement might start sending out search parties again.

So the two of us shook hands and I thanked him for his hospitality and for showing me the caves.

'You must drop by again, Your Grace,' he said.

'I will,' I assured him and set off across the fields.

*

December 13th

*

I seem to find the less I eat the livelier I become. Each rejected savoury gives me an extra charge of vim. All these years I have thought it was food which kept me going – the fuel for my body's fire. Now I am not so sure. Recently I went for a whole day without eating a single thing and when I woke the following morning felt just as bright as a button. Mealtimes have begun to slip by without even a hint of appetite stirring in me. Some days the thought of a sandwich is enough to make me sick.

But it is not as if I am starving myself. Yesterday I ate a pear and two dry scones. Today I have already had an onion pastry and shall not be in the least surprised if I have something else before I retire. Have vowed to forgo meat of all kinds and must say I am feeling better for it. Mental faculties are a deal sharper. Each day now there are moments when I become so altogether pure I begin to float away.

*

Have been forced to discontinue my custom of standing-on-my-head, which is a bitter disappointment as I am certain that gravity is the natural way to encourage extra blood to the brain. I recently immersed myself so successfully in meditation that I dozed off for a moment or two. When I came round I was out by ninety degrees – had gone from vertical to horizontal, bringing a curtain and an Elgin vase down with me. Mrs Pledger was quite insistent I give the whole thing up there and then.

So, as an alternative means of invigoration, I have taken up what my father used to call 'the hot and cold treatment', which, in plain English, is simply the practice of jumping straight out of a hot bath and into a cold. It does wonders for the complexion, giving a body the ruddiest glow. Clement is not keen on the idea – I suppose it rather rubs up against his own philosophies – but I am proud to say that in my old age I am learning to dig my heels in and so every day now he fills one bath for me with scalding water and another with ice-cold. Unfortunately, there is only the one tub in my own bathroom so we have to draw the cold one in a bathroom down the hall.

Now, I cannot pretend that leaping into a cold bath is an altogether relaxing experience, especially when one has been stewing-in-a-pot only seconds before, but there is no denying that it wakes the body up with an almighty jolt. My heart sometimes takes twenty minutes to return to its pedestrian plod.

From one bathroom to the other is a good fifty- or sixty-yard trot and it has become necessary to seal off the whole landing by hanging up blankets at both ends. This follows an unfortunate incident when a housemaid happened to come round the corner with a pile of towels as I was going down the corridor at full-pelt. The poor girl almost leapt down the stairs in fright and had to be carted to my study by Clement and given a brandy to bring her round. We had to send her home. But the sight of a naked old man must be very alarming to one of such tender years. Especially when he is haring towards you for all he is worth.

So, as I say, we now take the precaution of hanging up blankets. And, in order to clear the area, Clement strikes a small gong just before I go.

✻

This afternoon I went on another walkabout, setting out along the East wing and then venturing off down other corridors. By some deft little twisting and turning I came across an unfamiliar flight of stairs and, following them, found a tiny storeroom which I had not come across before. It was no more than ten foot by twenty, in what used to be the servants' quarters, and with nothing in it but a stack of chests and boxes and a collapsed bedstead. The contents of the boxes were mostly broken or in poor condition. In one was an ancient rug, stored in peppercorns; in another, a hammock and several pairs of flattened shoes. There was an ivory chess set with two pieces missing, a dented sports cup and a Chinaman's hat.

I cannot honestly say I know what I am after on these little expeditions of mine, but have convinced myself that in some forgotten corner of the house there sits an item which will make sense of my recent spiritual hurly-burly.

Whatever form this enigmatic object might take, I can safely say it was not unearthed today, though I did come across a rather curious wooden microscope, wrapped in linen, and three boxes of glass slides. No idea who they belonged to. I do not recall acquiring them myself. All the same, I brought the whole lot back to my bedroom, feeling quite pleased with my little find.

Sat myself down at my table and took the slides from their neat little tins but as I removed the tissue paper found that most were cracked or shattered and only one set was intact. The box was marked

HYMENOPTERA
Honey Bee
Apis mellifica
– drone –

Each slide was individually labelled, indicating the part of the bee it contained . . . 'third leg', 'mandible', 'hind wing' and so forth.

I held one of the slides up and, even without the microscope, could make out the tiny fragment of the long-dead bee. Each slide was, in fact, two identical glass wafers with the bee-part sandwiched in between, held in what looked to me like a flattened drop of the bee's own amber honey.

I gave the microscope a quick dusting-down and moved the table over to the window where there was a little more light.

The scope itself is no more than ten inches tall and turned from a beautiful dark wood – walnut, perhaps – squat but curvaceous, like a tiny stair banister, and fitted at one end with three crooked brass legs. Each leg is welded onto a thick brass ring which, when turned, effectively raises or lowers the height of the microscope, thereby allowing the operator to bring the object into focus.

I placed a sheet of paper on the table top, selected a slide and slipped it under the lens. The microscope was cold against the bag of flesh beneath my eye – a sensation which stirred in me memories of my old telescope. But with this instrument I looked not up, up, up at the distant stars, but down, very deeply down, and found myself suddenly in the troubling company of gargantuan insect limbs.

A single wing was veined like a leaf – more a construction of glass and steel than a part of a once-living thing.

The 'first leg' becomes bristly and muscular under the microscope . . . gnarled with all manner of knots and joints. A massive spring for his alighting, for flicking the fellow up in the air . . .

In this manner I examined each tiny component of the dismembered honey bee. Scrutinized him; made him whole again, limb by furry limb. When he was restored he was a frightening creature. He sat hugely in my mind and seemed much angered as he licked his scalpel wounds.

There is something about him I do not care for. He is not the friendly type. After peering at him down the scope for five or ten minutes I had to jog around the room to shake him from my head.

When I eventually returned the slides to their little box I added it and the microscope to my slowly-growing shrine. At present it consists of:

Sanderson's map;
Peak's note;
the *Ancient Chinese Healing* man;
Gray's Anatomy (and various other books);
a wind-up monkey;
my father's clog-shaped pipe.

Mr Hendley's Account

It must have been quite early in the morning, for I was only out at the Pykes, which is the gatehouse just this side of Clumber near the top of my round. I had dropped them off a letter and was climbing back on my bicycle when I saw him at the entrance to the tunnel, standing and watching and not saying a word. His not talking made me a bit uncomfortable, so I said, 'Morning,' to him to try and bring him round. He nodded at me then he slowly come over. He come right over and started inspecting my bike. Asking all sorts of questions, like if the saddle was especially comfortable and what sort of speed the thing could make.

I remember him looking up at me, excited all of a sudden, and asking what I reckoned to a cycle down the tunnel. Said we could take it in turns or I could sit on the saddle and he could do the pedalling. Well, I didn't want to get myself in trouble, but I said no, because I never did like tunnels, nor any dark place come to that, so there was no way he was going to get me down there without a fuss. Besides, I had my whole round in front of me and I didn't have the time to be loaning out my bike.

Well, of course, he wasn't altogether happy with my answer. He went very quiet again. Then he asked if he could just sit on the thing for a minute, to see what it felt like. To be honest, I was still a mite suspicious. Thought he might try and pedal off with it. But I thought who am I to stop a Duke from sitting on my bike? So I let him have a go.

He sat there with his hands on the handlebars and nodded to himself and said it seemed very good indeed. Said he had always fancied being a postman and looked rather enviously over at my sack. He seemed to get a little melancholy, which, I have to say, rather baffled me. I should have thought a man with his money could be just about whatever he chose to be.

Anyway, I told him I really should be getting on my way again and he eventually climbed off the bike and handed it back. He said goodbye and turned and went on his way. He didn't hang about, by any means. Last time I saw him he was disappearing down his tunnel. That was the only time I came across him. He did seem a bit of a rum old chap.

From His Grace's Journal

DECEMBER 15TH

*

He is all root and branch and foliage, with bright red berry-eyes. He creaks and crackles as he creeps along and frightens the birds away. He has stalked the Wilderness as long as I can remember, sneaking from tree to tree the whole year round, waiting for a small boy to wander close enough to be dragged back into the undergrowth.

A man of scratches and of tangled bramble, he is, all in a nasty knot. But when he wishes, the Berry Man can scatter himself into a hundred disparate parts and a prying eye would see nothing but the same leaves and twigs as lie on any woodland floor. But once the prying eye has passed on the Berry Man draws himself back in. The scraps of bark slowly shift along the ground and are reintroduced to each other; the chill wind shuffles him into shape. The vines wind around him and bind him up until he stands broad and tall again.

Sometimes he wears the antlers of a broken branch, sometimes he wears a thorny crown. Some days he is a skinny man, made up of nothing but bark-stripped twigs. Other days he has an ivy belly, packed with wriggling worms. One day he has mossy eyebrows, the next a hornet's nest-hat. Ever changing, always insecty, made from whatever comes to hand.

But you'll not hear a whisper out of him. The Berry Man has no tongue in his head. When he is angry he just takes to spinning. Spins so fast he pulls the whole wood in. He spins until the whole world is nothing but a whirling dervish of rattling leaves.

*

All my life the Berry Man has occupied the Wilderness. He is as much a part of the place as the trees. Mother and Father believed in him with a passion. They introduced me to him when I was very small. I remember them saying how if I strayed into his territory he would take me off and whip me with the switches of his arms. A year or two later I believe I suggested that perhaps the Berry Man was only make-believe after all, but they both looked at me most gravely and slowly shook their heads.

A child is expert at frightening himself, his mind primed to imagine the most terrible things, and I cannot now say for certain how much of my Berry Man was inherited from my parents and how much I conceived myself. Certainly I have retained a particularly vivid picture of a little boy (who looks very much like me) running through the Wilderness. The boy has no flesh left on his body for he has been caught and thrashed by the flailing arms of the Berry Man. Right through my childhood this picture served as a warning to keep well clear of that wood.

I was so convinced of the awful creature's existence that once or twice I thought I saw him, squatting among the bushes at the edge of the wood, watching me as I hurried by. All these years later, I still find myself walking half a mile out of my way to avoid that dreadful place. I do not really expect to be confronted by some leafy creature, yet always find some dim excuse to take a different route. The ghouls which haunt our childhood are not easily shaken off.

*

I was out on my constitutional this morning, with a young terrier who had repeatedly misbehaved. So much so that I had lost all my patience and put him on a leash. I must have been cold or damp and heading home in something of a hurry, for I had chosen to return by way of the Wilderness.

We were thirty yards or so from the old wood and I was keeping my mind busy with as many trifling thoughts as I could think up, when I became convinced that a pair of eyes were trained on me. Felt their gaze wash up and down my spine. I turned and scanned the woods from one end to the other. Most of the trees were leafless and they were all a winter-grey and I had just about assured myself that I was mistaken when I caught sight of a face, peering grimly from a bush. I leapt back and almost tripped over the dog, which started him barking and jumping all around.

The face in the bushes looked left and right. The leaves around him twitched. Then all at once, with a swish, the branches parted and he came racing out of the woods. He was nothing but a blur of thrashing limbs and I would have run myself had I not been all tied up with the blasted dog. The Berry Man scythed through the high grass towards me. His steps made a terrible whipping sound. After all these years, I thought, the Berry Man has grown tired of waiting and broken cover to come and snatch me away.

I was frantically trying to untangle myself when I saw how the Berry Man was, in fact, not headed for me at all but was running down the hill towards the lake. I saw also how there was something troublesome in his gait; some hindrance, as if one leg was shorter than the other. And in that instant, when I realized that this was not the Berry Man but some fleeing, limping lad, I found all my courage restored to me; found I had a sudden abundance of it.

'Ho!' I shouted after him. 'Ho, there!'

But he continued limping hastily away from me and in a

minute he was hobbling onto the bridge across the lake with me and the barking dog quite a way behind. Now, I am not overly fond of running and would most likely have given up the chase if I had not that moment spotted one of my keepers coming along the track on the far side of the lake. He was a big fellow and very familiar but his name had momentarily slipped my mind, so I called out,

'Ho, there! Keeper! Stop the boy!'

And in a thrice he had dropped his shoulder bag and was barging his way through the iron gates and came running onto the bridge at such a pitch that the hobbling boy found himself trapped between the two of us. I slowed my pace a little and pulled on the leash to try and quieten the dog. And now the boy was all in a fluster, glancing first towards the keeper, who continued to bore down on him on one side, and then right back at me. And for a moment I thought he recognized just how old and bandy I was and how easily he might knock me down and I felt all my courage drain away again and I wished I had let him go. The lad was turning one way, then the other, and working himself up into a right old state. Then, to my horror, I saw how he had started scrambling up the low wall which runs along the length of the bridge.

'No, boy!' I shouted at him, but he was like a rabbit, and carried on clambering for all he was worth. He dragged his lame leg up onto the wall beside him, stood and hurled himself at the lake. But the keeper had come along behind him, made a lunge and grabbed him by his arm.

By the time I caught them up the keeper had dragged the boy down from the wall and dumped him on the ground, where he now thrashed his arms and legs about and made an awful grunting sound.

'Calm down, boy. Calm yourself!' I shouted, but it did not the slightest good.

The dog was still barking and baring his teeth and the poor boy had his hands up in front of his face as if the keeper and I were all set to give him the stick. The whole scene was so chaotic that I was obliged to give the dog a smack to shut him up, and it was another minute after he had swallowed his bark before the lad finally drew his terrible sobbing to a close. When he drew his fingers down from his face I saw that there was indeed something wrong with him. His head seemed to have too much jawbone about it, if that makes any sense. It was as if his eyes and nose and mouth had been put together not quite right.

'Nobody is going to hurt you,' I told him, but he stared nervously down at the keeper's grip on him. When it was released the boy's moans just about abated and the three of us were able to lean, panting, against the wall of the bridge while the dog looked stupidly on and, not knowing how best to deal with the situation, I suggested the boy come up to the house.

It was a maid who recognized him as one of the Linklater sons. They apparently live out near Cuckney village, so I sent a footman to their cottage, post-haste. While we were waiting on him I had Mrs Pledger make us a pot of tea and a few rounds of cinnamon toast and asked Clement if he would join us, as the man's very presence can soothe the most agitated scene. So the whole gang of us trooped into the downstairs study and sat around in silence while the poor lad drank his tea. He was very thirsty and supped it up most lustily and I was sure his fumbling grip would crack the china cup, or that his huge jaw would take a bite out of it. He looked to me no more than twelve years old but his hands and forearms were as thick as a thatcher's. One of his shoulders was a little hunched-up so that he appeared not to be able to turn his head as easily as he might have liked. And the sole on his left shoe, I noticed, was built up an extra inch or two, so that the whole leg tended to hang rather sorrily from his hip.

If there were no more tears then there were no words either. He must have sat there without a whisper for getting on half an hour, taking self-conscious sips from his cup of tea until I thought it must be freezing-cold. The rest of us made some attempt at conversation while snatching occasional glances at him across the room, until at last I got word that my footman had returned with another of the Linklater boys.

I dismissed Clement and the keeper and once they were out of the way asked our guest to be shown in. As he entered the room I kept an eye on his younger brother, to see how he would react, and though he remained seated and stared most fixedly at the dregs in the bottom of his cup, I could see that he had clearly registered his brother and, I thought, begun to tremble a little. The lad who came in had only a year or two on his brother – was no more than fifteen years old himself. The same mousy coloured hair sprang from his head. He even had a few whiskers on his chin. I suppose I was expecting some sort of introduction, but he simply nodded in my direction and marched straight past me towards his kin, taking his hand from his jacket pocket as he did so, and moving with such determination and velocity I wondered what humiliating punishment I was about to be a witness to. By now the lame brother had got up from his chair and stood with his big head hanging down and his cup and saucer still clutched in his hand. He was panting now and I thought his shoulders had begun to shake up and down again. Yet when the older boy reached him he simply took his cup and saucer, set them down on a table, put his arms around his brother's shoulders and pulled him to him in a loving embrace.

Straight away the young thatcher started sobbing like a

baby, while his brother gently stroked his head and I must say that as I stood there observing them it was all I could do to stop myself joining in.

'I must apologize for my brother,' said the older boy. 'He must have wandered onto your estate.'

I nodded my head then shook it once or twice and waved my hands vaguely in the air.

'You see, he likes to look around, sir. Always has done. His curiosity sometimes gets the better of him.'

I told him not to mention it and that no harm had been done, and that I only hoped we had not frightened the boy too much with all our carrying-on. To try and put us at our ease I introduced myself. The older brother told me his name was Duncan and, easing his damp-eyed brother off his shoulder, added, 'And this is Doctor.'

'Doctor ... Ah.' I tried digesting the information, but I simply couldn't keep it down. 'He is a doctor, you say?'

'He is the seventh son of a seventh son, you see, sir, so that is his given name. It is an old tradition. Sevens being lucky. It makes him special, you see.'

All this was announced most matter-of-factly, as if it were common knowledge, but I felt sure I detected also a note of pride in his being the bearer of such exotic news.

The whole idea was, of course, quite fantastic. I was obliged to ask Duncan how his brother's special qualities manifested themselves and was informed (in a most ingenuous tone) how he was frequently consulted by local people, as an oracle or prophet might have been in ancient times. I found all this rather hard to imagine as I had yet to hear the boy utter a single word and when he referred again to Doctor's 'rare faculties' I felt compelled to ask for an example of them.

'Well, for instance, if you give him the date and the month and the year you were born he can tell you which day of the week it was.' He then added, 'It doesn't matter how many years ago it was.'

I allowed the implication of this last comment to sink in a little and was about to furnish young Doctor with the required information and generally try him out when he sort of shuddered, took a gulp of air and spluttered out,

'Wednesday,' then was silent again.

Incredible! I stared at one brother, then the other. I had *indeed* been born on a Wednesday. I remember my mother saying so. I was trying to work out how on earth he might have guessed it, when he added in a whisper,

'March 12th, 1828.'

I was absolutely dumbstruck. His brother turned and saw from my expression that the young prophet was right on the mark again.

'Now then...' he said to himself. 'He's never done that before.'

*

I ordered more toast from Mrs Pledger and the pair of them stayed on for a good half hour, Duncan proving to be very good company but Doctor, unfortunately, having nothing more to say. At some point in the conversation I discovered that Duncan is, in fact, the younger of the two.

'It's a common mistake,' he told me. 'He is very boyish-looking, is he not?'

We were all gathered at the front door and the two of them were just about on their way when Doctor hesitated and ground to a halt halfway down the steps. He stared anxiously at his boots for a few seconds and grimaced and shifted from foot to foot. Duncan went over, put an arm round his shoulder and asked him what was wrong. Doctor chewed on his cheek a little before finally surrendering a solitary, mangled word.

'Underwood,' he muttered in my direction.

I begged the young fellow's pardon.

'Underwood,' he said again.

Well, neither Duncan nor myself had heard of any such fellow and after we had stood around in silence for a minute were obliged to leave it at that. But as they set off down the driveway Doctor turned briefly back to me and with his good arm pointed towards the Wilderness, where I had first mistaken him for The Berry Man.

*

DECEMBER 19TH

*

The weather this month has been very bad. We have had just about everything thrown our way. These last few days especially have been some of the coldest for a long while, with a great deal of frost and snow. Icicles, some of them six foot long, have been hanging off all the gutters and Clement has had to lean from the windows with a broom to knock them down, which was a shame for they were most impressive but necessary, lest they fall and cleave some unfortunate chap in two.

Every pipe in the house is frozen-up – the staff have had to fetch water from the well – and when the thaw eventually comes around I have no doubt we shall have a hundred leaks on our hands. But what the cold weather has also brought with it is the freezing-up of the lake. Very rare. It is nothing but one great crystal slab with a surface as smooth as glass.

The day it first froze over there were children knocking at the back door at dawn, after permission to skate. Now it would be the meanest of old men who would deny folk a pleasure which came so cheaply to him, and once word got round that the lake was open people came from all over, with their ice-skates tucked under their arm. From first light until last thing at night any number have been out on the ice, all of them slowly spinning in a giant human wheel. Courting couples, their arms crossed before them, glide gently left then right; whole families make chains, each member holding on to the waist of the one in front, as their many-headed, many-legged creatures go snaking over the solid lake.

All this I have observed from an upstairs study and this very afternoon I watched musicians troop across the snow and set up on the benches at the ice's edge. They played their fiddles and whistles and squeeze-boxes until their fingers must have been numb from the cold. But while they played I caught the odd half-familiar fragment of a tune, which was brought to me on the breeze.

I stood there for a while this evening with the window open an inch or two to let the music in. The moon was up and around the lake several dozen lamps were hung on poles. They formed a glowing oasis in the night which I was admiring when Clement appeared at my side. We both stood there quietly for a moment, watching the distant figures swinging under the stars.

'The lake is very busy tonight,' I said.

Clement nodded. A distant cheer found its way through to us.

'O, yes,' I said, 'they are having a gay old time.'

As I turned to face him I noticed how Clement stood rather strangely – almost Napoleon-like – with one arm tucked inside the front of his jacket. For a second I thought he had perhaps burnt his arm and had it bandaged, but as I watched he slowly withdrew it and there, in his hand, were a pair of ancient skates.

When the penny finally dropped I stepped back, aghast,

saying, 'O no, Clement, I couldn't possibly. No, I really don't think I could.'

But old Clement deposited the skates into my outstretched hands, which had the effect of momentarily silencing me.

I turned them over.

'I mean to say, Clement, that a skate would be very pleasant,' I went on, 'but you know how I am not one for the crowds.'

Well, he swept out of the room at such speed that if I had not known him better I might have thought he had taken offence. I made a closer examination of the old skates. A most unsophisticated pair they were. Very heavy. Little more than a pair of old bread knives bound together with straps. I was still looking them over when Clement swept back through the door with a heap of clothes in his arms. These he dumped on the rug before me and proceeded to pick out various jackets and mittens and woollen caps.

Then Clement dragged from the heap a ten-foot huckaback scarf and set about winding it around my neck, so that when he had finally done wrapping and tucking only my old man's eyes were left peeping out.

I looked at my reflection and, in a muffled voice, said, 'If I fall, Clement, I shall bounce back up,' and padded my prodigious girth with mittened hands.

It was in this state of woolly incognito that Clement sent me out into the night, a lantern clamped in one hand, my ancient ice-skates in the other.

It must have been several days since I last ventured outside, for the fresh air made me come over quite giddy. The world had been charmed by snow and ice and all the trees were whitely gowned. Every fold in the land glowed in the moonlight, as if the clouds had given in to gravity and tumbled from the sky.

My boots made a fresh path towards the lake, each footfall

packing down the snow with a creak. The voices grew steadily louder and the distant figures slowly took shape and in time I found myself at the edge of the frozen lake, hanging my lantern with the others on an alder branch. The hearty babble of all the skating strangers washed around me, their dreamy locomotion drew me in.

As I strapped my skates to the soles of my boots I leant against a rowing boat, which was half in and half out of the ice. It was a second before I spotted on its bench a young child, every inch of him swaddled in coats and scarves, just like me. I assumed he had been put there by his parents while they were both out on the ice, being too much of a mite to skate himself. To his credit, he seemed to wait most patiently. I nodded my bandaged head at him and he nodded back.

'Are mother and father out taking a spin?' I asked.

From his jacket pocket he produced a half-eaten apple.

'App-le,' he said, as if offering me a bite.

'Good boy,' I answered and patted him on the head, then I turned, drew in a draught of chilly air and cast myself out onto the ice.

I had not skated for many a year and my arms were rather inclined to flail about. But after a while I began to find my balance, then some confidence and quite soon felt I was making some modest contribution to that great turning, stirring mass.

As everyone swept round in the circle a space was left in the middle of the lake where, now and then, an especially gifted skater would show off his skating skills. A man in a balaclava executed an impressive figure of eight, the blades of his skates making a hissing sound as they cut into the ice. Then a young girl – no more than fourteen years old – took the stage and slowly wound herself up into a tight little spin, gradually drawing her arms and feet into her so that she was soon spinning on a sixpence and sending out a fine white spray. Her audience gave her a round of applause but she continued to spin furiously on, until I feared she would cut right through the ice and disappear into the lake below. Then she suddenly cast a leg out and with a graceful backward slide emerged from the blur and in no time had rejoined her more sedate skating companions.

But though I am old and bow-legged I did not envy her. For I was brimming with the simple pleasure of skating with my fellow man. O, we swung and we sang and we gathered speed, did so many anticlockwise circuits I thought we had escaped the grasp of Time. I was lost in a skating-ceilidh. It was Fellowship, without a doubt.

You see, I have been thinking about my baker, Ignatius Peak, and his enviable religious zeal. I recall how 'Fellowship' was the biggest bee in his bonnet. And, indeed, what could be a worthier pursuit than harmony with one's fellow man? But out on the ice tonight I felt as if I had found my own version of it. It rather crept up on me. I was a stranger, skating among other strangers. Nobody said a word. Yet between us we seemed to stir up enough fellowship for the whole wide world.

*

DECEMBER 21ST

*

I believe I may have found what I have been looking for – Mr Fowler's head. As I write this he stares blindly across the study, in meditation many leagues deep. If the tortured fellow in *Gray's Anatomy* had attained an air of resignation then it is indifference – profound indifference – Mr Fowler's creamy head personifies. How can I put it? He is passive yet full of prospect. Silent, but like an unstruck bell.

These past few weeks I have undertaken several house-safaris and on a number of occasions climbed the stairs to fumble in the attic's airless gloom, but my only trophies so far have been the odd book, a wind-up monkey and a bee in several parts. Sensing a fresh approach was necessary if I was to succeed where I had previously failed, I gave my tactics a thorough review: rather than wander up and down the corridors, I decided to pull back from the problem and come at it more objectively.

Rigged myself out, as usual, in beaver and sable coat then strode purposefully down the Great Stairs to sally forth into the frosty morn. On the porch I did a bit of marching on the spot to warm me up, then weighed anchor, swung to starboard and took the narrow gravel path which skirts the house. For it was my intention this morning to circumambulate the place; a task which, I believe I am right in saying, I have never previously carried out. One tends always to approach one's home or leave it, rather than go around and around. But there is something magical about a circle and the act of circling itself seems to generate all sorts of powerful stuff.

Once I had embarked on this mission, however, I discovered that keeping close to the house would not be as easily executed as I might have hoped. I was constantly finding walls and hedges and flower beds in my way. But by some mindful orienteering and a little clambering here and there I managed to go some way towards accomplishing the task I had set myself.

How instructive to look *at* my house instead of *from* it. I did not immediately recognize the balcony where I have recently taken to stargazing and smoking my pipe, nor the bay window of my bathroom, come to that. It demands, I now see, a special sort of thinking to match up the picture one has of the inside of a room with how it might look from *without*. The same might be said about journeys to and from a place . . . that when one travels in each direction one might sometimes just as well be covering different ground.

My aim today, however, was to turn up some room or annexe which had previously eluded me, so as I tramped along the path and scaled the occasional wall I continually scanned the house. I was approaching the barometer tower and beginning to puff and pant and wonder, frankly, if I had not dreamt up for myself another fool's errand when I rounded a corner and came upon a place which had entirely slipped my mind.

There are times when I am quietly impressed by my powers of forgetfulness. In this instance they had brought about the disappearance of a whole host of bricks and mortar. A sizeable building, so no mean feat. But as I stood there staring at it, its mental equivalent slowly re-emerged in my mind. Wasn't this the place my grandfather once whistled for me his favourite tunes? I believe it was. The longer I stared at the outhouse the more my memory's muscle was restored, so that in time I could recall with some certainty how it had originally served as a stable block before the riding school went up. It was like bumping into an old acquaintance.

The building is not connected to the house and stands, I should say, a good twenty yards clear of it. Over the years it has become ivy-covered and introverted-looking. A sapling now sprouts from its roof. I spotted an old gardener nearby, pushing a creaking barrow towards a smouldering fire, and called out to him. He gave not the slightest hint that he had heard me and seemed to carry on his way undisturbed. But as I continued to observe the fellow I saw how he leaned a little to the left, slowly swung his barrow over a few degrees and, in his own time, wheeled his pile of rotting leaves in my direction.

He pulled up and let his barrow down. He had an unlit pipe in his mouth. I asked if he knew anything about the old stables, which obliged him to push his cap back on his bald head.

'I believe they are used for storage, Your Grace,' he said.

Well, the door was bolted but was not padlocked. Its wooden stalls were all intact. Not much effort had been made to clean the place up for the floor was still strewn with strawdust and the sweet pungency of horses seemed still to hang in the air, though the only evidence of the building's former use was a pair of cobwebbed cartwheels which leant against the far wall.

Like a policeman I investigated, my breath making their own small clouds, until I came across an aged staircase, tucked away in a corner. I went up it with considerable caution, each step creaking painfully as it bore my weight, to come out in a low loft, beneath the naked tiles of the roof. Somewhere, behind a rafter, a bird rustled in its nest.

The room was bare but for a few tea chests which huddled together in a corner. Of these, two were empty, the others containing old tools, a broken sundial and a coil of stinking rope. But sliding the cover off the last one I found myself face to face with Fowler's porcelain head. I imagine he had been packed away in a bed of springy straw but the intervening years had withered it and only a few blackened strands of the stuff now clung to his eyes and mouth. I peered down at him in his wooden box. He stared back at me with his strange sightless eyes.

'I remember you,' I said.

All through my childhood that head sat on a mahogany chest of drawers in the corner of my father's study and I had no reason to doubt it had rested there since the very dawn of time. The bust utterly fascinated me, with his bald, inscribed cranium and his vacant gaze. Once, while my father sat at his desk, writing, I silently climbed the chair next to the cabinet and slowly reached out a hand. My finger was hardly an inch from the porcelain when my father said,

'You must not touch him, boy.'

I froze right there on tiptoe with my finger in midair.

'Touching is forbidden,' he added, then returned to his paperwork.

And now, all these years later, that same head stared up at me from a damp old crate and stirred in me a whole world of forgotten thoughts. The head was identical in every detail – except size, for it seemed strangely diminished, as if the years had worn it away. He nestled uncomfortably in the old straw, like a creature in cold hibernation.

His skull was covered with the same curious inscriptions. The porcelain was as inviting as it had always been. But my father was no longer there to scold me and I was no longer a worried young boy and I found myself reaching a hand into the crate . . . tentatively, as if towards a cornered animal.

When my fingertips were less than an inch from the porcelain they froze. I listened for the voice of my father, booming down the years. But he was quiet and too distant. And my finger touched the skull.

'Cold,' I whispered into the cold air.

With the cuff of my sable I wiped the window pane and located my gardener, fifty feet away. Managed to open the window without it coming away from its hinges and called down to him, to ask if he might lend a hand. Again, there was nothing in his attitude to suggest he had heard me – he did not look up, there was no discernible shift in direction or speed – so that I was considering calling out a second time when I saw how he was, in fact, banking slightly to the left and, in a roundabout way, wheeling his creaking barrow towards the stable door below.

The bust is no more than a foot and a half tall, but I was anxious no harm should come to it and did not trust myself to carry it all the way round to the front of the house. So when we were safely down the stable stairs my gardener (whose name, I discovered, was George) suggested I place it in his barrow with his decomposing leaves. Then he wheeled it gently around the network of paths, with me walking by his side.

'Is it heavy, George?' I asked him as we went along.

'No, Your Grace,' said George. 'It is just right.'

When we reached the front steps George lowered his barrow and offered to carry the head into the house for me. I thanked him for the offer but told him I thought I should be able to manage the rest of the way, took the head up in my arms like a baby from a perambulator and went carefully back up to my rooms.

*

The plinth is inscribed . . .

'PHRENOLOGY'

BY

L. N. FOWLER

From the base I note that he hails from Staffordshire.

A damp cloth cleaned the dirt and rotten straw from his face. He is about as good as new. He sits in his shadowy corner, pondering the same intractable puzzles he has always pondered.

Nothing seems to come or go between him and the world. His thoughts are buried deep in the pot. He might almost be a member of some shaven-headed tribe who communicate silently and on a different plane. But what lends his appearance such peculiarity are the lines which map out his skull. His face is blank but his cranium is parcelled and labelled like so many cuts of meat. Friendship, Approbativeness, Mirthfulness. All the things which fail to register on his face.

I wonder if this is the fellow. My long-lost phrenological man.

*

DECEMBER 22ND

*

First thing this morning I sent a note to Mellor.

> Mellor,
>> PHRENOLOGY
>> – information required.

And in no time the reply came back ...

> Your Grace,
>> Information available
>> – you are always welcome.

So after a lunch of buttered comfrey greens and a slice of seedie-cake I called down to Grimshaw, had him hitch up a coach and bring it round to the tunnels' landing stage.

My sable has become a little damp, lately. Smelt a bit mouldy when I put it on today, so swapped it for a redingote and cape and even forwent the beaver (I found I was in no mood for hats). Then, with one hand on the banister and the other round Fowler's head, I slowly made my way down the back staircase to the tunnels below. Clement roped a rug or two down in the dumb waiter and we were still sorting ourselves out when Grimshaw came trundling around the bend, looking very smart in knee boots, gauntlets and goggles.

189

Clement sat with his back to the horses and I settled Fowler's head down next to me among the tartan rugs. Then, with Grimshaw under strict instruction to avoid every pot-hole along the way, we set off for Holbeck village.

The floating boy grows in confidence. He came along for the ride, for most of the journey quite content to hover at the same speed as us just outside the carriage door. Like the moon on a crystal-clear night, he was, keeping up with us and peeping in. But when we neared the end of the tunnel he decided to slip inside the coach. He is a sly fellow and no mistake – always receding from view. Like the eye-detritus of hair and such which obscures my vision on sunny days. Always skimming off into the periphery and impossible to pin down.

I did manage to snatch a glimpse of him today before he ducked out of sight. He is a tiny fellow, not much more than a babe-in-arms. His flesh is the same colour as Fowler's head – luminous-white, like the clouds – which made such an impression on me that, without meaning to, I blurted out, 'Both so very white,' which caused Clement to give me a most quizzical look. I had to pretend I had nodded off for a second and was talking in my sleep.

When we reached Holbeck I asked Clement and Grimshaw to wait in the carriage and assured them I would not be long. Gingerly made my way up Mellor's garden path with Fowler's head peeping over one shoulder and the boy-in-the-moon floating on the other. The Reverend, clean shaven this time, opened the door straight away, saying, 'I see you have brought a friend along,' and I was stumped for a second as to which of my creamy companions he referred to.

At the edge of the sea of knick-knack laden tables I became worried lest I trip and smash my phrenology head. Asked Mellor if he would mind playing St Christopher.

'Not at all, Your Grace,' he said, and took him from me

with admirable sureness (which I attributed to his many christenings) then he was off, gracefully weaving his rotund little body through the maze of book-towers and fragile glassware towards the fireside, while I did my best to stay on his tail. As we picked our way through the debris, Fowler's head peered back at me over Mellor's shoulder and a song of wonderful whiteness composed itself in my mind.

When we were seated and had cups of tea in our hands, Mellor allowed himself a closer look at the head. He seemed very pleased.

'So what's your knowledge of Phrenology, Your Grace?' he asked.

'Of the philosophy, next to nothing,' I admitted, but went on to tell him how, as a child, my head had been measured (very roughly, I might add) by some old gent with bony fingers, while my mother and father looked concernedly on. I recalled the phrenologist taking from his case a huge pair of callipers which he proceeded to place over my skull. I can still see me perching on my wobbly stool, overflowing with apprehension, convinced that at any moment the old fellow was going to plunge the tips of those callipers right into my temples.

'Very fashionable at one time,' said Mellor. 'You will have heard, perhaps, that Her Majesty had a phrenologist measure each of her offspring's heads?'

He is a regular treasure-chest of information, is Mellor. A walking, talking book. And, without the least bit of prompting on my part, I found myself the recipient of what turned out to be a great torrent of the stuff. This particular torrent was all to do with the science of Phrenology – the chap who had originally come up with it (named *suchandsuch*) and how the science had first spread across Europe (by two other fellows) then across the Atlantic (by some other chap). Names and dates swept all around me, as well as the marching feet of large committees of medical men – some of whom were in favour of phrenology, but most of whom were decidedly against – until finally it was all I could do to hang on to the arms of my chair and try and keep myself from being washed away.

How much of this impressive oration was spontaneous and how much had been prepared I could not say. It is quite possible the Reverend had been cramming from some textbook right up until the moment I knocked at his front door. On the other hand, it might simply be that his is one of those minds which drinks up every drop of information it is offered and has no trouble in later pouring it back out. Either way, I just about managed to withstand Mellor's assault on me without either falling asleep or falling off my chair and came out clutching what I reckon to be the gist of the matter ... namely, that phrenology was an attempt to gauge an individual's character by recording the various bumps and hollows on that person's head. Each bump, depending on its whereabouts, suggests a predominance of a particular quality – Hope, Spirituality, Firmness, etc. – so that by consulting a map (or a model, like Fowler's head) the phrenologist can assess the head in hand.

'Not many of the old fellows left kicking about, Your Grace,' said Mellor. 'The whole caboodle fell out of favour some years ago.'

Then he paused and looked me squarely in the eyes.

'Beg your pardon in asking, Your Grace, but where does this sudden interest in phrenology spring from?'

Fowler's head sat coyly in Mellor's lap. The pair of them stared silently at me. If I had not known and trusted them both so well I might have imagined they were ganging-up on me.

The silence spread across the prickly room. I took the opportunity to look around for my boy-in-the-moon. I searched every last inch of my periphery but found he had slipped away.

'I have given the matter a good deal of thought,' I heard me say, 'and have concluded that what I need is a good head-man.'

The Reverend nodded slowly at me, gently placed Fowler on the rug and hupped himself out of his chair. He then proceeded to spend the next five minutes clinging to the rock face of his bookshelves, picking over their spines with a tilted head. He hum-hummed to himself and ground his teeth and paused only to draw out some huge leathery slab. As the minutes crept by and the book-hunt pressed on I thought I saw him grow increasingly discouraged, until at last he stepped back from one shelf with an expression of great suspicion on his face – as if the books had been guilty of conspiring against him. He turned slowly, slowly . . . listening, it seemed, for the scurrying footfalls of his prey's retreat.

'Ah-ha,' he said, and pounced upon a seemingly-innocent table. He wrestled briefly with its pile of papers, whipped out a cardboard folder from its base and left the whole precarious structure swaying from side to side.

He returned, removing a single sheet from the file.

'Here she is,' he said, and dropped it in my lap.

The paper was all yellowed with age and eaten away at the edges, but the illustration was perfectly intact. And what a strange and exotic picture, to be sure – a cross-section of a head, much like Fowler's, but nothing like as mundanely numbered or named. At first I thought it was some sort of head-hotel, for in each compartment miniature folk posed, in representation of all the characteristics of Man. Here in tableau-form were Self-Esteem (a proud couple strolling in the country) and Suavity (some slippery-looking fellow, drawing the reader in with a crooked finger). Here was

Combativeness, personified by two boxers ... in fact, all the human qualities, good and bad, with a man or woman acting them out in their own little cell.

'Wonderful,' I told the Reverend.

'A gift,' he replied, before adding, 'Not very rare.'

I thanked him all the same and was already planning how it might fit into my shrine. I continued to examine the picture while I got around to asking if he might know where I might find a good head-man.

I waited a second before looking up. When I did so I found he had fixed me with a wry expression.

'A head-man? Well, as I said, Your Grace – phrenologists are very much a dying breed. But, if pressed, I would have to say Edinburgh. That's where the last of them retreated to.'

'Edinburgh,' I said.

'I know a professor there. An old friend of mine ... I could introduce you. I'm sure he'd see you straight.'

'And are there tunnels to Edinburgh?' I asked.

He shook his head.

'Not yet, Your Grace.'

This was a big disappointment. I rather hoped there might have been.

'Edinburgh,' I said. 'Very well.'

I was making ready to leave when the Reverend caught me by my coat sleeve and whispered excitedly in my ear.

'Before you go, I must show you my latest acquisition.'

And he trotted off to burrow in some corner, returning with what I first took to be a pair of thick spectacles which had a strip of card attached. He was fairly beaming as he handed the strange contraption over.

'Try them on,' he said.

Well, I slipped the things over my nose and as I did so, a photograph came into view. But – how extraordinary! – one with lifelike depth of field. A young boy sat with an open book in his lap, yet the table in the foreground and the wall behind seemed to exist on quite separate planes. Remarkable! As I moved my head from side to side I could even sense some parallax. For the sake of it I peeped over the glasses at the piece of card and saw two identical photographs, side by side, but when I looked back through the glasses they merged into a single, startling image with all dimensions accounted for.

'Stereoscopic,' announced Mellor over my shoulder.

'Very good,' I said. 'And what is the scene?'

'"A boy, reflecting",' he told me. 'What do you say to that?'

When I left I had my new phrenology head-map under one arm, all rolled up and tied with string, and Fowler's porcelain head under the other. Clement and Grimshaw sat stiffly in the carriage, wrapped in the tartan rugs. I must say, they looked quite cold.

Mrs Pledger's Account

It has long been a tradition at Welbeck that on Christmas Eve every employee of the House and estate drop by with their families in the afternoon. Nothing much, just a stand-up buffet in the ballroom and some games for the little ones. But mainly just an excuse for a get-together and the opportunity to wish each other well.

So, around three o'clock His Grace comes down for ten minutes or so, to help ladle out the punch. He was never one to make a speech or draw attention to himself and it is not as if anyone expected it. But when one year he joined in a game of dominoes with some of the children it was talked about for weeks on end. Just a little thing like that, you see, but it goes a very long way.

Well, me and the girls had put some effort into it the last time round. We'd made a big potato salad, brought up some smoked hams and laid it all out on the best tablecloths. But it had got to three o'clock, then quarter past and half past with nobody having seen hide nor hair of His Grace. So Clement goes off and searches for him and eventually tracks him down in some corner of his rooms with his books and charts. Tries to get him down, to show his face just for a second, but His Grace says that he is busy and to leave him alone.

Well, some of us see him every day of our lives but for others it might be the only time they will see him from one year to the next and when it becomes clear His Grace is not to make an appearance people begin to drift away. And all this time he was upstairs reading. What is one to make of that?

It was later on that His Grace came down and apologized. Said he had not realized that it was Christmas Eve and was quite upset. But when a fellow forgets it's Christmas something is definitely wrong. It's not just the effort. It's people's feelings I'm talking about.

From His Grace's Journal

*

By eight o'clock this morning we were on the platform at Worksop station with time enough to stand and watch the train come rolling in. There was an unholy commotion of steam and brakes before it juddered to a halt and blocked out what little light had previously illuminated the place. I was helped up into my carriage by Clement, who then heaved himself and the baggage in after me; he swung my cases easily up onto the racks and generally fussed about the place. I must say I had not expected the carriage to be so luxuriously fitted-out. The last time I travelled by train it was little more than a wooden box with a leaking roof, but now there are curtains and cushions and carpets and even a mirror in which to comb one's hair.

I had on my William IV coat with its high moon pockets and deep collar and a letter of introduction from Mellor tucked away somewhere. On the seat beside me I placed my knapsack which had in it a vegetable pie, some fruit and pastries and a flask of hot sweet tea. It had been my intention to travel to Edinburgh alone and to stand on my own two feet, but I had come under pressure from various quarters to allow Clement to come along. It was Mrs Pledger who pointed out that my shirts and trousers would need pressing after spending the best part of a day crammed in their cases, and that though there may be no end of boot-cleaners in our hotel there is slim chance they will know one end of a boot from the other. So I relented, on the strict understanding that he travel up in a separate carriage and generally keep out of sight, so that anyone coming upon me these next few days might think me a regular and independent man about town.

Clement was now back on the platform, checking departure times with various railwaymen and working himself up into a right old state. And now he was back in the carriage and checking me for the journey and now very reluctant to close the door.

I shooed him away with my cane until he finally relinquished the door. Then a guard came along and slammed it shut and Clement loped off to his own carriage. Then somewhere down the platform a whistle was blown and a second later the whole contraption made an awful lurch, followed by a series of smaller, more frequent lurches until my tiny, fancily-furnished room began to carry me away. I poked my head out of the window to watch the station slide by and saw Clement two carriages back down the train, looking anxiously up at me. I shouted at him to put his head in and eventually he did as he was told. I suppose he just wants to be sure of me. But he needn't have worried for I had my floating boy for company.

The engine dragged us through the town, coughing and spluttering most unhealthily, but gradually managed to clear its lungs and soon we were out of Worksop and generally flying along. The wheels squealed on the tracks beneath me like little pigs and through the window the hills took to rising and falling in great earthy waves and, what with farms and cows slipping past as if on greased wheels, I must admit I began to feel a little sick. Drew the curtains to try and quell the queasiness and took deep breaths until some composure had been regained.

Clement had taken the precaution of fixing a sign to my door which read

ESPECIALLY RESERVED

so that passengers waiting to board at stations along the way would be discouraged from barging in on me.

Well, we seemed to call in on just about every town and village in the North of England; forever pulling to or pulling away. There was a little porthole by the curtained window and at the first few stations I stood on the seat and peered out to watch the people come and go. Huge trunks were being wheeled in every direction and there were kisses and handshakes and embraces and much waving of handkerchiefs as we set off. But I soon tired of spying on these anonymous leave-takings and as the stations grew steadily further apart I slipped slowly into a not unpleasant torpor.

An hour or two later, I ate some pie.

Although I was very nicely curtained-away and cordoned-off, at every stop the station's noises still bundled their way in. Countless calls of 'Take care!' and 'Write ... Promise to write!' came through to me, along with 'Give my love to suchandsuch...' – all punctuated by the shrill comma of the guard's whistle and the clatter of slamming doors.

I found myself unintentionally eavesdropping on these hurried farewells and began to note how, mingling with the voices of the returning Scots, one could make out the local accents and how, as we ventured further north, these slowly shifted from one brogue to the next.

The boy in the bubble floated up by the luggage rack with his back turned most defiantly towards me. I thought perhaps he bore me a grudge of some sort; an idea which I proposed to him, but which received no reply. He is not a very talkative chap.

We had been travelling for several hours and I was

beginning to feel thoroughly bored. So bored, in fact, that while I knew we were still a good way from Edinburgh, I resolved to leave the curtains open at the next stop and as we sped across a viaduct I slipped my arm out of the open window and removed the sign which Clement had fixed to the door. I told myself that if Fate decides that I should have travelling companions then so be it. I had a sudden desire to be in the company of my fellow man.

By Newcastle my fellow man had taken the shape of a young mother and her twins (a boy and girl, aged about five years old) and a severe-looking chap in his fifties with an over-waxed moustache. My hopes of some camaraderie between fellow travellers were dashed immediately: the young woman was almost too exhausted to lift her children up onto the seats and the attitude of the gentleman who sat down next to me made it quite plain that conversation was the last thing on his mind. After our initial greetings I think not a single word was exchanged. The children were the epitome of good behaviour, only piping up once or twice, but each time met by a vicious glance from the evil Moustache Man. So imposing was his presence that I became aware how my own gaze had rationed itself to the smallest plot of carpeted floor, my eyes barely daring to stray from it. At the time I wondered (as indeed I wonder now) how we can allow one person to get away with so wilfully and malevolently imposing himself on a situation and generally poisoning the atmosphere. Perhaps it is the strangeness of modern travel which cultivates such dismal isolation in its human freight.

The train brought us right alongside the North Sea, which was a wonderful brackeny-brown and so utterly sharp and shiny it looked to have been hacked out of flint. If I had been on my own I might have opened up the window and drawn great draughts of the sea air into me. As it was, all five of us stared rather balefully at it before returning our gazes to their prison cells.

Soon after, one of the twins let out a terrific yawn, totally debilitating its little owner. It was then a wonder to see the speed at which the same condition struck down the rest of us, though we adults hid ours behind raised palms and subjected them to such terrible compression as to squeeze all the pleasure out of them. Even so, the young one's yawn swept round the carriage like a contagious infection, bouncing from seat to seat just like a ball. And very soon, we all found ourselves vacant-eyed and full of sighs, as we surrendered to the motion of the train. And we adults were all slowly reduced to infants, each one of us rocked in our mother's arms, so that while we failed to come together in conversation in the first place we found ourselves united in sleep at the last.

*

EDINBURGH, JANUARY 7TH

*

A free day before visiting Professor Bannister so Clement and I spent the morning touring the town. As we trailed up and down the windy streets, going from tea-house on to tailor, I noticed how strangely everybody appears to be dressing these days – hats and collars so meanly cut. Felt quite old-fashioned and over-fancy in my burnous and tall hat and my shirt with its double frill.

After lunch, on Mellor's recommendation, we visited the famous Camera Obscura, which is right at the top of the High Street just outside the Castle gates. It is a chubby sort of tower, a little like a lighthouse, but has a half-timbered air about it and a wholly wooden hat.

Mellor had become highly animated when telling me about the place, saying how he never visited Edinburgh without calling in at the Camera. So, having located it, we went straight in and up to a tiny counter where I paid our pennies to a woman dressed from head to toe in tweed. She congratulated us on choosing such a breezy day for our visit as all the morning cloud had been blown away, thereby guaranteeing, she insisted, a particularly spectacular show. Heartened by this news we set off up the stone steps – hundreds of them, there were, like marching to the top of the world – to emerge, at last, on a high terrace where three other gentlemen stood, smoking and taking in the view. And what a prospect! – so grand and gratifying it alone was worth the effort and the entrance fee.

The Camera shares the Castle's great chunk of rock, so we had an almost perfect panorama of the vertiginous city below.

'So many spires,' I said to Clement, who nodded vaguely in reply.

Indeed, there looked to be one on just about every street corner, puncturing the firmament. The nearest clouds were banked up on the horizon several miles away and the sky was a most heavenly hue, lending all the roofs and churches an even frostier sharpness and making one's eyes prickle with delight. I had counted well over a dozen spires and steeples and had plenty more to go, when the woman in tweed (and a magnificent pair of brogues, I might add) came puffing up the steps.

'This way, gentlemen, if you please,' she announced.

She opened up a door off the terrace and waved us into a wooden room, which from the outside looked like a tall windowless gazebo or a bathing-machine with the wheels removed.

Now, I must admit that as we were herded towards that tiny room I had not the least idea what to expect. The Reverend Mellor, whilst heartily promoting the Camera

Obscura and even endeavouring to describe the mechanics involved, had left me with no abiding notion as to what the occasion might actually entail. So, finding myself in a small round room with only a high ceiling to distinguish it, I will admit I was a trifle disappointed. If we were to bear witness to a visual demonstration of the magnitude and beauty which the Reverend had led me to expect, then surely, I mused, some major gadgetry would have to be drafted in.

As these thoughts drifted around my head the woman in tweed closed the door behind her, then took a minute or two to introduce us to the basic principles of the Camera. I was not overly impressed and took some satisfaction from seeing another chap stifle a yawn. But when she reached over and began to dim the lamps I was suddenly all eyes and ears as it dawned on me I might be about to endure another session as claustrophobic as the one in Mellor's cave. So in those last moments before we were completely engulfed in darkness I made quite sure I had located the door's precise whereabouts, in case I was gripped by another fearful attack and had to make a sudden and embarrassing dash for it. 'Small wonder this is such a favourite of Mellor's,' I thought to myself, as my stomach tied itself in a familiar panicky knot and the darkness swept up from the corners and covered the room and its inhabitants with its gloomy cloak.

But, as in the cave, one moment I was on the verge of absolute terror, with my own child's voice screaming in my ear, and the next I found myself landed on the other side of the abyss. Somehow the knot in my stomach had been magically undone and I was keen and lucid again.

Like my co-spectators I rested my hands on a circular railing and looked down on a broad concave table – perfectly smooth and white – whilst the woman in tweed pressed on with her practised intonation about the room in which we stood. With one hand she had hold of a long wooden rod which hung down from the high ceiling and as our eyes accustomed themselves to the dark she gradually became more visible. Her hands and face had about them a ghostly luminosity. She twisted the rod, saying, '. . . the same principle as the camera. A tiny aperture in the roof allows an image to be cast on the dish below . . .'

And indeed, as her incantation washed over me I saw the first outlines of a picture take shape. I saw trees – the trees of the nearby gardens, their branches slowly coming into focus, whilst behind, the whole length of Princes Street was emerging from the mist. It was as if we were witnessing, from a bird's-eye view, the very making of Edinburgh. For a minute I was quite overcome with emotion and when I snatched a glance at my fellows found my own astonishment reflected there. Like characters in a Rembrandt their faces shone with the dish's milky light.

I looked back to the dish just in time to see the whole picture suddenly slip on its axis, accompanied by the creaking of the tweedy woman's rod as it was twisted in her grip. The castle swung into view.

'Hurrah,' cried one of the other gentlemen.

'The Fortress,' announced our guide.

Every detail was sharp as a pin now and I was thinking how remarkably like a photograph this image was – a very round and colourful one at that – when a seagull sailed right across the shallow bowl and the scene was suddenly brought to life. Well, the whole company burst into startled laughter. One or two started chattering excitedly.

'What we see,' announced our guide, as if to calm us, 'is not fixed but a living image of the world outside.'

So there we stood, in the belly of a breathing camera, as the whole city leaked into us through a single beam of light. Yet the vision it cast among us was not in any way frozen but as real and vivid as could be.

As we watched that white dish and clung to our railing we were transported through each of the city's three hundred and sixty degrees. Here were horse-drawn trolleys inching up the High Street, past street pedlars with their baskets laid out – all the trade and transport of a working city, with the deep sea standing by.

The whole of Edinburgh was poured into the bowl before us, as if we were ringside angels, yet was conjured out of nothing more than a couple of lenses and a small hole in the roof.

*

When we emerged blinking into the daylight I honestly felt as if I had sat in the lap of the gods. And for the rest of the day, as we carried on with our sightseeing, I found I had to keep the odd giggle from slipping out.

*

EDINBURGH, JANUARY 8TH

*

'Professor Bannister,' I say, holding out my hand.

'Come, come,' says the tall fellow, and waves a finger in my face like a metronome. 'William, if you please.'

I was in the very bowels of the University's Anatomy Department, meeting the man around whom this whole trip had been arranged and, judging by the deference bestowed upon him by his students and colleagues outside his office and the capaciousness within, he must be a singularly important chap, for he had sofas and armchairs and an aged chaise, not to mention a vast writing desk with a green leather top.

The Professor set about impressing upon me what old friends he and Mellor were. And, for a while, we juggled between us the pleasantries such occasions demand, regarding train journeys and the dampness of Edinburgh, before we returned to our mutual friend.

'Is he still round?' asked Bannister.

'Very round,' I replied, which seemed to please him no end.

'Excellent,' he said most earnestly, and ushered me into a chair.

I should, I think, make some reference to my host's extraordinary height, as this greatly occupied my mind at the time, in that having taken his own seat he proceeded to cross his long legs with such far-reaching swiftness I worried he might inadvertently cut me down.

'Heads, is it?' said William Bannister, waving my letter of introduction at me. 'Mellor says it's heads you want.'

'Information, rather than the heads themselves,' I replied, rather lamely. 'I am ... working on a project to do with heads.'

He smiled at me, slid down into his chair a foot or two, made a church and steeple with his fingers and perched his chin on top. In retrospect, I appreciate that his silence most likely denoted a man who was ordering his thoughts (for I soon discovered he had no shortage of them), but at the time I wondered if he hadn't simply drawn a blank. The only animation about the man was the huge foot which balanced on the kneecap and waggled madly, as if all his energy had congregated there. He sized me up for another minute, pursed his lips, then finally let loose.

And I must say he turned out to be about as full of head-information as a man could possibly wish: how a head might be judged and measured, for example, or how it might be broken and repaired. In fact, it soon became clear that, like his old friend Mellor, Professor Bannister was a wordy fount and once his tongue had properly got into its stride it left me struggling far behind.

Unfortunately, his monologue seemed to me quite tedious, being marred in two different ways. Firstly, the *tone*, which was academic and totally humourless (no anecdotes, which will often keep my interest up). Secondly, the *sheer magnitude* of the thing for, stored in his skull, he seemed to have information equivalent to several dozen regular headfuls and in no time my own rather small, unacademic head was filled right to the brim.

After twenty minutes I was so thoroughly saturated I began to wonder if he did not perhaps have some work he should be returning to and my only participation had been whittled right down to the odd nod or grunt, to signify I was still awake. Then, right in the middle of this very erudite and thoroughly boring flood of words, my ear caught hold of a vaguely familiar term. A phrase I must have come across in one of my medical dictionaries.

'Trepanning?' I said (putting something of stick in the Professor's spokes). 'Now what is that all about?'

Well, at first he was quite floored by my interruption. He looked like a man who had just been snapped out of an hypnotic trance.

'A hole in the head, Your Grace,' he said. 'A man-made hole.'

And an arm reached out to a distant desk, scrabbled among the papers for a second or two, before scissoring back and dropping into my lap a yellowed, jawless skull.

'Well held, sir,' said Bannister.

I turned the thing cautiously in my hands. I was beginning to understand why Bannister and Mellor are such firm friends – both are such wordy fellows and both enjoy sporting with bones.

Having a dead man's head rolling in my hands made me feel a little strange, but I was determined not to be outdone and managed to gamely ask, 'And who is this fellow, then?'

'That is *Homo erectus amazonas*, Your Grace. We found him down in Brazil.'

I had a good long look at what was left of him – I had never met a Brazilian before – and gently ran a finger along the fine fissures where the different continents of the skull had merged.

'If you care to look at the crown,' Bannister told me from the depths of his chair, 'you'll find a hole about three-quarters of an inch wide.'

Indeed I did.

'Now, while we medical men find these holes very handy for carrying old skulls about the place – one's middle finger fitting so snugly inside – there are a good many in our profession who claim that such holes are, in fact, the result of primitive surgery...'

'But why would a Brazilian consent to having a hole made in his skull?' I asked.

'Well now, Your Grace, that's a fair question, for there's no evidence that the fellow consented to any such thing. But it is commonly held that such operations were undertaken in order to release Evil Spirits.'

I looked down at the dried old husk in my hands. Whatever once possessed it had long since upped and gone.

'Tell me, William,' I said, continuing to look down at the skull, 'are men still trepanned today?'

'O, plenty. Plenty of them. I should say there are several hundred people currently walking about with some sort of hole-in-the-head. Though not for spiritual reasons, of course, but to relieve a haemorrhage perhaps or to allow us to have a poke around. But, to answer your question ... Yes, Your Grace. We still like to make the odd hole or two.'

Bannister was now so far down in his armchair he was practically horizontal, with his legs stretched out before him and his feet crossed neatly at the ankles. I was anticipating another verbal onslaught when, quite without warning, an arm swung out from his body and came at me like the boom on a boat. I had to duck down out of the way as it swept around the room. When it finally came to rest I saw how the finger at the end of it was pointing towards a glass cabinet on the other side of the room.

'Have a gander at my old John Weiss,' said Bannister.

So I made my way over to the cabinet and found behind the glass a slim case, about ten inches by five. In its open mouth lay a row of evilly-gleaming instruments.

'A trepanning kit, Your Grace,' said Bannister, coming alongside. 'A little out of date, but beautifully made, wouldn't you say?'

It certainly was. Like terrible jewellery; each piece very snug in its own velvet bed. The centrepiece resembling a small carpenter's drill – but not so modest – with a finely turned wooden handle at one end and all glinting metal at the other. Its own little army of apostles lined up on either side. But I was baffled by a tiny brush and a phial of oil which lay in their own little concavities.

'For lubrication,' Bannister explained.

I was so completely taken with this macabre machinery that I asked the Professor where one might purchase such a trepanation kit. But he was quite emphatic that such things were not commonly available to non-medical folk, so I said no more on the matter.

*

Bannister took me out to his dining club for luncheon, which was entirely unexpected and very kind indeed. I have had very little appetite lately, the food in the hotel being far too fancy, but when we were seated and served and Bannister launched into another incomprehensible monologue (something to do with carbon this time, I think) I rather found myself tucking in. We had a thick broth, grilled trout, spicy plum pudding and a bottle of sweet red wine. I was sleepily spooning the plum stones in the bottom of my bowl when some sort of rumpus went off at the table to my right.

There was the scraping of chair legs, the clatter of abandoned cutlery and the sound of conversations being hastily brought to a halt – in other words, that particular atmosphere which usually precedes some sort of fight. I was still trying to identify the protagonists (and praying the mêlée would not spread and engulf any innocent by-standers, such as myself) when Bannister suddenly sprang up from the table, sending his chair skittering off across the floor.

I had not the slightest idea how he had been drawn into it. Perhaps looks and glances had been exchanged. But in a couple of strides he was at the next table, had a fellow by the throat and was pushing him right back in his chair. The chap with Bannister's hands clamped on his windpipe was flat on his back in no time at all, whereupon Bannister jumped on top of him, sat on his chest and pinned his arms down with his long legs. Then his hand went hard down into the fellow's face. Screams now came from all parts of the room and one woman (who I took to be the fellow's wife) tugged vainly at Bannister's shoulder as he drove his fingers down into the fellow's throat.

When his hand came back up it had a piece of pork fat dangling from the fingers. It was very white and very wet. Bannister dropped it into a nearby saucer, then helped the unfortunate diner back to his feet.

'Thank you, sir. Thank you,' said the red-faced fellow. 'The damned thing got caught right under my tongue.'

But Bannister merely bowed a restrained little bow and returned to the table, while the rest of the room babbled admiringly.

'Some people simply refuse to chew their food,' he confided in me, wiping the grease from his fingers with his napkin.

The dining room slowly restored itself. The conversation

settled, the broken crockery was cleared away. The chap who had got the chop fat lodged in his gullet came by to shake my companion's hand and heap yet more praise on him.

When he was finally out of the way Bannister got to his feet.

'Well, onward and upward,' he announced. 'What says Your Grace?'

I said that 'onward and upward' sounded like good advice. So we collected our coats and hats at the cloakroom and went out into the already-darkening day.

*

That morning Bannister had suggested I look around his Special Collection, the implication being that this was something of an honour for a layman such as myself. By the time we emerged from the dining club, however, I would have been happy to go back to my hotel and spend the rest of the afternoon in bed. But, as I have already mentioned, William Bannister is very keen on remembering those details others might be inclined to forget. So, with his long arm around my shoulders, I found myself escorted back to the Anatomy Department and being led left and right and right and left and eventually down into the deepest depths of the place.

At the bottom of the steps stood a pair of doors with frosted windows which I thought very pretty indeed, and I might have stood there admiring their wintry sparkle a good while longer had Bannister not given me a smart shove towards them.

'You should find everything labelled,' he told me. 'Enjoy yourself,' and disappeared back up the steps.

It was not long before I was regretting having eaten such a substantial lunch or, come to that, having lunched at all. The vast white room was much too brightly lit and the bottles and jars and glass cases all gleamed like great chunks of ice. But as I made my way among them I recoiled not from the piercing light and its many reflections but from the overwhelming, all-pervading smell. The air was awash with formaldehyde – was warm and sticky with the stuff – so that, advancing down that first aisle of exhibits, I wondered if, by the time I came to leave the place, my own organs might not be as pickled as those on show.

That atmosphere of profound liquidity encouraged in me the notion that I made my way through some underwater world, for I found myself in the company of entities so wet and strange they would have looked more at home on an ocean bed. I could have read my *Gray's Anatomy* cover to cover a thousand times without preparing myself in the least. The lasting impression was of my having come upon an awful carnage, the result, perhaps, of a terrible explosion, which had scattered its victims into several hundred jars.

Handling the bones of an Ancient Brazilian may be fairly gruesome but coming face to face with his descendants' bottled brawn is something else again. Man had never seemed to me so mortal, had never seemed so sad. For as I slowly padded through that vast stinking room the voice which spoke to me most intelligently was a melancholy one – seemed to seep right through the thick glass jars.

Having never previously come across a man's vitals I was hardly likely to recognize them. Thus, here (the label assured me), suspended in alcohol, was a human heart, looking like nothing but a soft black stone. Here was a sectioned kidney, like a mushroom ready for the frying pan. All around me the innermost, most secret pieces of man were laid bare, hanging slack and horribly sodden in their prison-jars.

A Cumberland sausage of intestine.

A single eyeball dangling in fleshy mid-trajectory.

A human tongue, long enough to choke a man, coiled up like an eel.

And a brain – a man's brain, for goodness' sake! – with all

the contours of a bloated walnut. And not the ocean-blue I had always imagined but a dismal, pasty grey.

A curious construction, marked 'broncho-pulmonary', sat atop a pedestal in a fancy bell jar and which, after much puzzled label-reading, I finally understood as being an intricate representation of the interior of a lung. Again, I found my own picture of a body's mechanics well wide of the mark. The inside of my lung is apparently less like the branches of a leafless tree and more like a coral bouquet. Yet even this beautiful, bizarre lung-tiara, I thought, seemed to sparkle in a mournful way.

The whole collection evoked in me tremendous feeling. Certainly there was horror in those glass cases and some peculiar pulchritude to admire, but above all else I sensed that every organ was drenched in the same sad concentrate and that disappointment filled every last vessel.

I had wandered up and down those humid aisles for getting on half an hour and, rather surprisingly, my lunch had stayed where it was, when the following idea occurred to me . . .

Is it not possible to take all these marinaded pieces and reintroduce them to one another? To recreate out of all these miserable, disparate parts one frail but functioning human being?

But the answer was all too apparent.

No, of course it is not possible. He has been unwhole for far too long. If he was put back together there would be no making sense of him. He would be an altogether too vinegary man.

By now, I had had enough of the place and was making my way towards the door, eager to fill my lungs with fresh air, when I came across an exhibit which struck such a deep chord in me that it stopped me in my tracks. Through the jar's inch-thick glass I saw what appeared to be a tiny but perfectly-formed child. The little fellow was all hunched-over. His bald head was bowed in meditation, his hands rested delicately on his knees. He seemed to float in an entirely different world to me, looked to be scowling with concentration. But from under his right knee I saw that there dangled an umbilicus, which hung uselessly like a disconnected pipe. And at that moment I realized that he had, in fact, never lived outside the confines of his mother's belly – was but a foetus of a child. He must have gone straight from the warmth of the womb to the awful chill of the jar, effectively living and dying without ever having breathed a mouthful of air.

How close he had come to being born or the circumstances of his death I could not tell. The label made no mention of these facts. Yet he had on his head a smattering of hair, had fingernails and neat little toes . . . all the detail of a born boychild.

There was something familiar in his luminosity. Something in the magnification of the water and the glass. I looked in on him, hoping he might unfold himself and look me in the eye. But he did nothing but peer down into the solution which buoyed his poor body up.

*

As I was sitting here in my hotel room and recording the entry above I was reminded, no doubt by all the meaty imagery, of the one time I saw a rabbit being prepared for the pot.

I happened to call in on one of my gatekeepers and found him sharpening up a knife for the job. I remember the rabbit hanging forlornly in the corner from a hook on one of the kitchen's beams and my keeper going over and gently lifting it down and laying it on the table top. The prospect of a rabbit-skinning quite intrigued me, so I asked if he would mind me staying to see how it was done.

I reckon I must have thought back to that day a hundred different times in an attempt to get a hold on that transformation; trying to locate the precise moment when the rabbit ceases to be a creature and becomes nothing more than a piece of meat. Certainly, when one looks upon a dead rabbit one easily senses the difference between it and the rabbits which live and breathe. Its head hangs too heavily, its limbs are limp, it is too deeply asleep. Yet one somehow imagines the situation might be resolvable. As if the rabbit has just temporarily lost its quick. One feels that if one could only summon up in one's lungs some essential heat or spirit one might breathe some life back into it.

But to see the rabbit stripped of its fur and see its flesh bloodily gleam is to admit to some important threshold having been crossed and that only a genius with a needle and thread could return this animal to its previous form. I recall the fur being peeled back with care (even kindness), as if helping an aged relative off with her coat. The leg-joints were neatly bent and tucked in order to ease them out.

Only when the creature's head is detached from the body can one say with certainty that the process is complete. For when the cleaver strikes cleanly through the neck and its awful edge is sunk in the chopping block, then both parts of the bloody rabbit must know how significantly they have been rent. And when the head is gone we have no eyes, either conscious or unconscious, and it is there that we plumb for life.

When the belly is slit open and the innards are removed (although, to be perfectly honest, I cannot now recall at which point in the proceedings this took place) we are, without doubt, in the domain of the butcher, not the open field. And by the time the keeper had done with his twitching knife and gone off in search of herbs and onions to accompany the grey-red chunks into the pot, what I looked upon was not a rabbit but most definitely rabbit-meat (which, not surprisingly, I have never had much fancy for).

✳

EDINBURGH, JANUARY 9TH

✳

Last night, when I was all tucked-up in bed with the light out and just beginning to drift away, I caught a glimpse of the most distant, yet heartfelt memory. A recollection of some moment before my birth. There I was in my mother's belly; warm. My whole world very close to me. Yet there was something else – something important. Some other aspect which has slipped away. It is hard to find words to describe a time before words were available to me. But I have no doubt that what I momentarily caught hold of was a memory of the womb.

✳

This morning I decided to stroll up to the Castle and break in a new pair of boots. Allowed Clement to come along, on the understanding that he walk several yards behind. I think the wind must have been behind us for we reached our destination in no time at all and finding I still had a little spirit to spare I left Clement at a chop house and carried on down the High Street to pick up some tobacco.

Bought a 'Visitor's Guide to the City' from an old woman on the corner of Bank Street and was pleased to find it contained a folded map – very simple, about two foot wide. The old lady, who wore a pair of spectacles with one lens missing, said it was by far the best street map of Edinburgh ... of such quality that it had won an award.

'What sort of award?' I asked her.

'A map award,' she replied.

No doubt. Well, I asked if she knew a good tobacconist in the neighbourhood. A straightforward question, one would have thought, but one which provoked in her no end of personal discord and face-pulling before she finally reached some tentative agreement with herself. Having firmed up her directions she informed me how if I took the next-but-one passage off to the right and descended two long flights of steps I should come out right opposite one of the best tobacco shops in town.

Well, I thanked her, set off and, as directed, turned right at the second passage along the way. So confident was I of my imminently entering the tobacco shop and hearing the 'ding-a-ling' of the bell above my head that I had gone down, I think, three flights of steps and was climbing a fourth before I sensed that I might have gone awry.

Twenty yards further down the passageway I found myself at the wrong end of a cul-de-sac. A huge iron gate stood before me, bound by a rusty chain and lock. At this point I felt distinctly worried. No, why should I lie? Panic is what I felt. I saw at once how that old crone had led me – a stranger in town and about as green as the hills – into an easy trap and how, any minute now, some great lumbering nephew of hers would descend on me, club me on the noggin and rob me of every last penny in my purse.

So I filled my lungs in preparation for a desperate cry for help and my head prepared itself to be clubbed. I waited ... then waited a minute longer. The lumbering youth must have forgotten our violent little tryst, so I set off back down the steps as fast as my old legs would go.

When I descended that first flight on returning I saw a

passageway off to the left which I must have gone straight past before. It looked long and dark and full of drips. Was it possible that the old woman had included an extra turn in her instructions and that I had not taken it in? Perhaps she had meant to mention it but had omitted it and the mistake was on her side? Either way, I decided to follow the passage for a minute or two and that if the tobacco shop had not given itself up by then, I would simply turn myself around and come straight back.

Well, I can only imagine that I took another left or right which went unaccounted when I tried to return. For within five minutes I was feeling as if I were the object of some practical joke, whereby a half-dozen stagehands constantly switched the set between my going and coming back. The passage walls, however, seemed quite solid and not like the set of a play at all. My bearings found no tally in their surroundings. In other words, I was completely lost.

Then I suddenly remembered my award-winning map and got it out and studied it very hard, as if the sheer intensity of my gaze might draw from it the information I required. But, of course, a map is absolutely useless unless one can say for certain whereabouts one is on it, and as there was not a single street sign on the walls around me I might as well have held up a blank sheet of paper and tried to set a course from that.

Well, I must have bounced around those passageways for getting on three-quarters of an hour, with that map flapping uselessly in one hand. My mind became the debating chamber for two fiercely dissenting voices ... one reassuring me that I would be out of this awful stone maze the next minute, the other screaming that I would never get out alive.

All this time I did not come across a single other soul. It was bitterly cold and every door and window was firmly shut. If I had been wandering across a desert, I thought to myself, I would have about as much hope of finding a helping hand. Tenement buildings towered all around me and every once in a while I would come out into their yards. No doubt there were people within a few feet of me who knew this labyrinth like the back of their hand, but they were too busy warming them by their firesides to be bothered with an old man's distant halloos. The only signs of life were an occasional baby's cry or the distant bark of a dog, which echoed up and down the empty passageways. Given the choice, I think I would have elected to hear nothing but my own footsteps than those eerie, anxious sounds.

I trekked up cobbled valley and down cobbled dale. Turned myself about so many times I became dizzy and forgot which city I was in. I had marched myself deep into a state of exhausted fretfulness when I came out suddenly into broad daylight on a narrow footbridge which spanned a busy road below. Beneath my feet, on the floor of that city-canyon, the street was hectic with carriages and shopping-folk, all flowing merrily along. But my footbridge leapt straight across it, to disappear into a dark passageway on the other side.

As I peered hungrily down at all that humanity I noticed a row of three or four tiny shops. In the middle of them I saw one whose windows housed many mounds of freshly-rolled tobacco and many shelves of pipes. I saw the door of the shop open, heard the bell faintly ring and the proprietor, in a neat white apron, step out into the street. He looked left and right, as if he expected me, checked his watch, then turned to go back into his shop.

I shouted – at the top of my voice I shouted – so loud I felt sure I would set in motion tobacco-avalanches in his window display.

'Halloa! Below there!' I yelled through cupped hands.

But the tobacconist disappeared. As he closed the door I heard the bell briefly jingle again but it was soon gathered up and washed away by the wind and wheels and horses' hoofs.

I pushed myself back from the railing and there and then consigned myself to being for ever stuck up in the sky.

✳

It would be as impossible for me now to explain how I managed to extract myself from that conundrum as it would be to explain how I became lost at the start. Certainly it was not due to any resourcefulness or calculation on my part and, though it is strange to hear myself say it, I can't help but feel that some piece of me is still trapped in those passageways ... doomed to wander, exhausted, for evermore. The rest of me suddenly found itself pitched back onto the High Street, as if the malevolent force which had held me for its entertainment had at last grown tired and spat me out.

By now the very idea of tobacco repulsed me. So I brushed myself down and, in the poorest condition, set off to try and find old Clement. On my way I passed the spot where the old lady with one lens in her spectacles had stood with her visitor's guides. If she had still been there I might have had a good old shout at her, though I am not sure what I would have shouted, or if I would have had the energy to shout for long.

✳

EDINBURGH, JANUARY 10TH

✳

It must have been late afternoon when I came across the bleak little cemetery at Greyfriars'. The air particles which had held the daylight were being slowly vacated and made cold.

I strolled between the gravestones in their weathered gowns of green and brown and read the epitaphs of horse-dealers, pulpit orators and medical men. Took some comfort from the fact that even the most patronizing, puffed-up doctors do not escape the earth's deadly pull.

Sat on a bench and pulled my coat about me and watched the world slip through gradations of grey, a change so incremental in its nature that it was as if my own lungs were bringing it about. I remember pondering how an Edinburgh dusk might be different to an English one and chewing over corresponding matters of light and dark and, one way or another, reached such a zenith of enlightenment that I inadvertently drifted off.

I must have tumbled in the shallows of unconsciousness for quite a while, for when I came to things were altogether darker and chillier. My left leg, which was crossed over my right leg, was completely senseless and my fingers, which had formed a small cairn on my knee's hilltop, were similarly numb.

I carefully set about disentangling my frozen joints, thinking how this is becoming something of a habit with me, when I became conscious of the most heavenly music slowly pouring over me. A whole host of celestial voices were singing their Praises Be, as if welcoming me to the kingdom in the sky. The graveyard was utterly dark and dank but my mind was filling up with light. And though the air particles remained tight and empty, they had become enlivened and quivered amongst themselves.

It was some time before I gathered my wits and understood that the glorious sound which had stirred me emanated from the church behind my back. The choir was rehearsing the harmonies of 'Father Who Didst Fashion Me' and had not quite reached the end of the second verse when they were pulled up by their master's muffled voice and, after a short pause, made to recommence with the first line of that same verse.

I was stamping some life back into my dead leg and

rubbing some heat back into the palms of my hands when I saw just how marvellously the church was lit up, so that all the tableaux in the stained-glass windows radiated from the candlelight within. The saints, the angels and even the lambs – all brimmed with a heavenly glow. It was as if a great ship had stolen up behind me, with its cargo of hallelujas and kindly light. And no one else there to witness its arrival – just me and the grudging graves. I was struck by how a church's windows might be admired from outside as well as in, and I stopped my stamping to watch as the blues and purples were gently coaxed from the glass by the choir.

I was sitting up in the bath back at the hotel with Clement scrubbing my back before the significance of my experience in Greyfriars' cemetery truly came home to me. That here, if I could only put my finger on it, was a demonstration of the duality of man. We are not, as I had feared, simply a camera obscura – just a spectator of the light of the world. No. We are both the camera obscura and the lighthouse. We receive light and we send it out.

*

Edinburgh, January 11th

*

Called in again on Bannister. He did not answer his door. In fact, he had rather carelessly left the thing unlocked. I was in and out without anybody paying me much attention. Perhaps they think me some learned old gent.

Skipped down the stairs and was halfway back to the hotel before I realized I had cut my hand on the glass. Bandaged it with my handkerchief.

Clement wanted to know how I had come to hurt myself. Told him I had taken a fall. Packed up my bags without too much interference from him and we got to the station with hardly a minute to spare.

✳

JANUARY 12TH

✳

Home again. The estate looks even colder and more wretched than before.

Unpacked and bathed and was back in my old routines within a couple of hours.

A month ago, I was quite convinced how my own body, or some element in it, was intent on bringing me down.

I see now how it is upstairs I am akilter – my mind which is askew.

✳

JANUARY 20TH

✳

Out onto the balcony late last night. The wind was all around. Fished out my father's Dutch clog pipe from my pocket but found it broken in two. Must have sat on it. So I stood there in my slippers and leaned against the balustrade and let the breeze billow in my dressing gown and whistle in my ears.

A while later – perhaps an hour or so – a strange mist crept in from the lake. It rolled silently over the orderly lawns and seeped right through the hedges. I stood and watched it thicken up, watched it lap against the walls below. And quite soon the whole house was adrift in it and beginning to gently creak and sway. And we were advancing through a milky sea, with me in my slippers at the helm.

The clouds stole back at some point to reveal a sky alive with painful stars. And I became cold and tired and empty and my legs began to ache. I felt lost in the world and lonely and found no purchase in the mist below. So I took a reading from the heavens, set a course for the Cotswolds and retired to bed.

*

In the night I had a terrible vision.

> I saw a small ship with twenty men aboard, trawling off some Icelandic shore. The nets had been cast and the crew stood by to heave in the evening's catch. But the captain, who was up on the bridge and whose company I shared, saw that something was amiss. The compass was twitching in its glass and the vessel shifted towards starboard of its own accord.
>
> Orders were given to bring her back about but the young man wrestling with the wheel complained that his efforts all came to naught. He turned to the captain. 'It's the North Pole,' he cried. 'It is pulling us in.'
>
> Then I am no longer alongside the captain but floating high above the sea in the cold night air.
>
> I hear men wailing, calling out in the darkness. Some jump overboard into the freezing waves. And I see how it is the magnetism of the pole which has got a hold of the metal ship and begins to haul her inexorably in. And that when they reach the North Pole the compass will be spinning and the ship will be torn apart in the jaws of the ice.

*

This morning, peering at myself in the mirror, I noticed a mole on my left shoulder which I had never seen before and, turning, saw how it was just one of a considerable scattering, spread diagonally across my back. A great constellation of freckles, stretching from my shoulder right down to my waist.

Is it possible, I wonder, that there might be some correspondence between these moles and the stars I watch at night?
There is something undeniably Orion-like about that cluster
just beneath my shoulder blade.

The next time I am out on the balcony at night I shall
compare them. I shall use a mirror.

✻

January 24th

✻

A grey and tedious day today. Nothing worth noting at all
with the exception of a letter from Professor Bannister
(threatening me with all manner of things, including police-
men, which I chose to ignore) and an experiment I undertook
in an idle moment, as I sat at table waiting for lunch to arrive.

Found my attention drawn towards a jug of water, about
two foot in front of me. No doubt the same jug which has sat
there every day for the last ten or twenty years. Today,
however, I noticed how its little spout was turned up and
away from me most contemptuously and how, when I moved
my head to get a better view of it, the water in its belly threw
back all sorts of refracted and untrustworthy light.

My first thought was to put something in it. Put something
in the water and spoil its fun. I thought, 'If there is mashed
potato on my plate when lunch arrives I shall drop a spoonful
straight in.' But then I thought, 'No, not mashed potato. I
shall harness the energy of my mind to send the blasted thing
whistling across the table and crashing to the floor.'

I should mention that, for quite some time now, I have
been wondering if it might not be possible for a man to cause
objects to move by using the power of his mind. (I have some
notes somewhere.) So I went straight ahead and concentrated

227

my attention on that patronizing jug, glaring at it with undiluted fury and bringing to the boil such quantities of psychic energy that my ears were soon as warm as toast. I glared and I stared and grunted, but my efforts were all in vain. The damned jug did not budge a single inch, which was, of course, deeply humiliating. Outwitted by a common jug!

When my lunch finally arrived I told Mrs Pledger that I was sick of the sight of the water jug and asked it to be removed at once. I now wonder, however, if the experiment's failure might be down to not just my mental shortcomings but an unusually stubborn jug.

Lying in bed this evening, I eyed all the phials and bottles on my bedside table which contain all my preparations and powders and pills. How merrily they jangled against each other as a maid strolled past my door. I feel sure this has some bearing on the water jug business, though I cannot think just what.

*

JANUARY 28TH

*

Most of it fades or falls away. We are more like Mr Snow than we care to think. But the odd memory, or sliver of it, perseveres. Nags away, like a stone in the shoe.

It is as if it has been stalking me since I first disturbed it in the Deer Park in the mist but even if I had known it was closing in on me I somehow doubt I would have been able to get out of its way. It had a fair old head of steam on it, had momentum on its side.

I happened to pick up my *Gray's Anatomy*, as I am in the habit of doing, and it fell open at the title page, where I clearly saw the name 'Carter', who is credited for all the illustrations in the book. I was not aware that the name had so profoundly registered in me – I must have picked that book up a dozen times before – and was half out of my chair to poke at the dying fire when I became suddenly aware of something moving powerfully in on me . . .

I froze. I listened hard. Something inside me stirred. As if a whole series of forgotten cogs had been set in motion; some deep-sunk machinery in my memory fired-up by the name in the book.

My free hand clung to the mantelpiece and I felt my presence in the room diminish. I heard a voice cry 'Carter' down all the years. Then,

I am a boy again, in the old family carriage, come to a halt on the beach with the mist creeping in.

My father has his head out of the window. The driver argues with another man, whom I cannot see. I do not understand what they are saying. All I hear are the voices to-and fro-ing towards a crescendo, before suddenly giving out.

A man with a long branch in his hand and a leather cap on his head passes the carriage window, heading back the way we came.

'Carter,' my father calls after him.

This Carter-man with his cap and his stick means nothing to me. I only know that I wish he would stay. I watch him marching off into the mist across the cold flat sand and when he has been all but swallowed up by the mist I see him turn and shout,

'This way. For the very last time.'

He waits a second, then turns and is gone.

I believe my mother is crying. Her tears start off some tears in me. After a minute she says, 'Not to worry. Not to worry.' But it is no good, for we are all of us worrying a very great deal.

Then my father pulls himself back into the carriage and gives me an unconvincing smile. He tells us how our driver is

certain he knows the way. And as if to back him up the brake is let out and we are moving again. We travel through the mist, which goes a little way towards relieving me. And I concentrate all my attention on the sand thrown up by the wheels, so as not to be frightened by my mother's tears and my father's unconvincing smile.

So successfully do I wrap myself up in my own small world that I have almost forgotten to be afraid. My father is talking and watching the sand with me and my mother has dried her eyes. But then the carriage suddenly comes to a dreadful halt and my precious sand stops flying for good.

My father has his head out in the mist again, which now carries on it the smell of the sea.

The driver is saying to my father, 'Sir, I think perhaps we should turn about.'

My hand has the poker in a fierce grip, as if I am about to do someone some terrible mischief. But whatever machinery previously stirred in me has all but seized-up again and I am left clinging to the mantelpiece, staring into the fire.

I prod and I poke at the embers, but they refuse to come back to life.

A Housemaid's Account

Three things always stick in my mind about him ... You're quite sure it is all right for me to speak? ... Well, the first is when I had only been at the house a month or two and was still finding my way about and I was right down in the basement and heading for the kitchens, I suppose, when I came across him in the shadows, sitting on a step.

He seemed to think my name was Rosie. There's no knowing where he got that idea from. But I had been warned by Mrs Pledger that he was confused enough to begin with and that in such an event it was probably best not to bother to put him right.

Well, he asked me where the trolleys had got to. I should explain that between the kitchens and the lifts up to the dining room is a fair old stretch, so there are tramlines set into the flags of the basement corridors and when the food is ready to go upstairs it is put inside the metal carts, then wheeled down the tracks. So I understood that these were the carts the old Duke was after, but seeing as how I did not know where they were kept I told him, in my politest voice, that I supposed that they were all locked up and I was about to carry on my way when he jumped up and grabbed me by my hand and insisted that I help him hunt them down.

Well, to be honest, I hoped we would not find them. I was very nervous about the whole affair and not half as pleased as he was when we came across one, tucked in a corner, just by the cupboards off the main corridor. Well, having found the cart I made my excuses and was all set to leave again but the old Duke ... beg your pardon, His Grace ... was having none of it and insisted I help him out.

Well, he ... Oh, I don't quite know how to put it ... but he made me ... made me ... push the cart up and down ... with him inside. He climbed inside the cart, where the plates and tureens would normally go, and had me push him up and down the corridors ... at speed.

There I've said it. Oh, dear ... You'll have to excuse me a second ... Oh, my goodness ... What a to-do.

The second thing ... now what was the second thing? Oh, yes. That they discovered His Grace ... and I should say here that I was not personally present at this one, but my good friend Molly was and she's no reason to lie ... but that they found him one morning in the dumb waiter which we use to bring the coal up from below. Just sitting there when they pulled it up, he was. All squashed up in the coal lift, with his face as black as you like.

Molly told me she was all set to scream – as indeed you would be – but he raised a finger to his lips so she never got the chance. He said that if she listened very hard she would hear the coal miners far below. Said you could hear them digging up the coal.

Well, she asked to be taken off coal duty after that one. Said she'd rather sweep the mausoleum every morning than risk another episode like that.

The third and final thing which stays with me, and the last thing I want to mention here, happened really not that long ago when I was coming in to work one morning, at the very crack of dawn. I was almost at the house and thinking to myself how the world was freshening up and was very much looking forward to spring when I saw a strange shape hanging from a tree. Very peculiar. I thought to myself, it looks just like a man. And of course it *was* a man. It was the

Duke himself, caught by his trousers. Just dangling from a tree.

I went to the bottom and shouted up to him. Asked if he required assistance of any sort. And he explained that he had been checking on the bud situation and that he appeared to have got his trousers snagged. I asked if he had been there very long and he said that he did not think so, but that whatever it was I intended doing I should hurry up because there was no knowing how long his trousers would hold out. It was a fair old drop.

So I went and called Clement, who came running. We had to fetch a ladder to get him down.

Yes, that last one will certainly stay with me. His Grace hanging from a tree.

From His Grace's Journal

*

I must be over-tired or in some way nervously exhausted. Something is certainly up with me, for I have recently been afflicted with what I can only describe as 'imaginings' – brief slippages of the mind. Spent the whole morning worrying about the memories of church spires I brought back from Edinburgh and how they have been scratching away at the inside of my skull. Then this afternoon had a very bad session with that head-picture Mellor gave me – the phrenology chart with Man's characteristics laid out in tableaux of tiny men.

I had it pinned on the wall above my shrine and stood there meditating on the various rooms within the head. I went slowly from one room to another and everything was right as rain, when I thought I saw one of the little chaps wriggling in his seat. Nothing much, just the straightening-out of the back a fellow does after he has been sitting for too long at a time. When I looked back at him he was perfectly still again, but now sat, I felt, a little more stiffly, as if he was holding his breath. I waited, did not take my eyes off him until, at last, he let out a tiny sigh.

The next thing I spotted was an old lady in the next compartment who scratched her head, just as cool as you like. Then a young girl in the room above her bent down to adjust the lace of her shoe. At this point I stepped back from the

235

picture and saw how all the little figures had become minutely animated and how all now went about their chores. 'How marvellous,' I thought. 'Such harmony. Each inhabitant happy in his own four walls.'

But as I watched, the grim fellow in the room marked Acquisitiveness (a miser counting his piles of coin) leaned back in his chair and took a long look about him, until his gaze lit on Tunefulness' maiden, who gently strummed her guitar. The miser's gaze now turned distinctly lecherous. He sneaked a glance over each shoulder and got to his feet. Then, without a by-your-leave, he took up his walking stick and started to smash right through the separating wall and in no time was upon the maiden and looking her up and down in the most wicked way.

Meanwhile, the fox in nearby Secretiveness had started scratching at the wall, having sensed that on the other side Cautiousness' plump hen brooded over her clutch of eggs. The fox had soon scratched a hole for himself and squeezed right through; had got the bird by its throat and was shaking it this way and that.

And now Combativeness' burly pugilists heard Tunefulness screaming and broke their bout to listen for a moment or two and when they realized that the poor girl was in distress, began battering their bare fists towards her cries. And very soon they were through and upon the miser, one holding him down while the other struck him in the face, whereupon Benevolence's good Samaritan heard the miser moaning and abandoned the care of his patient to join the fisticuffs below.

Destructiveness' big cat caught a whiff of Alimentiveness' succulent joint of meat and started clawing its way through to it. Philoprogenitiveness' loving father, it seemed, had grown bored with his wife and child and began to look lustily across at Friendship's embracing girls.

Elsewhere, I saw Amativeness' cherub fix an arrow to his bow and train it on the fox with the hen in its mouth, while Conscientiousness doggedly held his scales in the air and looked impotently on.

The whole head was in a state of anarchy, walls were being torn down everywhere as the façade of civilization slipped aside to reveal Man's savage nature beneath.

※

FEBRUARY 15TH

※

I have been working on a theory, quite unusual and primarily to do with bones.

First of all, I must say that not nearly enough is made of bones. I reckon they are all too frequently overlooked. When one considers how every creature which walks the earth leaves behind its own set of ribs and hips and tibia-fibias, one begins to grasp just how many bones there must be scattered about the place. The world, one might say, is nothing more than a vast burial ground on which we are invited to briefly picnic.

But my thoughts have been focused mainly on whalebones, which are, it goes without saying, the biggest in the world. How many whales are there, altogether? Millions, to be sure. The question, therefore, is: what happens to all those whalebones once their owners have passed away? They cannot all of them be picked clean by tiny scavengers and left to rot on the ocean bed. If that were the case there would by now be great piles of them poking out of the oceans everywhere. Shipping would have been brought to a halt.

No. The truth is that they are somehow organized – laid out in lines to form some sort of World Bone Network. Who is in charge of the enterprise? An international committee, presumably. No doubt the French are involved. As far as I can tell, this network consists of both longitudinal and latitudinal bone-lines, the majority of which are under the sea. On land this vast net is buried deep underground.

The purpose of this bone arrangement? I am not yet certain, but have narrowed down the options to . . .

    (i) some sort of 'brace'. A way of cradling the Earth, to stop it splitting and coming apart from old age;

   (ii) some powerful means of communication, via tremors, between governments;

  (iii) bars of a prison. The world is but a cage.

I note all the above in order to prevent them drifting off into the ether, but also as a means of introducing another aspect of this whole business which has recently come to my attention . . .

At four o'clock this afternoon it occurred to me that Mrs Pledger is, in fact, a ship and that all the house's little gusts and zephyrs are what fill her skirts and blow her from room to room. It was only her breezing into my rooms this lunchtime with a bowl of minestrone in her hand which finally provoked in me this nautical connection. She was tacking her way around a sofa, plotting her course by way of Fowler's head on the mantelpiece to the north and the bureau to the east. As she approached I thought to myself, 'There must be a good deal of hidden rigging to keep her so navigable and trim.'

I watched with interest as she dropped anchor on the fireside rug and placed my soup on the table by my chair. As she bent down her bosomy cargo swung into view, all splendidly girdled and packed, and when she saw how I was spying her she gave me one of her frostier looks. Things were now falling very neatly into place, so I gave her a cheeky little wink. It was my way of saying, 'The game is up, Mrs Pledger!'

But she wasn't for coming clean. O, no. She became all tight-lipped and hoity-toity. I could see I was going to have to squeeze the truth right out of her.

'You're a sizeable lady, Mrs Pledger,' I told her, and waited to see how this little observation went down. She stared at me but not a word came out of her, so I continued. 'Be kind enough, Mrs Pledger, to tell me about the bones.'

She did her best to assume some incredulous air but it was quite plain I had caught her out. 'And which bones might they be, Your Grace?' she replied, reddening.

'Why, the whalebones that hold us all together,' I countered calmly, and leaning over toward her, added, 'And maybe the secret ones, Mrs Pledger, which keep you so shapely-looking.'

She was properly horror-stricken. I leaned back triumphantly in my chair.

I believe I might well be the first mortal man to understand the significance of the whalebones which are stitched in every woman's corset. For all I know, Mrs Pledger is, at this very moment, down in the kitchens sending out signals to the bone organizations. Perhaps *this* is why women are so peculiar. They are all in league with the whales.

Whatever lies at the bottom of this whole business – and I must say I believe there is still a great deal to dig up – it was clear from Mrs Pledger's reaction that I had struck a nerve. A whole lifetime of bone-secretion exposed!

I gave her another big wink then watched as she marched straight across the room. She stopped by a fruit bowl, picked up an orange; turned and threw it at me. It was headed right between my eyes. I ducked down too late, it bounced off the top of my head and landed smack in the middle of my soup.

We were both silent for a moment.

'Excellent shot, Mrs Pledger,' I announced.

She swept out of the room, leaving the whole place rocking in her wake.

Now, I have no problem having in my employ a woman who is up to her ears in bones. Mrs Pledger is a very fine woman – I have always said as much – and I sincerely hope that her paymasters do not punish her for being found out. After all, we are none of us entirely guiltless in that department; we all hide our bones away.

The orange bobbed in the remains of my minestrone.

'Fruit in my soup again,' I said.

✻

FEBRUARY 19TH

✻

I have been poorly as long as I can remember. Upstairs as well as down. Long before this pain set off on its travels something nagged at me. Something has always nagged.

The problem, I am slowly beginning to understand, is that we are all prisoners of our own skin. Our bodies, with their incredible capacities, are also the gaols in which we are sentenced to languish. Our ribs are the bars of our tiny cells. We are entombed in flesh and blood.

Sooner or later our body's frailties begin to drag us down and we have no choice but to go. Illness, when it strikes, is a torture we are bound to suffer. We cannot be removed.

As often as not my own feelings are a mystery to me. Most days, the best I can hope for is to weather them, to endeavour not to get washed away. How wonderful it would be to let the mind roam freely, unencumbered by the fetters of skin and bone. To be able to come together and communicate with all the other souls.

I am, I now see, two very different people. The mind and

the bag of bones it heaves behind. The body, I suppose, is a sort of vessel. The next man might regard it as a temple but, then, what a foul and decrepit ruin in which to worship.

What I long for is transcendence. To let the deepest part of me rise up and breathe the air. It is the awful separateness of life, foisted on me by flesh, which I have slowly come to detest.

All I want is to let a little light in. To let a little of me out into the world.

✻

February 24th

✻

The razor felt strange in my hand. Unfamiliar. The scissors too. So excited that my whole body itched. Something very odd about being beardless after so many bearded years. My neck now feels absolutely naked. As fleshy as a freshly-plucked goose.

The scissors took the bulk of it off in a couple of minutes – clumps of white hair, tumbling into the sink. Small bushy balls of the stuff resting on the porcelain, then flushed away with a twitch of the tap. Me left looking almost bruised, battered. But then, after the soap and the razor, a little less fierce. My neck has collapsed while it has been hidden from view. A baggy abundance of chalky skin hanging over a pair of straining guys.

So, all in all, I must say quite a surprise, which is more or less what I expected. The chin not the one I buried under the bristles all those years ago. The dimple disappeared. How curious to be reintroduced to oneself. To find one's most intimate relationship changed.

When I first started snipping away at the hair on my head

I had a fit of giggles. Simply couldn't help myself. Like trimming away at the clouds. Felt quite light-headed and as I lathered it up (a wonderful feeling) had further giggles to quell. Had to breathe slowly and get a grip on myself. Just my eyes staring back at me. Calmness. Calm.

My whole dome a-froth, with just the odd blossom of blood where I nicked myself. The razor's rasp very loud around the ears. Shaved away from them, so that if I slipped I would not lop them off. Left the old eyebrows well alone and, before I knew it, was rinsing away the soapy-suds.

I may have missed the odd little tuft or two, around the back of the head. I will need another mirror for that. But finally, there I am – a genuinely shocking sight. No longer laughing. A withered stump of a man. Thought I might suddenly start crying, like a baby.

Talcum-powdered the whole thing, so as to cover up the tiny scars and try to distract myself. Then, for a minute or two, sat in the bedroom and busied myself, pretending to read. Rose and returned to the mirror.

Much calmer now. Less giddy. Not worried like I was before. Stood there at the mantelpiece mirror, saying, 'Yes. The right thing to do.' And then, suddenly, I saw it. It leapt right out at me. To the right of my reflection sat Fowler's porcelain head with his usual inscrutable look and, what with my own head so white from the talcum, the two of us looked like kin. How strange. It would never have occurred to me. All I lacked were his labels and dividing lines.

Undid my gown and went over to the full-length mirror. Removed my trousers. What a white old man. Stared at me until I became a stranger. And in time I saw projected onto the flesh the *Ancient Chinese Healing* chart, with all its tributaries running up and down my arms and legs.

I imagined my belly, packed with Mrs Pledger's various herbs. Saw me stuffed full of them, like a turkey.

I saw the same organs the Oakley sisters had seen in me, the sleepy fish.

And in the middle of all this I saw the bone-tree, my very own skeleton-man.

With my white head perched on top, just like Fowler's, and those two eyes staring back at me from the void, I saw myself as some sort of living synthesis. An amalgamation of all the maps of man.

✻

FEBRUARY 25TH

✻

I locked myself in my bedroom and walked around awhile. Unlocked the door, called out, 'Do not disturb,' then stood there while the words went galloping up and down the hall. I was already quite inebriated, having consumed a quarter of a bottle of brandy. Perhaps even staggered a little as I ushered me back into my room and locked the door behind. I had not yet crossed that threshold into flailing drunkenness, but was in no doubt that I was by now sufficiently anaesthetized.

Slumped down at my dressing table, where all the towels and instruments were laid out. The mirror which usually sits on the mantel I had placed flat on the table top. I tilted the middle of the dressing table's triptych of mirrors forward, at an angle of some forty-five degrees, and leaned my head between them both, which was a little like inserting one's head into a lion's open mouth. With a slight adjustment to the upper mirror the top of my head swung into view. The brandy bottle was close at hand in case I needed another swig.

I remember tapping the top of my skull with a finger before I started. The flesh was pliant and warm. Then I picked up the scalpel and made the first incision – about two inches in length – from back to front. I pressed down until I felt the blade scrape against bone. It made a grinding sound in my ears. Almost immediately blood welled up from the neat little line; a single black-red bead rolling forward and another one rolling back. I made a second incision, roughly the same length, which perfectly bisected the first, so that I now had a cross – a bleeding cross at that – on the crown of my head.

There was pain, certainly, but it was distant and somewhat blurred. I took a couple of gulps from the brandy bottle, and waited for the alcohol to find its way into my veins. Then I positioned myself between the mirrors again, reached up with both hands and carefully peeled back the four pointed flaps of skin. It was as if I was opening out an envelope, the flesh dragging a little as each fold reluctantly came away. There was pain, as I say, but it was secondary to a curious coolness and was dulled by my fascination. When I had done, the effect was quite fetching – like four petals on an exotic plant.

I mopped at my head with a towel (which went up white and came back very red) and succeeded in soaking up enough of the small pool of blood to reveal a startling flash of bone.

I fixed Bannister's trepan together. I had practised holding it several times. For all its finely-worked woods and metals and the plush upholstery of its case the implement is essentially little more than a corkscrew, the significant difference being the tiny-toothed circular bit which I now fitted to the end.

I had chosen one with a diameter of three-quarters of an inch, with a depth of about an inch and a half. I considered taking another swig of brandy but decided more alcohol might affect the steadiness of my hand. So, with the aid of my mirrors, I inserted the trepan in the very eye of that bloody blossom and slowly began to turn. The sound of the bit scraping out its circle made a terrible groaning sound – like a chair dragged across a bare floor – which resonated right through me, especially through my jaw and teeth.

One's skull, I discovered, is surprisingly hardy. More like teak than the shell of an egg. After three or four minutes both my arms were completely drained and I had to bring them down and rest them a while. When I paused that first time I removed the trepan and could clearly see the ring it had cut in my skull. I recommenced a few minutes later, having oiled the bit with the tiny brush, and found it fitted easily back into the groove.

The next time I rested I found I could actually leave the tool in my skull (or, rather, that it would not easily come out). So I sat there at the dressing table for a minute and took another swig of brandy, with that corkscrew poking out of my head. In all, I think I must have stopped and rested my arms about half a dozen times in this way, the whole operation lasting somewhere in the region of half an hour. Certainly, the deeper I drilled down into me, the harder each turn became. The operation also produced a rather acrid smell, which I did my best to ignore.

As time went by I became quite exhausted and began to wonder if I would ever finish the job. Once or twice a nauseous wave swept through me and I had to hold on to the dressing table until it passed. The trepan became very sticky with blood and I think I had paused to wipe my hands when I heard a tiny hissing sound.

I pushed on with the infernal winding – my head fairly throbbing now – until I felt the tool lurch a little to one side. I continued to carefully wind the apparatus – slowly now – and, by jiggling it a little, managed to extract the instrument from my head. In the end of the trepan I found a circular piece of bloody bone. I was through! I had uncorked myself! Had finally managed to break down that wall between myself and the outside world.

I sat back in the chair. A little dizziness, perhaps, but vision surprisingly steady. An assortment of wheezes and sucking sounds emanated from my head. I could feel tiny pockets of air creeping under my skull and at one point watched as a bloody bubble slowly inflated itself, right over the hole, before disappearing with a pop.

I can only describe the overall sensation as being somehow similar to the tide coming in.

Once I had restored some sort of equilibrium I raised a tentative hand to my head and very gently inserted a finger into the hole. It was quite deep and wet, like an inkwell. My finger went down until it eventually touched something moist and warm. Was that really my little box of tricks? Was that the terrible fruit?

Bandaged myself up, went into the bathroom and vomited several times. Dozed in an armchair for an hour or two. Woke and recorded this entry. Have applied a little ointment to the wound. Am about to pack myself off to bed.

*

FEBRUARY 26TH

*

I hear voices. Beautiful voices. Voices all around. Last night, as I sat by the fire putting a fresh bandage on my head, I picked out the distant voice of a young woman reading a bedtime story to her child – a tale of a boy and a girl who get lost in a wood. The mother's voice was pure amber. It shone across the night. I saw her perched on the edge of her child's bed, wearing a dress of many pinks and blues. Pictured her perfectly in her cottage, all those miles away.

Sounds which had previously hid from my ears now shyly make themselves known. This morning I heard a young boy whistling as he strolled along a lane. The song danced among the hedgerows before winging its way to me.

I hear a maid down in the laundry, asking how much starch she should add to the water. Hear a young girl knocking on a neighbour's door and asking if her friend may come out to play.

But what came creeping in a little later and what most uplifts me are all the natural sounds. The heaving of the daffodil bulbs, unravelling beneath the thawing soil. The mighty heartbeat of every oak.

The seasons sweep about me. 'Prepare' is whispered down every root and vine. The great conspiracy of spring is almost on us. The buds have all been primed.

*

I must have fallen asleep in the flower beds. I remember my creeping out in the night. I believe I was listening for something. Perhaps I was being a sentry. My only recollection is my lying down on the cold, hard earth and looking up at the ocean of stars. The pruned stems of the roses pointed out the stars for me and were like branches of tiny trees. I remember imagining I was a very big fellow on the floor of a stark, empty wood.

When I came to the night had been swept from the sky and the stars had been moved along, but they had left their twinkling in a fine frost which had fastened itself to the bare roses and the fellow who lay below.

Getting to my feet took me several minutes. Bones extremely stiff. My trousers had a boardlike consistency but, once I had plucked myself from the roses, I felt altogether quite healthy and fit. Sneaked back up to my bedroom. Slept until almost four.

*

Mrs Pledger found some discarded bandages this morning and left a message asking what was up. I explained down the pipe that I had had a minor accident. She asked if I needed a doctor. I replied that I did not.

*

FEBRUARY 28TH

*

I have in my hand a chalky coin. A small disk from my very own skull. I scrubbed and scrubbed away at it until it came up white.

Question— How many coins make up a man? How much is your average man worth?

This coin bought me my freedom. (There's a thought.) I just opened up my purse and took it out. In so doing I managed finally to heave back the door which opens on to the world. And now parts of the world come through to me which had previously been out of reach. In return, my thoughts go out into the world. It is a fair exchange.

I am doing so much wondering these days. Wondering full-time. This morning I wondered what I should do with my coin. Pickle it, perhaps? Or have it framed? Give it to someone as a gift, maybe? Who then? Clement? Mellor? A child? I decided the best thing would be to bury it. Put it deeply in the ground. There are Roman coins down there, I hear. I shall simply add one of my own.

The wound is healing up very well. Some pain, but it goes out of me and does not hang around, although I sometimes see its shadow. I have put some lint on the wound and a bandage, which goes round and round, under my jaw and over my head. It stops me talking (except through my teeth, like a bad dog) which is no great sacrifice. I now converse with the world in other ways and, I might add, with a good deal more success.

I have decided not to let my staff see me. I think they would be alarmed. Perhaps later, when things have settled down. Meanwhile, I have asked for my meals to be left outside my door. I wrote a note to Clement. One day, the whole world will send notes to one another. Our pockets will overflow with them.

Clement brought some stew, just now. I felt him approaching, one warm footfall over the other. Heard him thinking at the door. Eventually he came to a decision and crept away like a bear. I have not touched the stew.

*

MARCH 1ST

*

Dawn was but an inkling as I tiptoed from the house. My first time out in many days. I wore a woollen bonnet.

Is it milder? I think it is milder, although my wound still aches somewhat. If it is not yet milder, there is the prospect of mildness. Mildness is at hand.

Strange, but when I gauged myself at the edge of the Wilderness I found hardly a trace of fear. An ounce of apprehension, maybe, but nothing more. Nothing flighty.

Clambered through the creaking fence and eased myself into the foliage. Crept forward. Stealthily, just like a fox. Winter still insisted; an old darkness lingered among the bushes and the trees. The ground surrendered beneath my boots – like walking on an old damp mattress. But such richness all a-brimming. Such leafy promise everywhere.

Made my way deeper into the wood. Not a single bird sang. Took the trowel from my coat pocket, knelt and plunged it in. The soil was like black pudding. Very moist and many worms. Dug up a dozen trowelfuls, then brought out my handkerchief. Carefully unfolded the four corners and removed my bit of bone.

Placed it into the cold hole. I remember holding it there a while. I believe I may have said a few words. The occasion would have called for them. I replaced the earth over the bone-coin then gently patted it down.

Wandered for a while, touching fern and branch, then rested on a stone. Found a twig to scrape the soil from under my finger-nails. Warmed a smudge of earth between finger and thumb.

'Are you alive?' I said.

As I rose, the stone seemed to shift under me. I looked down at the thing. With a little effort I managed to haul it over and found myself staring into what looked very much like a well. Had no matches with me but stared long enough into it to make out a raggedy flight of stone steps. So, not a well at all but some sort of shaft. And it slowly came upon me how it was the place where the old monks' tunnel emerged. The modest passage which is the great-great-ancestor to my own subterranean lanes.

Had I a lamp I might have taken a step or two down it but resolved instead to come at it from the other end. Returned to my rooms without being spotted. Cantered much of the way.

*

MARCH 2ND

*

Left a note for Clement . . .

Please remove all chains from entrance to monks' tunnel. Also, please note that, for the foreseeable future, I shall be communicating with all members of the staff via messages such as this.

Slipped it under the door into the corridor and within half an hour felt Clement heading this way. Heard him gently unfolding the note and in my mind's eye saw his face – at first puzzled, then slowly crumpling. After a minute a rough piece of paper appeared under my door with, *Is Your Grace ill?* scribbled on it in pencil.

'Not at all,' I whispered at the door.

Another note.

Then why does Your Grace hide away?

There was no satisfactory way of answering this last question, so I let the tight, round silence speak for itself and after a minute or two he left me alone.

I have my voices to be getting along with. I find that if I come within twenty yards of another mortal their thoughts tend to interfere with my own. Yesterday I heard a farmer in Derbyshire complaining about his dinner. 'This meat is too tough,' he said.

*

March 3rd

*

Blew down the tube around ten o'clock tonight and Clement came puffing up the stairs. I had posted a note requesting a lit lantern and, five minutes later, he deposited one outside my door, with a note of his own suggesting I wrap up warm. Took the stairwell through the door by my fireplace and went down, down, darkly down.

The chains to the monks' tunnel lay neatly coiled on the ground. I raised my lamp and headed in. The tunnel is a very long and narrow affair, apparently hacked right out of the earth. Its floor is littered with many mounds of crusted dirt where the roof has come away. Halfway along, where it dips a little, there is a huge patch of flowering mould, about fifteen foot long in total and the same colour as crême caramel. After a while I began to feel cold and tired, so to pass the time I imagined myself as a monk, tramping down that same tunnel several centuries before, in sandals with open toes. Composed a sort of madrigal. My lamp pumped out its meagre light and the darkness comprehendeth it not. It was as if I advanced in my own box of light, with darkness fore and aft. It slowly receded before me and came along behind.

Eventually my feet came down upon paving stones and I could tell by the change in temperature and the quality of the air that I was in the Wilderness. I came to the bottom of the old steps. The stone over the entrance was ajar, as I had left it, and a slice of moonlight shone through. I shouldered it open and the night air slid slowly in. Then, like a natural man, I crept out of the cold earth and into the mumbling wood.

*

MARCH 4TH

*

I eat just about next-to-nothing these days and sleep right through the afternoons. But each morning, before the aching dawn, I take my private stairwell down to the grotto and, with my lantern out before me, creep undergroundly out to the Wilderness. Down the earthy-reeking tunnel I go, with the spirits of the bony monks.

Have recently been giving some thought to clothing and begin to grasp how, for far too long, collar studs and cuff links have been keeping me locked-up. How, since infancy, I have been bound by belts and buttons, by too-tight jackets and over-starched shirts. Fairly got myself in a tangle with it. I became angry and stamped about the place. So now, on my nightly trips down the monks' tunnel, I pause at the bottom of the stone steps before emerging and remove every last constricting thread. Only the insects bear witness to this ceremonial casting-off. The earth finds nothing wrong with me.

In the Wilderness the lost moments give themselves up. The terrible grinding between Past and Future is quietened, calmed. There is something at work in the soil – something industrious – which fills up every last atom, emboldens the very bark on the trees. It gives the insects their tiny intensity, the birds the courage to call.

But all the little Lucifers are also out there, with their little forks and their eager grins. One of them told me how he fancied looking at my blood. But I find a modest garland of ivy keeps them at a distance. I knocked it up in no time and wear it with pride.

The last hour before daylight is the hour I love most. I go between the trees. My bare feet listen and Nature's ticking clock comes through to me. I hear the fixing of bayonets. I hear the buds contemplate their cannonade.

A Second Footman's Account

About this time I began to receive messages. Slipped under my door in the middle of the night and waiting for me when I got up.

The first one I got was on a Tuesday.

> The moon is, in fact, a hole in the sky. Consider.

or something along those lines. Well, I must say I considered it for quite a while, but it still meant nothing to me.

I didn't mention it to anybody at first. I was rather hoping it might be from one of the girls. A late 'Be my Valentine'. But the next night I got another one which said something like,

> What is that state of mind we call "consciousness"
> if not the constant emerging from a tunnel?

and then I knew it had to be His Grace.

I must have said something to one of the other lads on the Wednesday, most likely, who said he'd just received his first that very morning, written on a scrap of paper and slid under his door, just like mine. His had something to do with sarsaparilla. *Sarsaparilla – fact or fiction?* I think it was.

It turns out we were nearly all of us getting them. Maggie Taylor claims she opened her door and saw him scampering away.

He must have been using the secret passages he had put in for the tunnels. I should know because one of them goes right past my room and sometimes I would hear him sneaking about. That's a very peculiar feeling, I should say, to be lying in your bed late at night and hear someone creeping up and down between the walls.

From His Grace's Journal

MARCH 5TH

*

Out in the Wilderness late last night or very early this morning. The moonlight came down through the trees and dappled me but there was some mist to be waded through. I stopped to relieve myself against a bush. When I looked about to see where I might go stalking next, my eyes came to rest on an ivy-coated rock some twenty yards away which was picked out by the moon.

I approached, naked, garlanded, thinking, 'It is a very slim rock ... No, not a rock at all. Too square and upright for a rock.' And even then some instinct warned me. Some doomy inner-voice started up.

I tugged at the ivy but it bound the stone like string. Was reluctant to give its secret up. But I persisted and found that the stone beneath was smooth and flat with perfectly finished corners. This was no natural rock, crouched in the undergrowth. This was the headstone to a grave.

And horror quickly filled me up. I was weeping before the first word was revealed. Slid my fingernails under the moss and tore it back. There was twisting and snapping as I hacked it away. But I kept on tearing, desperately tearing until the headstone was bare. And I saw my own birth date chiselled in the stone.

I heard me say, 'I am a dead man.'
Read the words,

OUR BELOVED SON
BORN
MARCH 12 1828
DROWNED
1832

and the sky presses right down onto me. And I am running for all I am worth.

I run through the mist just like a madman. Then I am out of the woods and into an open field. As I run I let out a miserable groan, but it will not fill my ears. I am an old man trying to outrun a memory, but my footsteps only drum it up. And now the memory is almost on me. Looming up. Slowly descending. No mercy. Merciless.

The carriage has been abandoned and we are hurrying across the misty sands. My father has a hold of one of my hands and is dragging me forward as fast as I can go. Over my shoulder I see my mother, with her skirts all gathered up as she runs along. She holds the hand of another boy, about the same size as me.

The memory carries me through the early morning mist and sweeps me towards the house.

'Faster than a galloping horse' comes to me. An old man's face, right up to mine, saying, 'Just you mind that tide, boy. It comes in faster than a galloping horse.' And I finally understand what we are running from – Mother, Father, myself and the other boy.

As we run across the sand we trip and stumble. But we pick ourselves back up to go on stumbling some more. And my child's mind is full of that galloping horse, which is now the tide's messenger and brings the whole sea charging in. I hear its terrible hoofs hammer behind me. I imagine its terrified eye.

We are all of us breathless and exhausted. I trip and tumble to the sand again. My father hauls me up, saying, 'Come on, boy. Come on. Another minute and we'll be there.'

The mist is clearing and in the distance I see tiny cottages, set back from the shore. I am back on my feet and running for the blessed cottages, knowing we are almost there. And then the water is suddenly upon us. We are running through it. It races under me and sweeps ahead of me and makes me dizzy to look down at it.

'Don't stop, boy,' my father shouts at me. But now the water is all around. It has climbed my legs and, in a second, is almost up to my waist. I hear a shout, and turn to see my mother disappear into the sea. When she comes back up she is all drenched and bedraggled and the small boy no longer holds on to her hand. She stands there in her wet dress, looking all around.

'Where's my boy?' she screams. 'Where's my boy?'

And I go down. I am under the water. Every sound in the world has been washed away. And I see the small boy floating close by. The floating boy with his back turned towards me and his child's hair shifting in the stream. He turns ... slowly turns towards me. And when he finally faces me I see how his face is very much like my own. He is lost in thought. I reach out to touch him ... to touch the floating boy ... but the water grows cloudy and the tide rolls over us ... and the floating boy is carried away.

❉

The house is all in darkness. I grab a frock coat from the cloakroom and race straight up the stairs. But Mrs Pledger is on her way down in her slippers, with her lamp held out in front. She catches sight of me. Lets out a terrible scream.

'Your head, Your Grace!' she cries.

And then I am charging up and down the corridors and I

am bouncing from wall to wall. So late in the day yet I am still chasing, still searching for that one elusive thing. And I find myself at the door to the attic. Locked. I hammer at it with both hands. And now my hammering and Mrs Pledger's screaming have the landing filling up with staff. Their staring faces all lit with their candles and lamps. All wanting a little look-see at the mad, bald, beardless Duke.

They congregate at the bottom of the attic steps and watch me scratching, scratching at the door. Until at long last Clement – dear Clement – appears among the throng.

'The door's locked, Clement,' I call down to him. 'Where's the key, man? Where's the key?'

Mrs Pledger comes along beside him. Her eyes look straight at me but she speaks to Clement out of the side of her mouth. And I pay close attention to these sideways words.

'We have sent for Dr Cox,' they say.

And then I am filled up with all sorts of panicky feelings which make me rush at the faces, waving my arms about. And every last one of them is scattered, and the maids go shrieking down the corridors. I battle my way down to my bedroom door and the next minute I am back here in my hidey-hole, with the bolts all firmly locked.

I must have stood at the door a full five minutes, trying to catch my breath. And the noise in the house slowly subsided and there was less and less scurrying about, until at last I found myself wrapped in silence. All the beautiful voices had raised a finger to their lips.

I waited. O, I can be a patient man. I waited until one of the voices got around to whispering to me. And in time, deep inside, I felt some connection coming about. The planets slowly aligned themselves. I came over to the bureau and looked it up and down.

My fingers began working it over. Eager fingers, searching

out its little switches and nooks. But I was like the conch-boy who fails to produce a note. The thing just sat there, unmoved by my embrace. I covered every last inch, but it refused to let me in. And then my patience failed and I was in a frenzy again, kicking at it and howling and rocking the whole thing back and forth.

And as I rocked, the middle finger on my right hand found an unfamiliar purchase at the back. A square of wood which was loose and very well hidden away. I pressed it and deep inside the desk heard an old spring being triggered. A slim drawer popped out at me.

Two folded pieces of paper trembled in the tiny drawer. I reached in and picked them out. The first was a Christening Certificate. My name, in a barely legible hand. The name of another boy next to it. The word 'twins' somewhere.

The other was a Death Certificate, for the same boy, filed four years after the first. In a column on the far right of the paper I read, *Drowned, Grange-over-Sands*.

And then there is silence. A terrible silence. A cavernous pity with no way of filling it.

When I have finished setting down this entry I shall take the staircase to the tunnels. I shall go out into the Wilderness and wait to hear what is to be done.

Mr Walker's Account

Mostly I would use the bag-net or the gate-net or a simple trap or snare. Some nights I might take along a dog or ferret but very rarely would I take my father's old fowling gun. Too much noise and, of course, being caught with it would only make a bad situation worse. But it had been a moonlit night and I had a lucky feeling so I took the wretched thing along.

Well, I was about to head home and was moving up the hill from the lake, with the gun primed across my arm. I came up alongside the Wilderness, where I've had some success before, and decided I would have a look around.

I was in quite deep when I heard something stirring. Like a panting or a groaning sound. So I slowed right down and crouched there, very still, to see where the noise were coming from. Then, quite close by, there was the sound of grinding stone – an awful rumble, it was – no more than thirty feet away. Well, I did not dare move a muscle.

And I saw how he came up out of the ground. Crawling. A fleshy creature. Never seen anything like it before in my life. He came out on all fours and slowly turned himself about. Went over to a nearby stone, as if he might bask upon it. And by now I was sick with fear.

I was so afeard I must have shifted. A twig snapped under my boot. And the creature swung round to see what went on there. He looked all around him from the stone where he squatted and I saw how his eyes settled themselves on me.

On my life, I thought he were some sort of monster-man. I thought he were after doing me harm. And in a second I had brought the gun up and let it go. God have mercy on me, but that's what I did. And he flew up and back, twisting every way. And he fell back into the ferns.

When I was sure he was not moving I went up to him and turned him over with my foot – like he were nothing but a dog – and straight away I saw how it were a man that I had shot. An ordinary man, but bald and naked, with a great hole in his chest where I had shot him, lying there among the leaves.

Author's note

Astute readers will have noticed that I used as my point of departure for this novel the life of the fifth Duke of Portland, William John Cavendish-Bentinck-Scott. They will also recognize just how swiftly and significantly the lives of the real and invented dukes diverge and the downright liberties which have been taken.

I am deeply indebted to the following people who, one way or another, helped me convert a handful of ideas into some sort of book . . .

Kevin Hendley, who first brought the story of the real duke to my attention and gave me his own guided tour of the estate; his parents, Tom and Win Hendley, who made me very welcome in their home while I was researching the project and his sister Diane for ferrying me about the place.

The Workshop Trader, Iris Exton, Caroline J. Bell, Doreen Smith, Jack Edson, Brenda Penney and Margaret Carter.

David J. Bradbury, a local historian and author of several publications on Welbeck Abbey.

The local studies departments at Worksop Library and Mansfield Library (where George Sanderson's map is on display); Miss F. Allen, The Hunterian Museum, London; Richard Sabin and Ben Spencer, The Natural History Museum; Professor M. H. Kaufman, Department of Anatomy, the University of Edinburgh and The Wellcome Institute.

The University of Nottingham Library for their kind permission in allowing me to reproduce the recipe for 'rheumatics' (ref: Pw K 2739) and the advertisement for 'Essence of beef' (ref: Pw K 786).

Joe Mollen, Tony and Mary Laing, Wendy Jilley, Ian Jackson and Adam Campbell for help with some of the more arcane details.

Rose Tremain for much-appreciated encouragement.

And, as always, my friend and mentor Peter Kiddle who got me chasing after the green man fifteen years ago.

Most of all, special thanks to Cath Laing for providing me with the time and space to indulge myself in the writing of this book.